READING
essentials
for the Pre-GED Student

Melissa L. Masi

with Stephanie Smith

THOMSON
★
ARCO

Australia • Canada • Mexico • Singapore • Spain • United Kingdom • United States

An ARCO Book

ARCO is a registered trademark of Thomson Learning, Inc., and is used herein under license by Peterson's.

About The Thomson Corporation and Peterson's

The Thomson Corporation, with 2002 revenues of $7.8 billion, is a global leader in providing integrated information solutions to business and professional customers. The Corporation's common shares are listed on the Toronto and New York stock exchanges (TSX: TOC; NYSE: TOC). Its learning businesses and brands serve the needs of individuals, learning institutions, corporations, and government agencies with products and services for both traditional and distributed learning. Peterson's (www.petersons.com) is a leading provider of education information and advice, with books and online resources focusing on education search, test preparation, and financial aid. Its Web site offers searchable databases and interactive tools for contacting educational institutions, online practice tests and instruction, and planning tools for securing financial aid. Peterson's serves 110 million education consumers annually.

For more information, contact Peterson's, 2000 Lenox Drive, Lawrenceville, NJ 08648; 800-338-3282; or find us on the World Wide Web at: www.petersons.com/about

Acknowledgments

From THE DIARY OF ANNE FRANK (play) by Frances Goodrich and Albert Hackett, copyright © 1956 by Albert Hackett, Francis Goodrich Hackett and Otto Frank. Used by permission of Random House, Inc.

From LORD OF THE FLIES by William Golding, copyright 1954, renewed © 1982 by William Gerald Golding. Used by permission of G.P. Putnam's Sons, a division of Penguin Group (USA) Inc.

From PLAINSONG by Kent Haruf, copyright © 1999 by Kent Haruf. Used by permission of Alfred A. Knopf, a division of Random House, Inc.

COPYRIGHT © 2003 Peterson's, a division of Thomson Learning, Inc.
Thomson Learning™ is a trademark used herein under license.

ALL RIGHTS RESERVED. No part of this work covered by the copyright herein may be reproduced or used in any form or by any means—graphic, electronic, or mechanical, including photocopying, recording, taping, Web distribution, or information storage and retrieval systems—without the prior written permission of the publisher.

For permission to use material from this text or product, contact us by
Phone: 800-730-2214
Fax: 800-730-2215
Web: www.thomsonrights.com

ISBN: 0-7689-1241-5

Printed in the United States of America

10 9 8 7 6 5 4 3 2 1   05 04 03

First Edition

Contents

Introduction v

Section I Evaluating Your Skills

Pretest 3

Section II Fiction

1 Novels and Short Stories 23
Comprehension 23
Main Idea and Inference 24
The Fine Detail 28
Sequencing 31
Point of View, Setting, Mood, and Tone 35
Compare and Contrast 42
Conflict 45
Drawing Conclusions and Predicting 49
Vocabulary in Context 53
Putting It All Together 57

Section III Nonfiction

2 Essays and Articles 67
Biographical Text 67
Essays 74
Magazine Articles 81
Media Review Articles 83

3 In the Workplace 91
Business-Related Documents 91
Brochures 97

Section IV Poetry and Drama

4 Poetry 103
Rhyme and Rhythm 103
Poetic Devices 108
Theme and Main Idea 110

5 Drama 117
Understanding a Drama 118
Comedy 118
Tragedy 122
Social Drama 126

Section V Reevaluating Your Skills

Posttest 1 133

Posttest 2 155

Section VI Appendices

A Word List 177

B About the GED 217

C Test-Taking Tips and Strategies 223

Introduction

You have taken a big step toward success on the GED Language Arts, Reading test by using this book. We know that you have a full, busy life and need a test-prep book that gives you fast and easy access to the skills that you need. We have created *Reading Essentials for the Pre-GED Student* with that in mind.

First, you are going to take the Pretest. The Pretest will help you figure out which areas on the Language Arts, Reading test you need the most help. The book is then divided into three review sections:

- Fiction
- Nonfiction
- Poetry and Drama

Each of these sections will teach you the reading comprehension skills that you will need to take the GED, including:

- Finding the meanings of unknown words in passages
- Identifying the main idea of a passage
- Finding details that identify the author's mood or tone
- Determining plot, setting, and tone
- Discovering how poets use language, rhyme, and rhythm
- Understanding how to read schedules and visual information

You'll also work with practice questions in these review sections. For every question, we have included a detailed answer explanation. After the review sections, you will take two Posttests to see how much you have learned. The first Posttest will be similar in level of difficulty to what you will study in this book. The second test will be harder, like the real GED Language Arts, Reading Test. Finally, we have included some test-taking tips and strategies in Appendix C to help you on test day as well as a list of frequently tested GED vocabulary words for you to learn.

About the GED Language Arts, Reading Test

The Language Arts, Reading Test contains 40 questions. You will have 65 minutes to answer them. The questions will be based on different kinds of reading passages. Each passage is between 250 and 400 words in length. The reading passages will include works of fiction, one poem, one piece of drama, and some nonfiction. The nonfiction will include one business-related document and at least one article or editorial concerning art or some other visual representation. There will be no visuals, such as charts or graphs, on the Language Arts, Reading Test. Of the reading passages on the test, 75 percent will be literary and 25 percent will be nonfiction. This means that 30 questions will be based on fiction, poetry, and drama, while 10 questions will be based on the remaining reading passages. Approximately 20 percent of the questions will require comprehension skills, 15 percent application skills, 30–35 percent analysis skills, and 30–35 percent synthesis skills. Let's take a look at each type of passage that you will read on the exam.

Fiction on the Language Arts, Reading Test

Works of fiction are simply written works that are made up or created by the author. They do not claim to be completely true or factual. Fiction can be in the form of a short story, novel, poem, or drama. On the Language Arts, Reading Test, your goals are to find the main idea of the passages, find and examine details, and make inferences.

The passages of fiction on the Language Arts, Reading Test may be from one of any number of time periods, including both classical and contemporary. In addition, the passages may be from a variety of authors, with each having a different ethnicity, age, and purpose for writing. Most of the fiction passages will be up to 400 words in length. Keep in mind that when you read the passages, you will be looking for things like the main idea along with details about the characters, setting, or mood. A 400-word passage is a very manageable piece of text; you should have little difficulty reading 400 words and remembering the information within the text. (To give you an idea of how long a 400-word passage is, there are approximately 400 words in these three paragraphs about fiction.)

Before you read a passage, you may want to skim over the questions so that you have an idea about what clues or information you should be looking for as you read the passage. Also, as you read the passage, you may want to underline parts of the passage that relate to the questions that you skimmed over before you began reading. As you read the fiction, remember that the questions will not ask you to identify some hidden meaning of the passage. Rather, the questions will require you to find the main idea, identify the tone, put items in a correct sequence, or predict a character's future action based on what you read. As long as you are familiar with the terms most often used with fiction and as long as you read the passage and find the main idea, mood, setting, and traits of the characters, you will be successful with the questions relating to the works of fiction. We will show you how to find these items in the chapter on Fiction.

Poetry on the Language Arts, Reading Test

The Language Arts, Reading Test will contain one poem that will be between 8 and 25 lines in length. As with the fiction passage, a poem of this length is very manageable. There is really no limit as to the type of poem that you will see. It may be a contemporary poem by a female author or it may be a classical poem by a classical poet. Regardless of the type of poem you encounter, the guidelines for reading and understanding it remain the same. Just as with fiction passages, you should glance at the questions before you read the poem so you know if you should be watching for symbolism, personification, or some other figurative language within the poem. Also, read the title of the poem and, after you have read the poem, think about how the title relates to the poem itself.

As you read the poem, you may try this helpful technique. To the side of the poem, rewrite the lines or stanzas in your own words so that you can refer back to your own summary of the poem when answering the questions. In addition, this helpful hint may help you organize your thoughts about the poem. Also, you may want to underline any examples of personification, alliteration, etc. within the lines of the poem so that you can quickly locate the examples if you need to refer to the poem. We will go over these types of items in the Poetry chapter. As with the fiction, the poetry selection will not contain an obscure double meaning or an extremely vague main idea.

Drama on the Language Arts, Reading Test

The Language Arts, Reading Test will contain one piece of drama. Although there is no line limit or word limit for the drama, you can expect the reading passage to be a reasonable length, comparable to the other reading passages on the test. As with the poem, the drama may be from one of any number of playwrights and time periods. Also like the poem, the same rules for understanding drama apply, regardless of the playwright or the time period in which it was written.

Browse the questions before you read the passage to get an idea of what to focus on while you read the passage. Also, try to get a visual image in your mind of the story that is being told in the reading passage. Pay close attention to the stage directions. They will help you visualize how and where the story of the drama is unfolding. Take note of the way the characters speak and act toward one another. The questions may require you to identify the relationship between particular characters. The questions relating to the drama may also require you to summarize the scene, identify the setting, place the scene in a greater context, or make some other inferences from the passage. The questions will not require you to have knowledge of other parts of the drama, but you may be required to predict the future actions of the characters based on the passage. In addition, the questions will not require you to identify details about the drama as minute as details within an excerpt of a novel or short story. We will go over these types of items in the Drama chapter.

Business-Related Documents on the Language Arts, Reading Test

The Language Arts, Reading Test will contain one business-related document. This document, which will be up to 400 words in length, may be a memo, an excerpt of a training manual, a business letter, or some other text that might be found in a business setting. The test will measure your ability to read a business communication and understand the point or purpose of the document. In a practical, real-world setting, a business communication is intended to give instructions, convey important information, or raise employee awareness concerning a particular issue. A misunderstanding of a business communication could have serious consequences in the business world. The business-related document on the test will be very similar to a real business communication. Therefore, the questions that relate to the document will require you to comprehend the overall meaning of the document and to make inferences that an employee might be required to make.

Before you read the document, take a look at the questions so that you know what to look for as you read. Next, consider the title or subject of the document; this should give you a clue as to the meaning or the context of the document. As you read, think about both the author and the audience. Also, think about the tone of the document. These clues will help you be successful with the questions relating to the document. We will go over these types of items in the Nonfiction chapter.

Commentary on the Language Arts, Reading Test

The Language Arts, Reading Test will include a reading passage that is a commentary or critique of another written work, a play or production, or even a work of art. If the commentary concerns a written work or a play, it will likely contain some description of the work. If the commentary concerns a work of art, it will likely contain a visual description of the art. As you read the commentary, try to imagine the story, the production, or the artwork. The questions may require you to draw conclusions based upon the description. The commentary will be written, of course, from a particular point of view based on the author's opinion. Since it is a work that is based on opinion, the commentary must not be mistaken for fact. The questions that relate to the commentary will measure your ability to make inferences about the thing that the author is talking about. The questions will also measure your ability to distinguish between fact and opinion. Keep these in mind as you read the commentary and answer the questions and you will be successful with the commentary on the test.

Practicing Language Arts, Reading Questions

Before you tackle the Pretest in the next chapter, try the following practice questions. The passages you will read below are much shorter than real GED passages, but they will give you a good idea of the types of passages you will find on the GED. Also, this will allow you to get a first-hand look at what kinds of questions you will see on the Pretest. Once you have completed the questions, check your answers on page xiii.

Item 1 refers to the following document, an excerpt from the novel *Moby Dick* by Herman Melville.

HOW DOES THIS MAN FEEL ABOUT THE SEA?

Line Call me Ishmael. Some years ago—never mind how long precisely—having little or no money in my purse, and nothing particular to interest me on shore, I thought I would sail about a little and see the watery part of the world. It is a way I have of driving off the spleen, and regulating the
(5) circulation. Whenever I find myself growing grim about the mouth; whenever it is a damp, drizzly November in my soul; whenever I find myself involuntarily pausing before coffin warehouses, and bringing up the rear of every funeral I meet; and especially whenever my hypos get such an upper hand of me, that it requires a strong moral principle to
(10) prevent me from deliberately stepping into the street, and methodically knocking people's hats off—then, I account it high time to get to sea as soon as I can.

   1. The author of the passage compares the sea to which of the following?

      (1) A coffin

      (2) Treatment for physical and emotional illnesses

      (3) A funeral procession

      (4) A watery world

      (5) A ship

Read the following poem, "Sonnet to Liberty," by Oscar Wilde and answer the question that follows.

WHAT ARE THE AUTHOR'S THOUGHTS ABOUT WAR?

Line Not that I love thy children, whose dull eyes
See nothing save their own unlovely woe,
Whose minds know nothing, nothing care to know,—
But that the roar of thy Democracies,
(5) Thy reigns of Terror, thy great Anarchies,
Mirror my wildest passions like the sea
And give my rage a brother—! Liberty!
For this sake only do thy dissonant cries
Delight my discreet soul, else might all kings
(10) By bloody knout or treacherous cannonades
Rob nations of their rights inviolate
And I remain unmoved—and yet, and yet,
These Christs that die upon the barricades,
God knows it I am with them, in some things.

2. In the passage above, the line "These Christs that die upon the barricades," is used as a metaphor for which of the following?

(1) The author's children

(2) The author's brother

(3) Democracies

(4) Liberty

(5) Soldiers who died for liberty

Read the following passage from Henrik Ibsen's play, *An Enemy of the People*.

WHAT IS THIS COUPLE'S PROBLEM?

Line **Dr. Stockmann:** Yes, yes, I see well enough; the whole lot of them in the town are cowards; not a man among them dares do anything for fear of the others. (*Throws the letter on to the table.*) But it doesn't matter to us, Katherine. We are going to sail away to the New World, and—
(5) **Mrs. Stockmann:** But, Thomas, are you sure we are well advised to take this step?
Dr. Stockmann: Are you suggesting that I should stay here, where they have pilloried me as an enemy of the people—branded me—broken my windows! And just look here, Katherine—they have torn a great rent in
(10) my black trousers too!
Mrs. Stockmann: Oh, dear!—and they are the best pair you have got!

Dr. Stockmann: You should never wear your best trousers when you go out to fight for freedom and truth. It is not that I care so much about the trousers, you know; you can always sew them up again for me. But that (15) the common herd should dare to make this attack on me, as if they were my equals—that is what I cannot, for the life of me, swallow!

Mrs. Stockmann: There is no doubt they have behaved very ill toward you, Thomas; but is that sufficient reason for our leaving our native country for good and all?

(20) **Dr. Stockmann:** If we went to another town, do you suppose we should not find the common people just as insolent as they are here? Depend upon it, there is not much to choose between them. Oh, well, let the curs snap—that is not the worst part of it. The worst is that, from one end of this country to the other, every man is the slave of his Party. Although, (25) as far as that goes, I daresay it is not much better in the free West either; the compact majority, and liberal public opinion, and all that infernal old bag of tricks are probably rampant there too. But there things are done on a larger scale, you see. They may kill you, but they won't put you to death by slow torture. They don't squeeze a free man's soul in (30) a vice, as they do here. And, if need be, one can live in solitude. (*Walks up and down.*) If only I knew where there was a virgin forest or a small South Sea island for sale, cheap—

Mrs. Stockmann: But think of the boys, Thomas!

Dr. Stockmann: (*Standing still.*) What a strange woman you are, (35) Katherine! Would you prefer to have the boys grow up in a society like this? You saw for yourself last night that half the population are out of their minds; and if the other half have not lost their senses, it is because they are mere brutes, with no sense to lose.

Mrs. Stockmann: But, Thomas dear, the imprudent things you said (40) had something to do with it, you know.

3. Which of the following is the best summary for the above passage?

   (1) A husband and wife are thinking about moving out of town because they are not getting along with the other people there.

   (2) A husband and wife have been declared Public Enemy #1.

   (3) A husband wants to leave his family and live in a forest.

   (4) A man is upset because he ripped his pants.

   (5) A man wants to go exploring in the New World with his wife.

Read the following critique of an art exhibit.

WAS THIS CRITIC INSPIRED?

Line The J.C. Smith Museum yesterday opened its latest exhibit, Art of the Midwest. The oil paintings of the exhibit showed little creativity and inspired but a yawn. The colors blended together like the shades of brown in a Midwestern cornfield in the midst of a drought. The sketches re-
(5) sembled those of my 11-year-old nephew in his fifth-grade art class. The sculptures displayed in the museum showed some promise and potential. However, they lack the excellent vision necessary to highlight a major exhibition. The one bright spot of the show was the exquisite watercolors of Midwestern farm scenes. The watercolors portrayed the everyday life on
(10) Midwestern farms with the grandeur of the great artists or our time.

4. Which of the following is probably true about the exhibit?

   (1) The author dislikes the Midwest.
   (2) The art at the exhibit was bad art.
   (3) The art at the exhibit was good art.
   (4) The author disliked most of the art at the exhibit.
   (5) The author disliked all of the art at the exhibit.

Read the following passage from an employee handbook.

WOODBURY SCHOOL FACULTY HANDBOOK

Section 4 Paragraph 3—Faculty Tutoring Students for Compensation
It is the policy of the Woodbury School that full-time and part-time faculty members be prohibited from tutoring Woodbury School students either during or after school hours. It is the belief of the Woodbury School that such tutoring would create a conflict of interest for the faculty member who would tutor. Woodbury School students should have ample opportunity for instruction and tutoring by Woodbury School faculty outside the classroom at no charge or fee in addition to the Woodbury School tuition. Instances of such tutoring shall warrant suspension or dismissal of the faculty member who collects pay for tutoring Woodbury School students.

---

5. Based on the passage above, which of the following might also be not allowed according to the faculty handbook?

   (1) A faculty member using a student as a babysitter
   (2) A faculty member buying raffle tickets from a student
   (3) A coach getting paid to instruct an athlete during the summer
   (4) A faculty member conducting a free exam review session after school hours
   (5) A faculty member hiring a student to cut the lawn

Answers

1. **The correct answer is (2), Treatment for physical and emotional illnesses.** The author says that he heads for the sea when he is feeling bad, emotionally and physically, because the sea makes him feel better.

2. **The correct answer is (5), Soldiers who died for liberty.** The "Christs" are the soldiers who died to save liberty.

3. **The correct answer is (1), A husband and wife are considering moving out of town because they are not getting along with the other people there.** The husband and wife are discouraged because the other people of the town are harassing them. So they are considering leaving.

4. **The correct answer is (4), The author disliked most of the art at the exhibit.** The author speaks unfavorably about all of the art except for the watercolors.

5. **The correct answer is (3), A coach getting paid to instruct an athlete during the summer.** Like a teacher tutoring a student for pay, a coach working with an athlete for pay would also be prohibited.

Once you get comfortable with the types of passages and questions you will see on the test, you will be more relaxed and confident when the time comes to take the GED Language Arts, Reading Test. So, are you ready to start? Then turn the page and begin your journey!

SECTION 1

Evaluating Your Skills

Pretest

Read each passage and answer the questions that follow. When you have finished the pretest, turn to page 16 to check your answers and see how well you did.

Questions 1–5 refer to the following passage, an excerpt from the novel *Anne of Green Gables* by Lucy Maud Montgomery.

WHY IS THIS GIRL HAPPY?

Line

Marilla looked at Anne and softened at the sight of the child's pale face, with its look of mute misery—the misery of a helpless little creature who finds itself once more caught in the trap from which it had escaped. Marilla felt an uncomfortable conviction

(5) that, if she denied the appeal of that look, it would haunt her to her dying day. Moreover, she did not fancy Mrs. Blewett. To hand a sensitive, "highstrung" child over to such a woman! No, she could not take the responsibility of doing that!

"Well, I don't know," she said slowly. "I didn't say that Matthew

(10) and I had absolutely decided that we wouldn't keep her. In fact I may say that Matthew is disposed to keep her. I think I'd better take her home again and talk it over with Matthew. I feel that I oughtn't to decide on anything without consulting him. If we make up our mind not to keep her, we'll bring or send her over to

(15) you tomorrow night. If we don't, you may know that she is going to stay with us."

During Marilla's speech, a sunrise had been dawning on Anne's face. First the look of despair faded out; then came a faint flush of hope; her eyes grew deep and bright as morning stars. The child

(20) was quite transfigured*; and, a moment later, when Mrs. Spencer and Mrs. Blewett went out in quest of a recipe the latter had come to borrow, she sprang up and flew across the room to Marilla.

_____

* Transfigured means changed or altered.

"Oh, Miss Cuthbert, did you really say that perhaps you would let me stay at Green Gables?" she said, in a breathless whisper, (25) as if speaking aloud might shatter the glorious possibility. "Did you really say it? Or did I only imagine that you did?"

"I think you'd better learn to control that imagination of yours, Anne, if you can't distinguish between what is real and what isn't," said Marilla crossly. "Yes, you did hear me say just that and (30) no more. It isn't decided yet, and perhaps we will conclude to let Mrs. Blewett take you after all."

"I'd rather go back to the orphanage than go to live with her," said Anne passionately. "She looks exactly like a—like a gimlet."

Marilla smothered a smile under the conviction that Anne must (35) be reproved for such a speech.

"A little girl like you should be ashamed of talking so about a lady and a stranger," she said severely. "Go back and sit down quietly and hold your tongue and behave as a good girl should."

"I'll try to do and be anything you want me, if you'll only keep (40) me," said Anne, returning meekly to her ottoman.

1. Which word best describes Anne?

   (1) Obnoxious

   (2) Kind

   (3) Frightened

   (4) Carefree

   (5) Honest

2. "Mrs. Spencer and Mrs. Blewett went out in quest of a recipe the latter had come to borrow" (lines 20–22) is an example of how

   (1) determined the women are to take Anne home.

   (2) disinterested the women are in getting custody of Anne.

   (3) brave the women are to go out in the dark.

   (4) strange the women are for wanting a new recipe.

   (5) skilled the women are at hiding their feelings.

3. Miss Cuthbert's reaction to Anne's calling Mrs. Blewett a "gimlet" (line 33) reveals that

   (1) Miss Cuthbert is amused by Anne's description but does not like name-calling.
   (2) Anne is not a nice person.
   (3) Miss Cuthbert does not really want Anne to live with her.
   (4) Miss Cuthbert agrees with everything that Anne says and encourages the girl to say more.
   (5) Anne is an unhappy child who will be miserable living with Miss Cuthbert.

4. With which of the following statements would Anne probably agree?

   (1) An orphanage is the worst place in the world to live.
   (2) Mrs. Blewett is a wonderful woman who works well with children.
   (3) Green Gables is the one place no child would want to stay.
   (4) Living at Green Gables is so appealing that Anne should try pleasing Miss Cuthbert.
   (5) A person should hide her feelings at all times.

5. What is the meaning of the phrase, "a sunrise had been dawning on Anne's face" (lines 17–18)?

   (1) The expression on Anne's face changes from sadness to happiness.
   (2) The expression on Anne's face changes from happiness to sadness.
   (3) Anne watches the sun come up as the women talk.
   (4) Anne wishes she could be outside playing in the sun.
   (5) Anne wants to be at Green Gables by dawn.

Questions 6–10 refer to the following poem, "If," by Rudyard Kipling.

WHAT IS A MAN?

Line   If you can keep your head when all about you
         Are losing theirs and blaming it on you;
         If you can trust yourself when all men doubt you,
         But make allowance for their doubting too;
(5)   If you can wait and not be tired by waiting,
         Or being lied about, don't deal in lies,
         Or being hated, don't give way to hating,
         And yet don't look too good, nor talk too wise:

         If you can dream—and not make dreams your master;
(10) If you can think—and not make thoughts your aim;
         If you can meet with Triumph and Disaster
         And treat those two imposters just the same;
         If you can bear to hear the truth you've spoken
         Twisted by knaves to make a trap for fools,
(15) Or watch the things you gave your life to, broken,
         And stoop and build 'em up with worn-out tools;

         If you can make one heap of all your winnings
         And risk it on one turn of pitch-and-toss,
         And lose, and start again at your beginnings
(20) And never breathe a word about your loss;
         If you can force your heart and nerve and sinew
         To serve your turn long after they are gone,
         And so hold on when there is nothing in you
         Except the Will which says to them: "Hold on!"

(25) If you can talk with crowds and keep your virtue,
         Or walk with kings—nor lose the common touch,
         If neither foes nor loving friends can hurt you,
         If all men count with you, but none too much;
         If you can fill the unforgiving minute
(30) With sixty seconds' worth of distance run—
         Yours is the Earth and everything that's in it,
         And—which is more—you'll be a Man, my son!

6. The two imposters are

   _____   _____

7. The words "don't deal in lies" mean that you should

   _____

8. Name three qualities that Kipling values in people:

   _____

   _____

   _____

9. Each situation described in this poem is a kind of

   (1) rule for living a virtuous life.

   (2) impossible contradiction.

   (3) dream.

   (4) quality common to young men.

   (5) dangerous pitfall.

10. What general statement is Kipling making?

    (1) Men are like kings.

    (2) The earth is owned by men who dream.

    (3) Maturity is difficult, but it can be achieved with these standards of conduct.

    (4) Always keep your head about you in difficult situations.

    (5) Life is intricate and complex.

Questions 11–14 refer to the following passage.

HOW DID THIS NATIONAL TRADITION EVOLVE?

Line The White House Easter Egg Roll is one of the oldest and most unique traditions in presidential history. The first White House Easter Egg Roll was held in 1878, with children playing games on the White House lawn. Soon the event evolved into a more elabo-
(5) rate affair, with bands, entertainers and food. In 1889, John Philip Sousa and a Marine Band performed for the children. Forty years later, Lou Hoover, wife of President Herbert Hoover, instituted folk and maypole dances to complement the egg-rolling. At her first Egg Roll in 1933, Eleanor Roosevelt greeted visitors
(10) and listeners alike for the first time over the radio, on a nationwide hookup. She also introduced more organized games. It was not until 1974 when the most famous event of modern Easter Egg Rolls, the egg-rolling race, was introduced with spoons borrowed from the White House kitchen. Subsequent celebrations included
(15) a circus and petting zoo in 1977 and exhibits of antique cars, Broadway shows and giant balloons in 1981. Egg hunt pits were introduced in 1981. Children would search straw pits for autographed wooden eggs.

 Presidents and their families have long enjoyed the White
(20) House's largest public celebration, and it has been customary for Presidents, First Ladies, their children, grandchildren and pets to attend the festivities. Among the most eagerly anticipated guests each year, of course, is the Easter Bunny. The White House Easter Bunny, usually a White House staffer dressed in a special
(25) White House rabbit suit, was introduced by Pat Nixon, wife of President Richard Nixon, in 1969. Strict guidelines prohibit the bunny from ever being seen without his costume head.

 On occasion, the Easter Egg Roll has been canceled, either due to inclement weather or in times of war. At these times, it is
(30) sometimes relocated to another Washington site, such as the National Zoo or to the Capitol. The longest hiatus was for World War II, followed by a White House renovation. When President Eisenhower reintroduced the Egg Roll in 1953, a whole generation of children had never experienced this treasured tradition.

11. Which of the following was part of the first Easter Egg Roll?

    (1) Music
    (2) Food
    (3) Games
    (4) Balloons
    (5) Dancing

12. Who was the first person to greet visitors to the Easter Egg Roll over the radio?

    (1) Eleanor Roosevelt
    (2) John Philip Sousa
    (3) Herbert Hoover
    (4) Lou Hoover
    (5) Pat Nixon

13. Which of the following is NOT listed as a customary visitor to the Easter Egg Roll?

    (1) Presidents
    (2) Senators
    (3) First Ladies
    (4) Pets of presidents
    (5) Children and grandchildren of presidents

14. Strict guidelines were created to prohibit

    (1) the Easter Bunny from attending the event.
    (2) Easter egg hunts.
    (3) citizens of the country from attending the egg roll.
    (4) the Easter Bunny from being seen without its costume head.
    (5) White House staffers from dressing up as the Easter Bunny.

Questions 15–19 refer to the following passage, an excerpt from the play *Mrs. Warren's Profession*, by George Bernard Shaw.

WHAT KIND OF WOMAN IS VIVIE?

Praed: I'm so glad your mother hasn't spoilt you!
Vivie: "How?"
Praed: "Well, in making you too conventional. You know, my dear Miss Warren, I am a born anarchist. I hate authority. It spoils the relations between parent and child; even between mother and daughter. I was always afraid that your mother would make you very conventional. It's such a relief to find that she hasn't."
Vivie: "Oh! Have I been behaving unconventionally?"
Praed: "Oh no: oh dear no. At least, not conventionally unconventionally." (*She nods and sits down. He goes on, with a cordial outburst*) "You modern young ladies are splendid: perfectly splendid!"
Vivie: (*Dubiously.*) "Eh?" (*Watching him with dawning disappointment as to the quality of his brains and character.*)
Praed: "When I was your age, young men and women were afraid of each other: there was no good fellowship. Nothing real. Only gallantry copied out of novels, and as vulgar and affected as it could be. Maidenly reserve! gentlemanly chivalry! always saying no when you meant yes! simple purgatory for shy and sincere souls."
Vivie: "Yes, I imagine there must have been a frightful waste of time."
Praed: "Oh, waste of life, waste of everything. But things are improving. Do you know, I have been in a positive state of excitement about meeting you ever since your magnificent achievements at Cambridge."
Vivie: "It doesn't pay. I wouldn't do it again for the same money."
Praed: (*Aghast.*) "The same money!"
Vivie: "Yes. Fifty pounds. Perhaps you don't know how it was. Mrs. Latham, my tutor, told my mother that I could distinguish myself in mathematics. I said flatly that it was not worth my while, but I offered to try for fifty pounds. She closed with me at that, after a little grumbling; and I was better than my bargain. But I wouldn't do it again for that. Two hundred pounds would have been nearer the mark."
Praed: (*Much damped.*) "Lord bless me! That's a very practical way of looking at it."
Vivie: "Did you expect to find me an unpractical person?"
Praed: "But surely it's practical to consider not only the work these honors cost, but also the culture they bring."

(40) **Vivie:** "Culture! My dear Mr. Praed: I'm supposed to know something about science; but I know nothing except the mathematics it involves. I can make calculations for engineers, electricians, insurance companies, and so on; but I know next to nothing about engineering or electricity or insurance. I don't even know arith-
(45) metic well. Outside mathematics, lawn tennis, eating, sleeping, cycling, and walking, I'm a more ignorant barbarian than any woman could possibly be."

Praed: (*Revolted.*) "What a monstrous, wicked, rascally system! I knew it! I felt at once that it meant destroying all that makes
(50) womanhood beautiful!"

Vivie: "I don't object to it on that score in the least. I shall turn it to a very good account, I assure you."

15. Who is older, Praed or Vivie?

_____

16. Vivie is very smart in what subject?

_____

Circle the best answer to the following questions.

17. Which gives the best meaning for the word *chivalry*?

- **(1)** Ancient items
- **(2)** A grave and serious manner
- **(3)** Behavior befitting of a knight; gallantry
- **(4)** Childish, immature behavior
- **(5)** Free-spirited acts

18. What do you learn about Vivie's mother?

- **(1)** She wants only the best for Vivie.
- **(2)** She is not really Vivie's real mother.
- **(3)** She is supportive of her daughter's ideas and independence.
- **(4)** She is biased toward Vivie's older brother.
- **(5)** She was once in love with Praed.

19. When Vivie says she "shall turn it to a very good account," she means that she

- **(1)** will invest her money wisely.
- **(2)** will use the skills she acquired in her future.
- **(3)** will turn her trophies over to her children.
- **(4)** will be leaving town.
- **(5)** is a good mother.

Questions 20–23 refer to the following workshop announcement and registration form.

STEP UP TO WRITING WORKSHOPS

2 LOCATIONS!   Cost $149

Monday, January 13   8 a.m. Registration (and continental breakfast)
Sherman Oaks   8:30 a.m. Workshop begins
Hyatt Regent Inn   3:30 p.m. Workshop ends
(213) 555-1289

LUNCH will be provided!

Tuesday, January 21   8:15 a.m. Registration (and continental breakfast)
Pasadena   8:45 a.m. Workshop begins
Marriot Grand   3:30 p.m. Workshop ends
(818) 555-4635

Join us for a day of creative writing techniques that will be sure to get your child motivated to write! Bring an open mind and lots of questions.

We promise to keep you as entertained as your child will be after we're done! Just see what others are saying about our program:

"*Step up to Writing* has turned my daughter into a successful student! I have tried nearly all the techniques and look forward to showing her classmates' parents how to use the same strategies with their kids. She looks forward to writing essays for English class now!"
          —Michelle Alacqua, mother of a 6th grader

"I used *Step up to Writing* to help my son write reports for his science class—it worked!"
          —Tobias Haley, father of an 8th grader

Fill out the following form for more information. Please indicate which workshop location and date you are interested in. Cut or tear this paper at the dotted line and drop the completed form in the mailbox for more information OR call us at 213-555-1234.

We look forward to hearing from you soon!

- -

Name _____   Child's School _____

Child's Grade Level _____   Phone # _____

E-mail _____

Location/Date Preference: _____   _____

20. What meals will be provided at the workshop?

_____

21. According to the testimonials, the writing workshop is

    (1) good for bilingual students.

    (2) bad for students who are failing their English class.

    (3) not useful in science classes.

    (4) good for parents whose children who are studying different subject areas and who are in different grades.

    (5) useful to parents who want to write books.

22. Which of the following information is NOT requested in order to obtain further information?

    (1) Name

    (2) Child's school

    (3) Student's grade level

    (4) Number of children the parent has

    (5) Location preference

23. If you go to the workshop on January 21, you should expect to arrive at the hotel for registration at

    (1) 8:30 a.m.

    (2) 8:15 a.m.

    (3) 8:45 a.m.

    (4) 9 a.m.

    (5) anytime before 10 a.m.

Questions 24–28 refer to the following passage from *The Awakening*, by Kate Chopin.

WHAT MAKES THIS WOMAN FREE?

Line
Edna had attempted all summer to learn to swim. She had received instructions from both the men and women; in some instances from the children. Robert had pursued a system of lessons almost daily; and he was nearly at the point of discouragement. A
(5) certain dread hung about her when she was in the water, unless there was a hand near by that might reach out and reassure her.

But that night she was like the little tottering, stumbling, clutching child, who suddenly realizes its powers, and walks for the first time alone, boldly and with overconfidence. She could
(10) have shouted for joy. She did shout for joy, as with a sweeping stroke or two she lifted her body to the surface of the water.

A feeling of *exultation* overtook her, as if some power had been given her to control the working of her body and her soul. She grew daring and reckless, overestimating her strength. She
(15) wanted to swim far out, where no woman had swum before.

"How easy it is!" she thought. "It is nothing," she said aloud; "why did I not discover before that it was nothing. Think of the time I have lost splashing about like a baby!" She would not join the groups in their sports and bouts, but intoxicated with her
(20) newly conquered power, she swam out alone.

24. Which of the following is the best title for this passage?

(1) "The Joy of Swimming"

(2) "The Fear of Swimming"

(3) "From Dread to Exultation"

(4) "Experiencing the First Taste of Freedom"

(5) "The Futility of Change"

25. The main idea in this passage is the importance of

(1) facing and overcoming fears.

(2) having strong relationships with others.

(3) experiencing new things.

(4) being free.

(5) giving in to your fears.

26. Which of the following is the best synonym for the word *exultation* in line 12?

    (1) Delight

    (2) Inspiration

    (3) Disappointment

    (4) Recklessness

    (5) Independence

27. The main conflict of this passage is between Edna and

    (1) herself.

    (2) Robert.

    (3) the sea.

    (4) her child.

    (5) God.

28. To what is Edna compared when she swims alone for the first time?

    (1) A child running on the beach

    (2) A child learning to walk

    (3) A fish that swims in the ocean

    (4) A man shouting for joy

    (5) A young person playing sports

Answers

See how well you did by checking your responses against the following answers.

1. **The correct answer is (5), Honest.** Anne's behavior indicates that she not only speaks what is on her mind but she also reveals her feelings through her body language. We do not find examples of Anne as *obnoxious* or *carefree*. In fact, she seems to be just the opposite. So choices (1) and (4) cannot be the answers. She is never actually described as *kind*, choice (2), in this passage, although it is possible that she is. The reader should get the feeling that Anne does not want to live with Mrs. Blewett, but she is not frightened of the woman.

2. **The correct answer is (2), how disinterested in getting custody of Anne the women are.** Although the author does not allow Mrs. Blewett to speak in this passage, the fact that she does not put up a fight when Miss Cuthbert denies her request to take Anne home indicates that she does not have much love for the child. There is no indication that choice (5) is true. There is no evidence of bravery or determination here, so choices (1) and (3) cannot be the answer. Although the women are in search of a recipe, there is no indication that this is strange behavior. Therefore, choice (4) is incorrect.

3. **The correct answer is (1), Miss Cuthbert is amused by Anne's description but does not want to condone name-calling.** The reader is told that Miss Cuthbert "smothered a smile under the conviction that Anne must be reproved for such a speech." The smile indicates that Miss Cuthbert thinks Anne's comments are funny. However, Miss Cuthbert knows that a child should be taught not to say things that are not polite. Miss Cuthbert may agree with Anne's description of Mrs. Blewett, but she does not encourage Anne to continue speaking. Therefore, choice (4) is incorrect. The other answer choices are either contradicted or unsupported by the story.

4. **The correct answer is (4), Living at Green Gables is so appealing that Anne should try pleasing Miss Cuthbert.** Anne states, "I'll try to do and be anything you want me, if you'll only keep me." It is obvious Anne will do whatever is necessary to please Miss Cuthbert and live at Green Gables. The other answer choices are contradicted by the story.

5. **The correct answer is (1), The expression on Anne's face changes from sadness to happiness.** The phrase indicated in the question is a metaphor. The happy expression on Anne's face is being compared to the light of the morning sun. Choice (2) conveys the opposite of what happens in the story. Anne may want to arrive at Green Gables in time for the sunrise, choice (5), but this is not stated in the selection. There is no evidence to support any of the other answer choices.

6. Triumph and Disaster are the two imposters (line 11).

7. The phrase "don't deal in lies" is a figure of speech. It means you should not tell lies, even when being lied to.

8. Any three of the following answers are acceptable: Kipling values calm-headedness (lines 1–2), honesty (line 6), humility (lines 8, 25, 26), a realistic nature (line 9), determination (lines 15 and 16), and a sense of purpose (lines 21–24).

9. **The correct answer is (1), rule for living a virtuous life.** These situations are not impossible contradictions, as choice (2) states. Nor are they dreams, choice (3), or dangerous pitfalls, choice (5). Kipling wants his son to have these traits, but he does not say they are traits common to young men, choice (4).

10. **The correct answer is (3), Maturity is difficult, but it can be achieved with these standards of conduct.** The poem deals with a son maturing into a man. Be careful of choice (5); although life is described as complex in this poem, the main theme is that for a boy to become a man he must follow these rules. Choices (1), (2), and (4) are all mentioned but are not the overall messages; they are merely minor points that are discussed within the context of the poem's theme.

11. **The correct answer is (3), Games.** In the second sentence, the author writes only that children played games at the first event in 1878. None of the other choices is mentioned in this section of the passage.

12. **The correct answer is (1), Eleanor Roosevelt.** The answer is directly stated in the first paragraph. At the 1933 Egg Roll, Eleanor Roosevelt greeted both visitors and listeners over the radio.

13. **The correct answer is (2), Senators.** All of the other answer choices are listed at the beginning of the third paragraph. Although the event is open to the public, there is no specific mention of Senators in the passage.

14. **The correct answer is (4), the Easter Bunny from being seen without its costume head.** The passage indicates that Pat Nixon introduced the White House Easter Bunny in 1969 and that a White House staffer dresses in a special rabbit suit. The last line of the second paragraph states that strict guidelines were created to ensure that the bunny would never be seen without its head. You can infer that this rule was created to prevent children from realizing that the Easter Bunny is really a person wearing a rabbit costume.

15. Praed is older. We know this because he says to Vivie "when I was your age" (line 14).

16. Vivie is exceptionally smart in mathematics (lines 29–30).

17. **The correct answer is (3), Behavior befitting of a knight; gallantry.** *Chivalry* is used to describe gallant behavior, as in the knights of the Middle Ages.

18. **The correct answer is (3), She is supportive of her daughter's ideas and independence.** We learn that Vivie's mom did not raise her to be too "conventional," as Praed had feared (line 6). We also know that Vivie was allowed to study mathematics in a time when little value was placed on educating women. Choices (2), (4), and (5) are not mentioned in the passage. Choice (1) is not supported by any specific details.

19. **The correct answer is (2), will use the skills she acquired in her future.** Vivie will use the skills she acquired from math study to her advantage in the future. It is the only answer choice that makes sense in the story.

20. Lunch and a continental breakfast will be provided at the workshop.

21. **The correct answer is (4), good for parents whose children are studying different subject areas and who are in different grades.** According to the testimonials, the parents of a sixth grader in an English class and an eighth grader in a science class were able to help their children with the techniques from the course.

22. **The correct answer is (4), Number of children the parent has.** There is no place on the form where it asks for the number of children.

23. **The correct answer is (2), 8:15 a.m.** Be sure to read the information for the correct workshop location.

24. **The correct answer is (4), "Experiencing the First Taste of Freedom."** This passage focuses on Edna's newfound freedom. It is not her ability to swim that is important but the feelings of accomplishment and freedom that exist as a result of that ability. Choices (2) and (5) are incorrect because they express situations opposite of the one explained in the passage. Edna is no longer afraid to swim and she has changed in a way that makes her feel like a stronger person. The Joy of Swimming, choice (1), and From Dread to Exultation, choice (3), are not the best answers because there is a deeper meaning to the story than simply Edna's ability to swim.

25. **The correct answer is (1), The importance of facing and overcoming fears.** Edna's feelings of satisfaction and freedom are a direct result of her ability to overcome her fear of the water. As long as she remains afraid, she cannot achieve independence.

26. **The correct answer is (1), Delight.** Edna is delighted by the new power she believes she has developed. Exultation means a great or triumphant joy, which is synonymous with delight.

27. **The correct answer is (1), between Edna and herself.** Throughout the passage, Edna must find comfort and peace within herself. She is not at odds with any of the other choices.

28. **The correct answer is (2), A child learning to walk.** The answer to this question is stated in the second paragraph of the passage. "But that night she was like the little tottering, stumbling, clutching child, who suddenly realizes its powers, and walks for the first time alone. . . ."

Now that you have checked your answers, use the following chart to see where you should focus your study. In each box in the Questions column, circle the question numbers that you answered incorrectly. Then count the number of wrong questions in each box. Write that number in the "Total Wrong" boxes. You will be able to determine which type of passage you need to work on the most by seeing which "Total Wrong" box has the largest number. You can then turn to the corresponding part of the book to study.

Questions	Total Wrong	Chapter
1, 2, 3, 4, 5		Fiction
24, 25, 26, 27, 28	_____	
11, 12, 13, 14		Nonfiction
20, 21, 22, 23	_____	
6, 7, 8, 9, 10	_____	Poetry
15, 16, 17, 18, 19	_____	Drama

SECTION II

Fiction

Novels and Short Stories   1

Comprehension

Many of the television shows you watch, like soap operas and sitcoms, let you escape into an imaginary world where an assortment of characters lead many different lives. These are **fictional** stories. Many books are fictional stories, too. Stephen King and Danielle Steele, for example, write fiction for adults. The bedtime stories you read to a child, like *Goodnight, Moon* and *Pat the Bunny*, and fantasy novels like the *Harry Potter* series are fictional stories for younger readers.

You read fiction to be entertained. What you may not realize is that when you read novels and short stories, your brain is busy at work. Not only do you use your imagination to picture the characters and events of the story as though you're watching a movie, but you also make predictions about what might happen next. You may make judgments about the characters and their behaviors. You connect events, like the way scenes in a movie fit together. All of this is called **comprehension**, which means that you understand what you read.

> One of the best ways to prepare for the GED Language Arts, Reading Test is to read! Find an author or a genre you like and put some time aside each day to read. Practice makes perfect!

To practice your fiction comprehension skills, in this chapter you will read passages from well known short stories and novels. The passages are taken from a variety of genres and time periods in literature, just as you will see on the GED Language Arts, Reading Test. Following each passage will be a set of questions. Just as the GED Language Arts, Reading exam, these will test your comprehension with twelve kinds of questions:

- Main Idea
- Inference
- Detail
- Sequence

- Point of View
- Setting
- Mood
- Compare/Contrast
- Conflict
- Drawing Conclusions
- Prediction
- Vocabulary in Context

Just like on the GED Language Arts, Reading Test, at the beginning of each passage you will see a **GUIDING QUESTION** in capital letters. These questions are meant to *guide you* in your reading; they are not necessarily questions that you will see in the question section after each passage. Use these guiding questions to help you comprehend, or understand, the passage as you read.

Not only will this chapter help you with fiction passages, what you learn will be useful for all types of GED Language Arts, Reading passages. So read carefully as we review the twelve types of questions.

Main Idea and Inference

The **main idea** of a paragraph or passage is the most important idea. Finding the main idea means you must sort through all of the passage's details until you find the most important one. The main idea is usually a general idea. Smaller details support it. For example, which of the following would most likely be the main idea of a passage?

George was a detailed and efficient worker.

George always answered all of his e-mails.

George took a half-hour lunch every day.

You are correct if you guessed the first statement, "George was a detailed and efficient worker." The other two statements are more specific; it is unlikely that an entire passage would be about George answering his e-mail or how long he takes to eat lunch. The idea that he is a detailed and efficient worker, however, could be supported with many other details about his work habits. These details could include how he always answered his e-mail and only took a half-hour lunch each day.

A main idea in fiction often is not *stated*. It is *suggested* or *implied*. You will need to read the passage carefully to get an idea of what the author is trying to tell you. From this information, you will figure out the main idea. Doing all of this is called **inference**.

NOVELS AND SHORT STORIES

> **Main idea questions can be managed easily if you follow these rules:**
> - Spot the focus of the selection (or paragraph) and look for it among the answer choices.
> - Main ideas usually are not stated. Put some extra thought into it.
> - "Okay" answers are not the same thing as "best" answers. You want to find the best one!
> - Look out for two-step main idea questions.

Read the following passages and answer the main idea questions that follow. And don't forget to read the GUIDING QUESTION in capital letters at the beginning of the passage! It could help you find the main idea.

The following passage is from *The Jungle* by Upton Sinclair.

HOW DO THESE PEOPLE CHANGE?

Line Jurgis was silent for a moment. "Do they know you live here—how you live?" he asked.

"Elzbieta knows," answered Marija. "I couldn't lie to her. And maybe the children have found out by this time. It's nothing to be
(5) ashamed of—we can't help it."

"And Tamoszius?" he asked. "Does he know?"

Marija shrugged her shoulders. "How do I know?" she said. "I haven't seen him for over a year. He got blood-poisoning and lost one finger, and couldn't play the violin any more; and then he
(10) went away."

Marija was standing in front of the glass, fastening her dress. Jurgis sat staring at her. He could hardly believe that she was the same woman he had known in the old days; she was so quiet—so hard! It struck fear to his heart to watch her.

(15) Then suddenly she gave a glance at him. "You look as if you had been having a rough time of it yourself," she said.

"I have," he answered. "I haven't a cent in my pockets, and nothing to do."

1. In the passage, Jurgis and Marija are discussing their current situations. By using inference, which of the following is the best main idea?

   (1) Tamoszius is a bad father.

   (2) Jurgis and Marija are in love.

   (3) Both characters have changed and are now in poor situations.

   (4) Marija is a hard worker.

   (5) Elzbieta knows about the situations they are in.

The correct answer is (3), Both characters have changed and are now in poor situations. The dialogue and inner thoughts of the characters let you know that this is the main idea. Clues to their poor situations include phrases such as "ashamed" and "haven't a cent." You also know that they have changed because Jurgis thinks of Marija in the old days, and Marija states that Jurgis is also currently having a rough time of it. Choices (1) and (2) are not mentioned in the passage. Choice (5) is too specific to be a main idea. Although choice (4) may be true, it is not supported by details in the passage.

The next passage is from "The Rules of the Game" by Stewart Edward White.

HOW DOES THE DENTIST GET HIS BUSINESS?

Line

"Never hurt a bit," the woman stammered.

Three more operations were conducted as quickly and as successfully. The audience was evidently impressed.

"How does he do it?" whispered Bob.

(5) "Cappers," explained Baker briefly. "He only fakes pulling a tooth. Watch him next time and you'll see that he doesn't actually pull an ounce."

"Suppose a real toothache comes up?"

"I think that is one now. Watch him."

(10) A young ranchman was making his way up the steps that led to the stage. His skin was tanned by long exposure to the California sun, and his cheek rounded into an unmistakable swelling.

"No fake about him," commented Baker.

He seated himself in the chair. Painless examined his jaw carefully.
(15) He started back, both hands spread in expostulation.

"My dear friend!" he cried, "you can save that tooth! It would be a crime to pull that tooth! Come to my office at ten tomorrow morning and I will see what can be done." He turned to the audience and for 10 minutes expounded on the doctrine of modern
(20) dentistry as it stands for saving a tooth whenever possible. Incidentally, he had much to say as to his skill in filling in bridgework and the marvelous painlessness thereof. The meeting broke up finally to the inspiring strains of a really good band. Bob and his friend, standing near the door, watched the audience file out.
(25) Some threw away their pink and blue tickets, but most stowed them carefully away.

"And everyone that goes to the 'luxurious offices' for the free dollar's worth will leave ten round iron one," said Baker.

After a moment the Painless One and the Wizard marched
(30) smartly out, serenely oblivious of the crowd. They stepped into a splendid red carriage and were whisked rapidly away.

"It pays to advertise," quoted Baker philosophically.

2. What can you infer about the Painless One's skills as a dentist?

   (1) He is learning much in school.

   (2) He relies on the Wizard to make diagnoses.

   (3) He is tops in his field.

   (4) He is a faker who swindles patients with false advertising.

   (5) He is as skilled as Baker.

   The correct answer is (4), He is a faker who swindles patients with false advertising. Through Baker's dialogue, we learn that the Painless One was only pulling out caps, not real teeth. When a man with a real toothache comes to the stage, the Painless One can only ask him to come to his office tomorrow. He hides his lack of skills by saying the man's tooth can and should be saved, not pulled out. Choices (1), (2), and (5) were not mentioned in the passage. Choice (3) is what the Painless One *wants* you to believe, but in reality the opposite is true.

3. What is the lesson that Bob learns after watching the Painless One's show?

   (1) A toothache can be painful if not properly treated.

   (2) Never let a friend pull a tooth.

   (3) All men are deceitful.

   (4) It is easy to make a profit off other people's pain.

   (5) Never trust a dentist who advertises.

   The correct answer is (4), It is easy to make a profit off other people's pain. Sometimes a main idea is the lesson learned, or the moral of the story. In this case, choice (4) is the closest description of the lesson learned by Bob in this passage. Since the Painless One and the Wizard were whisked away in luxury, their scam is obviously working. Bob sarcastically says, "It pays to advertise." None of the other choices correctly states the overall lesson learned.

Be careful of **EXTREME** words in answer choices. Words such as ALL, ALWAYS, NEVER, and MUST are dangerous because one little exception and the whole answer can be proved wrong. If possible, it is better to stick with less definite terms, such as CAN, MIGHT, MAY, SOME, USUALLY, and PROBABLY.

The Fine Detail

Detail questions come in many shapes and sizes:
- Some ask you to describe characters.
- Some provide support for conclusions.
- Some describe setting.
- Some ask you to determine their importance.

Luckily, detail questions can be answered just by looking back at the passage. Here are some examples of detail questions:

- Which details support the conclusion that dog owners are happier than cat owners?
- Which of the following details is least important to the setting of the story?
- Based on the details in the passage, which of the following is the best description of Mrs. Thomas?
- Which two places did Anna visit before she arrived at Jonathon's house?

It is always important in a detail question to **prove your answer**. No matter how good your memory is, you want to make sure that your answer can be proven by the details in the passage. Some answers may *look* right because they relate to the story in some way. The right answer, however, will be in the passage.

Detail questions can be answered easily by remembering these rules:

- Skim the selection to find the sentence or sentences that contain the answer.
- Understand the difference between the sequence of details in the passage and their sequence in real time.
- Read a sentence that contains information about a detail slowly and carefully.

The following passage is from the novel *Lord of the Flies* by William Golding. Again, don't forget to read the GUIDING QUESTION!

WHAT DOES THE ISLAND LOOK LIKE?

Line
It was roughly boat-shaped; humped near this end with behind them the jumbled descent to the shore. On either side rocks, cliffs, treetops, and a steep slope: forward there, the length of the boat, a tamer descent, tree-clad, with hints of pink: and then the
(5) jungly flat of the island, dense green, but drawn at the end to a pink tail. There, where the island petered out in water, was another island; a rock, almost detached, standing like a fort, facing them across the green with one bold, pink bastion.

The boys surveyed all this, then looked out to sea. They were
(10) high up and the afternoon had advanced; the view was not robbed of sharpness by mirage.

"That's a reef. A coral reef. I've seen pictures like that."

The reef enclosed more than one side of the island, lying perhaps a mile out and parallel to what they now thought of as their
(15) beach. The coral was scribbled in the sea as though a giant had bent down to reproduce the shape of the island in a flowing chalk line but tired before he had finished. Inside was peacock water, rocks and weeds showing as in an aquarium; outside was the dark blue of the sea. The tide was running so that long streaks of
(20) foam tailed away from the reef, and for a moment they felt that the boat was moving steadily astern.

Jack pointed down.

"That's where we landed."

Comprehension Check

Did you visualize the island as you read? Do you know what other structures are around the island? Do you know what approximate time it is?

- The island is roughly boat-shaped with cliffs on one end, some beaches around the sides, and a dense jungle in the middle. A long pink beach is on the far end.

- The pink beach stretches out to the water, where another smaller island sits. There is also a reef about a mile out around more than one side of the island.

- It is afternoon. (If you missed this detail, go back to the second paragraph.)

If you had trouble answering the questions above, read the passage again before answering the following detail questions.

1. The main island is described as being shaped like a(n)

   (1) tree.

   (2) coral reef.

   (3) boat.

   (4) mirage.

   (5) aquarium.

   The correct answer is (3), boat. Although all of the other objects are mentioned in the passage, the first sentence clearly states that the island "was roughly boat-shaped."

2. The other island can be found where

   (1) the reef began.

   (2) the main island petered out to a tail.

   (3) they had landed.

   (4) there was a fort.

   (5) the tide was running.

   The correct answer is (2), the main island petered out to a tail. The line reads, "There, where the island petered out in water, was another island." Choice (1) is wrong because we are not told exactly where the reef begins. Choice (3) is incorrect because where they landed is not specifically stated. Choice (4) is tricky because the smaller island is described *as* a fort, not as located *near* a fort. Choice (5) is wrong because the tide is described merely as running, causing streaks of foam by the reef; its location in relation to the other island is not described.

3. The terrain of the island could best be described as

   (1) a mix of dense jungle in the middle with some rocky cliffs and sandy shores.

   (2) mostly jungle, with streams and rivers.

   (3) long, smooth, sandy beaches.

   (4) beaches on all sides with a reef in the center.

   (5) flat and dotted with trees.

   The correct answer is (1), a mix of dense jungle in the middle with some rocky cliffs and sandy shores. Reread the first paragraph to get a good mental picture of the island. Draw it on scratch paper if it helps. The island is described as having "rocks, cliffs, treetops and a steep slope" on either side of where the boys are looking. That eliminates choices (3), (4), and (5). Streams and rivers are never mentioned, which eliminates choice (2). Since there is also "a tamer descent, tree-clad, with hints of pink" before the "jungly flat of the island, dense green, but drawn at the end to a pink tail," the reader can see that choice (1) is the best description of the mix of terrain on the island.

> So far, you have learned specific strategies to answer Main Idea and Detail questions. Here are some points to remember:
> - **Good readers** play a continual **movie** in their heads.
> - The **main idea** of a paragraph or passage is the most important idea.
> - A **main idea** in **fiction** is often not *stated* but *suggested* or *implied*.
> - Be careful of **EXTREME** words in answer choices.
> - **Prove your answer** in the passage in detail questions.
> - Use **guiding questions** wisely.

Sequencing

Suppose you were asked to describe your morning routine. You might say, "First, I make the bed. Then I get into the shower. After the shower, I brush my teeth. Later, I make coffee. After I put the filter in, I begin breakfast." This is an example of a **sequence of events**. As a reader, it is up to you to determine the order of events. Clue words like *first*, *second*, *later*, *then*, *while*, *before*, *during*, *after*, and *last* can help you. Even if these words do not appear in the passage, a sequence question will call for you to figure out the order of events.

Read the following passage and answer the questions that follow.

WHAT IS THE ORDER OF EVENTS?

Line Mabel was sitting in her living room when she heard the doorbell ring. Not expecting any visitors on a Tuesday evening, she scrunched up her face in confusion and put down her magazine. She was reading a very interesting article on signs that a rela-
(5) tionship was headed south and was curious to get to the quiz at the end. As she walked toward the front door she nearly tripped on a cat toy and she grumbled aloud at her pet as she kicked the fake mouse under the nearest piece of furniture. Peering through the little hole in her door, she called out, "Who is it?"

1. What was Mabel doing when the doorbell rang?

   (1) Cleaning up after her cat
   (2) Watching television
   (3) Taking a quiz in a magazine
   (4) Reading a magazine article
   (5) Sleeping

The correct answer is (4), Reading a magazine article. Be careful to check your answer in the passage. Do not rely on your memory because you might fall into a trap. For example, choice (3), *Taking a quiz in a magazine*, is mentioned in the passage, but it is something Mabel plans to do in the future. When the doorbell rings, she is still reading the article. Choices (2) and (5) are never mentioned in the passage, and choice (1) is something Mabel does as she walks toward the front door.

2. When Mabel called out, "Who is it?" what else was she doing at the same time?

   (1) Scrunching up her face

   (2) Kicking her cat's toy

   (3) Grumbling

   (4) Peering through the door hole

   (5) Reading in her living room

   The correct answer is (4), Peering through the door hole. The passage mentions in the last sentence that the first activity (peering) was happening as she called out. Mabel did perform the other actions in the answer choices, but they did not occur when she called out, as the question asked.

When Sequencing Is Not So Easy

Sometimes an author writes in an order that is not chronological (in the order of events). This may be done in several ways:

- Flashbacks (passages in which a character or the narrator thinks back to the past)
- Several characters are discussed in the same passage
- The sequence of events jumps into the future or into the past

Look for clue words such as *before* or *since* or phrases that might signal a flashback event or memory.

Read the following passages and answer the questions that follow.

WHAT WILL JEREMY DO?

Line
As Jeremy walked through the snow toward the factory, he saw his life as a blur. He remembered his marriage, the birth of his two beautiful daughters, the ceremony at the college, but the rest of the memories melted together like a fallen palate of paints.

(5) Why did he get married? Was it because she was the only one who laughed at his jokes? And why did they stop at two children instead of trying for a boy. A son: that's what he always wanted; a boy to keep the family name alive; a boy to play baseball with in the backyard.

(10) Jeremy kicked the snow as he walked. Great big heaps of powder flew into the air and stuck in his pant cuffs and around the edges of his shoes. His wife would surely scold him for his cold, wet socks. What awaited him at the other end of the field was a party for his best friend and coworker of twenty-five years. Were

(15) they really that old? He thought of his first day of work, age 18; he was so eager to learn and please his boss. He stopped for a minute and thought about turning and running. He could run for about a mile to the nearest bus station, and he wondered where in the world he might travel. There were plenty of cities in his

(20) state that he had never visited.

He looked at his watch. It was getting late. He continued walking steadily toward the party.

1. According to the passage, Jeremy looks at his watch

  (1) after he thinks about running to the bus station.

  (2) before he remembers his first day on the job.

  (3) while he kicks the snow.

  (4) as he leaves the house for the party.

  (5) before he gets his shoes wet.

The correct answer is (1), after he thinks about running to the bus station. The amount of details in the story and the memories Jeremy recalls make this passage tricky. Jeremy thinks about going to the bus station and where he would travel right before he looks at his watch and realizes it is getting late. The other four choices occur before he looks at his watch.

Read carefully to note when events occur. Take notes or jot down details that are important in the margins of your test booklet.

WILL HER SOUFFLÉ BE DONE IN TIME?

Line The label said that preparation time for the chocolate soufflé was 40 minutes. All the necessary ingredients were already laid out on her counter. Tanya had one hour before she had to leave for her brother's house, so she was cutting it close. After mixing the
(5) chocolate, milk, and sugar over a low heat, she began the flour mixture. She was careful not to drop any white powder on the counter or floor because she didn't think she would have enough time to clean up after herself, and she hated to think of leaving a dirty kitchen for tomorrow.
(10) When the ingredients to the second pot were all added, she stirred both pots on the stovetop. She knew she still needed to whip the eggs for the top, but not until the contents of the two pots were blended. Carefully, she poured the milk mixture into the flour mixture and then turned to beat the egg whites behind
(15) her on the counter. Hopefully, she would have time to change her clothes before she needed to leave. She turned on her new mixing bowl and went to work on the egg whites.

1. The first mixture that Tanya makes is

(1) the chocolate, milk, and sugar mixture.

(2) the flour mixture.

(3) the egg mixture.

(4) dropped on the floor.

(5) not for the soufflé.

The correct answer is (1), the chocolate, milk, and sugar mixture. The fourth sentence states, "After mixing the chocolate, milk, and sugar over a low heat, she began the flour mixture." This tells the reader that she made the chocolate mixture first. Therefore, choices (2) and (3) are not supported by the passage. Choices (4) and (5) are not stated in the passage.

Point of View, Setting, Mood, and Tone

As a reader, you should pay attention to more than just the actions in a passage. An author's word choice and sentence choice contribute to the main ideas, inferences, and conclusions. Every word chosen by an author is there for a reason. In this way, an author makes his writing more interesting by using various points of view, settings, moods, and tones.

Point of View

The **point of view** of the story lets the reader know the perspective from which the story is told. For example, the word "I" indicates a **first person** point of view, where the main character, the "I," tells the story. We see the story through the main character's eyes. Sometimes a story uses "she" and "her" and other pronouns that indicate a **third person** point of view. In the third person **limited** point of view, the author narrates events so the reader sees and hears characters in action but does not enter their minds and read their emotions. Another story might use an **omniscient** point of view, where the reader knows what *every* character is feeling or thinking. All three points of view contribute to the story in their own way.

Setting

Setting is very important to the message of a story as well. The setting is the time and place where the story occurs. While you read, look for details that indicate the time and place, or the *where* and the *when*. Pay attention to specific details, as if you were there in the story watching the characters and their activities.

Mood

The **mood** of a piece of fiction comes from how the author makes the reader feel. The mood can be gloomy, happy, sad, scary, or just about any other adjective that you might use to describe a person's mood. To find the mood of a passage, look for how the author describes the setting and characters and how he or she paces the action.

Tone

The **tone** is how the author's feelings come across on paper. Tone can be formal or informal, playful or serious, or hopeful or somber. It can be positive, negative, or neutral. This is where the author shows his attitude toward his subjects.

FICTION

> Here is a summary of what you have just learned:
> - **Point of view** lets the reader know the perspective from which the story is told. Choices: first, third limited, and third omniscient.
> - **Setting** is where and when the story takes place.
> - The **mood** of a piece of fiction comes from how the author makes the reader feel. Choices: gloomy, happy, sad, scary, etc.
> - **Tone** shows an author's attitude toward his subject. Choices: formal, informal, playful, serious, hopeful, somber, positive, negative, or neutral.

Let's practice point of view, setting, mood, and tone with some practice questions.

1. From what point of view are the following sentences told?

   "I had recently bought a power drill on sale at the mall. Therefore, I was not thrilled to let my neighbor borrow it since he had a habit of not returning borrowed items."

2. From what point of view are the following sentences told?

   "David was lonely, but he never realized that Jessica was lonely too. He continued talking to her, sensing a connection. She felt a connection on the same level."

3. From what point of view are the following sentences told?

   "Jimmy looked at Leigh. She returned his gaze as she stood up."

4. What can the reader infer about mood in the following sentences?

   "Mrs. Smith hurriedly drops butter into the pan, spins around, and pushes the pan roughly into the oven. Batter spills over as she slams the oven door shut."

5. What can the reader infer about mood from the following sentence?

   "Mr. Jones carefully measures the batter, gingerly carries the pan to the oven, and delicately closes the door."

6. A setting such as a hospital located in Innsbruck, Austria, during World War II might suggest a mood of?

7. A sentence reads, "Mary decided to become a defense lawyer, not realizing that she would have to sell her soul to the devil to be successful." What does this statement tell the reader about how the author feels about lawyers?

Answers

1. First person point of view. Notice the word "I" appears twice.
2. Third person omniscient point of view. See how we are privy to the thoughts and emotions of both characters? (*Privy* means we are allowed to know the information!)
3. Third person limited point of view. The author acts as a camera, only describing the actions of the characters, not their thoughts.
4. The mood is hurried, nervous, or confused.
5. The mood is calm and controlled.
6. The mood would probably be of pain and suffering.
7. The author's tone toward lawyers is not a favorable one; it is negative.

Did you get the right answers? Then move on to the following passage, which is from a short story written by Charlotte Perkins Gilman called "The Yellow Wallpaper." Don't forget to read the GUIDING QUESTION!

WHAT IS THE HOUSE LIKE?

Line A colonial mansion, a hereditary estate, I would say a haunted house, and reach the height of romance—but that would be asking too much of fate! Still, I will proudly declare that there is something queer about it. Why else should it be let so cheaply?
(5) And why have stood so long unattended? John laughs at me, of course, but one expects that in marriage. John is practical in the extreme. He has no patience with faith, an intense horror of superstition, and he scoffs openly at any talk of things not to be felt and seen and put down in figures.

1. The passage is told from the point of view of

   (1) John's daughter.
   (2) a caretaker to a mansion.
   (3) John's wife.
   (4) John's accountant.
   (5) John.

   The correct answer is (3), John's wife. The narrator says John laughs at her, which is expected in marriage. Therefore, the narrator is married to John.

2. The descriptions of the house present a mood of

   (1) discomfort.
   (2) pleasure.
   (3) sadness.
   (4) romance.
   (5) sarcasm.

   The correct answer is (1), discomfort. The wife uneasily asks questions about the house's availability and state of being unattended. She is not *pleased* or *sarcastic* because she talks about a haunted house and superstition. Choice (4), *romantic*, is how she wishes she could be in her description of the house, not what she feels in reality. Choice (3) is not the best answer because it is not as specific as choice (1).

Read the following passage from a story by Zutjaka-Sa called "Impressions of an Indian Childhood," and answer the questions that follow.

WHAT IS HER MOTHER LIKE?

Line

A wigwam of weather-stained canvas stood at the base of some irregularly ascending hills. A footpath wound its way gently down the sloping land till it reached the broad river bottom; creeping through the long swamp grasses that bent over it on either side,
(5) it came out on the edge of the Missouri.

Here, morning, noon, and evening, my mother came to draw water from the muddy stream for our household use. Always, when my mother started for the river, I stopped my play to run along with her. She was only of medium height. Often she was
(10) sad and silent, at which times her full arched lips were compressed into hard and bitter lines, and shadows fell under her black eyes. Then I clung to her hand and begged to know what made the tears fall.

"Hush; my little daughter must never talk about my tears;" and
(15) smiling through them, she patted my head and said, "Now let me see how fast you can run today." Whereupon I tore away at my highest possible speed, with my long black hair blowing in the breeze.

I was a wild little girl of seven. Loosely clad in a slip of brown
(20) buckskin, and light-footed with a pair of soft moccasins on my feet, I was as free as the wind that blew my hair, and no less spirited than a bounding deer. These were my mother's pride—my wild freedom and overflowing spirits. She taught me no fear save that of intruding myself upon others.

(25) Having gone many paces ahead I stopped, panting for breath, and laughing with glee as my mother watched my every movement. I was not wholly conscious of myself, but was more keenly alive to the fire within. It was as if I were the activity, and my hands and feet were only experiments for my spirit to work upon.

(30) Returning from the river, I tugged beside my mother, with my hand upon the bucket I believed I was carrying. One time, on such a return, I remember a bit of conversation we had. My grown-up cousin, Warca-Ziwin (Sunflower), who was then seventeen, always went to the river alone for water for her mother.
(35) Their wigwam was not far from ours; and I saw her daily going to and from the river. I admired my cousin greatly. So I said: "Mother, when I am tall as my cousin Warca-Ziwin, you shall not have to come for water. I will do it for you."

With a strange tremor in her voice, which I could not understand, she answered, "If the paleface does not take away from us the river we drink."

"Mother, who is this bad paleface?" I asked.

"My little daughter, he is a sham—a sickly sham! The bronzed Dakota is the only real man."

(45) I looked up into my mother's face while she spoke; and seeing her bite her lips, I knew she was unhappy. This aroused revenge in my small soul. Stamping my foot on the earth, I cried aloud, "I hate the paleface that makes my mother cry!"

Setting the pail of water on the ground, my mother stooped, (50) and stretching her left hand out on the level with my eyes, she placed her other arm about me; she pointed to the hill where my uncle and my only sister lay buried.

"There is what the paleface has done! Since then your father too has been buried in a hill nearer the rising sun. We were once (55) very happy. But the paleface has stolen our lands and driven us hither. Having defrauded us of our land, the paleface forced us away.

"Well, it happened on the day we moved camp that your sister and uncle were both very sick. Many others were ailing, but there (60) seemed to be no help. We traveled many days and nights; not in the grand happy way that we moved camp when I was a little girl, but we were driven, my child, driven like a herd of buffalo. With every step, your sister, who was not as large as you are now, shrieked with the painful jar until she was hoarse with crying. (65) She grew more and more feverish. Her little hands and cheeks were burning hot. Her little lips were parched and dry, but she would not drink the water I gave her. Then I discovered that her throat was swollen and red. My poor child, how I cried with her because the Great Spirit had forgotten us!

(70) "At last, when we reached this western country, on the first weary night your sister died. And soon your uncle died also, leaving a widow and an orphan daughter, your cousin Warca-Ziwin. Both your sister and uncle might have been happy with us today, had it not been for the heartless paleface."

(75) My mother was silent the rest of the way to our wigwam. Though I saw no tears in her eyes, I knew that was because I was with her. She seldom wept before me.

1. Which of the following details contributes LEAST to the mood of the passage?

    (1) "Often she was sad and silent, at which times her full arched lips were compressed into hard and bitter lines, and shadows fell under her black eyes."(lines 9–12)

    (2) "Having gone many paces ahead I stopped, panting for breath, and laughing with glee as my mother watched my every movement."(lines 25–27)

    (3) "With a strange tremor in her voice, which I could not understand, she answered."(lines 39–40)

    (4) "I looked up into my mother's face while she spoke; and seeing her bite her lips, I knew she was unhappy."(lines 45–46)

    (5) "My poor child, how I cried with her because the Great Spirit had forgotten us!"(lines 68–69)

    The correct answer is (2), "Having gone many paces ahead I stopped, panting for breath, and laughing with glee as my mother watched my every movement." This is the only choice that does not contribute directly to the sadness, anger, and regret felt by the characters. All of the other choices describe these feelings.

2. The setting of this passage is a

    (1) wigwam in an Indian village.
    (2) park on a springlike evening.
    (3) river bank near an Indian village.
    (4) dense forest in the summer afternoon.
    (5) steep hill.

    The correct answer is (3), river bank near an Indian village. We are told that the main character is following her mother as she walks to the "muddy stream" to draw water (line 7). The author continues to describe the area around the stream, but the main action of the selection takes place as the mother fetches a pail of water.

3. Based on the passage, the reader can assume that the main character is

    (1) scared and anxious.
    (2) young and inexperienced.
    (3) panicked and confused.
    (4) naïve and stupid.
    (5) perceptive and intelligent.

    The correct answer is (2), young and inexperienced. The main character is not yet old enough to fetch water from the river herself. Although she knows her mother is often unhappy, the main character is unaware of the magnitude of the hardships her mother has faced. There is no evidence in the passage that she is confused or scared (although both might be true). Choices (4) and (5) contain adjectives that are not supported by the passage.

Let's sum up what you have learned in the last two sections:

- Clue words like *first, second, later, then, while, before, during, after,* and *last* indicate **sequence**.

- The **point of view** of the story lets the reader know the perspective from which the story is told. It can be first, third limited, or third omniscient.

- **Setting** is very important to the message of a story—it tells the where and when of the story.

- The **mood** of a piece of fiction comes from how the author makes the reader feel. It can be gloomy, happy, sad, scary, or any other adjective that describes how a person might feel.

- The **tone** of a piece of fiction shows an author's attitude toward his subject. It can be formal, informal, playful, serious, hopeful, or somber. It can also be positive, negative, or neutral.

Compare and Contrast

Sometimes you will be asked to **compare,** in order to show how things are alike, or **contrast,** in order to show how things are different. Look at the **details** to determine the similarities and differences that are asked for in the question. In some questions, you will be required merely to **repeat** these details. Other questions may require you to make conclusions.

Read the following excerpt from *Little Women* by Louisa May Alcott.

WHO ARE THE LITTLE WOMEN?

Line As readers like to know 'how people look,' we will take this moment to give them a little sketch of the four sisters, who sat knitting away in the twilight, while the December snow fell quietly without, and the fire crackled cheerfully within. It was a comfort-
(5) able old room, though the carpet was faded and the furniture very plain; for a good picture or two hung on the walls, books filled the recesses, chrysanthemums and Christmas roses bloomed in the windows, and a pleasant atmosphere of home-peace pervaded it.

Margaret, the eldest of the four, was sixteen, and very pretty,
(10) being plump and fair, with large eyes, plenty of soft, brown hair, a sweet mouth, and white hands, of which she was rather vain.

Fifteen-year-old Jo was very tall, thin, and brown, and reminded one of a colt; for she never seemed to know what to do with her long limbs, which were very much in her way. She had a decided mouth, a comical nose, and sharp, grey eyes, which appeared to see everything and were by turns fierce, funny, or thoughtful. Her long, thick hair was her one beauty; but it was usually bundled in a net, to be out of her way. Round shoulders had Jo, big hands and feet, a fly-away look to her clothes, and the uncomfortable appearance of a girl who was rapidly shooting up into a woman, and didn't like it.

Elizabeth—or Beth, as everyone called her—was a rosy, smooth-haired, bright-eyed girl of thirteen, with a shy manner, a timid voice, and a peaceful expression, which was seldom disturbed. Her father called her 'Little Tranquility,' and the name suited her excellently; for she seemed to live in a happy world of her own, only venturing out to meet the few whom she trusted and loved.

Amy, though the youngest, was a most important person—in her own opinion at least. A regular snow-maiden, with blue eyes, and yellow hair, curling on her shoulders, pale and slender, and always carrying herself like a young lady mindful of her manners. What the characters of the four sisters were we will leave to be found out.

1. What are the major differences between the four sisters? In other words, **contrast** these characters.

   (A) Margaret: _____

   (B) Jo: _____

   (C) Beth: _____

   (D) Amy: _____

Answers

(A) Margaret is 16 years old, plump and fair, and has large eyes, plenty of soft, brown hair, a sweet mouth, and white hands. She is sometimes vain about her appearance.

(B) Jo is 15 years old and very tall, thin, and brown. She has long arms and legs (limbs), big hands and feet, a fly-away look to her clothes, and an uncomfortable appearance.

(C) Beth is 13 years old. She has a rosy complexion, smooth hair, and bright-eyes. She is shy and has a timid voice and peaceful expression.

(D) Amy's age is not given, but we know that she is the youngest sister. She has blue eyes and curly, yellow hair. Amy is pale and slender and always carries herself like a young lady who is mindful of her manners.

Compare/contrast questions can be cut down to size if you remember that they are only detail questions with an extra step. Note the steps:

1. **Look** at the two items in question.
2. **Note** specific details about each one.
3. **Decide** how the details of the two are similar or different.

Now try the following passage and questions.

WILL JUSTINE CATCH UP TO HER CLASSMATES?

Line   Justine glanced shyly around the room at her fellow students. To her left and right were faces that were younger than her, older than her, more wrinkled, less made up. It seemed as if they were all different in many ways. Only one statistic mattered to her,
(5) however; they were all faces of people who had a head start. She felt handicapped by her late arrival to the class. It was now the third week of class and these "peers" of hers were surely already more skilled than she. Perhaps if she had gotten her deposit check in earlier, she wouldn't be in this predicament. But she was
(10) in this predicament, and she made up her mind to make up for it. She would not be a failure at this point in her life.

    The girl next to Justine with lip piercings and fingers full of rings asked Justine for a pencil. As she reached into her bag, Justine thought proudly to herself that at least she was prepared.
(15) The girl next to her smiled in thanks and Justine glanced at her neighbor's notes. It didn't look like the class had taken too many notes without her. It would be easy to catch up. The class eagerly made their way to the clay slabs.

    Soon the teacher wouldn't even remember that she started the
(20) class late. Her pottery would be as good as anyone else's because she was a hard worker. She wanted this night out of the house to be much more than just a class. It would be a life experience.

1. Justine arrived for her first pottery class

    (1) with the new girl with lip piercings.

    (2) too late to get inside.

    (3) three weeks after the first class had begun.

    (4) and discovered she was the oldest person.

    (5) unprepared.

    The correct answer is (3), three weeks after the first class had begun. Justine tells us this detail in the first paragraph when she thinks of her "late arrival," being less "skilled" than the other students, and how it was the "third week of class."

2. In comparison to her classmates, Justine

    (1) is the youngest.

    (2) has more body piercings.

    (3) feels less eager to begin her pottery.

    (4) is a superior pottery maker.

    (5) feels less prepared.

    The correct answer is (5), feels less prepared. It is stated in the first paragraph that there are students both younger and older, so choice (1) cannot be correct. There is no information to support choices (2) or (4). We know Justine is eager to begin her pottery because of her positive attitude and determination, so choice (3) is incorrect.

Conflict

A **conflict** is a struggle between two opposing forces. There is conflict in everyone's daily life. Conflict forces us to make decisions. These decisions shape our lives. Think of how boring life would be without conflict!

Fiction is no different; characters develop and change through their conflicts. Since conflict causes the actions, it is one of the most important elements of stories, novels, and plays. Some of the best-known literary characters endure conflict—think of *Romeo and Juliet* or the captain in *Moby Dick*. There are two types of conflict: *internal* and *external*.

In an **external** conflict, a character struggles against an outside force, like an evil villain or a tornado. An **internal** conflict takes place within the character's mind. This is when a character struggles to make a decision, take action, or overcome a feeling. Questions on the GED Language Arts, Reading Test may be about both internal and external conflict.

Conquer conflict questions by remembering these points:

- Conflict can be found by reading carefully. Keep track of character traits and events.
- Characters are motivated by their feelings. Examine motivations to find deeper inner conflict.

The following passage is from the novel *The Blind Assassin* by Margaret Atwood.

SHOULD SHE GET MARRIED?

Line

"Why shouldn't I get married?"
"You're too young," she said.
"Mother was eighteen. Anyway I'm almost nineteen."
"But that was who she loved. She wanted to."

(5) "How do you know that I don't?" I said, exasperated.
That stopped her for a moment. "You can't *want* to," she cried, looking up at me. Her eyes were damp and pink: she'd been crying. This annoyed me: what right had she to be doing the crying? It ought to have been me, if anyone.

(10) "What I want isn't the point," I said harshly. "It's the only sensible thing. We don't have any money, or haven't you noticed? Would you like us to be thrown out on the street?"
"We could get jobs," she said.
"Don't be stupid," I said. "What would we do?"

(15) "Oh, we could do lots of things," she said vaguely. "We could be waitresses."
"We couldn't live on that. Waitresses make next to nothing. They have to grovel for tips. You don't know what anything costs," I said. It was like trying to explain arithmetic to a bird. "The fac-

(20) tories are closed, Avalon is falling to pieces, they're going to sell it; the banks are out for blood. Haven't you looked at Father? Haven't you *see* him? He's like an old man."
"It's for him, then," she said. "What you're doing. I guess that explains something. I guess it's brave."

(25) "I'm doing what I think is right," I said. I felt so virtuous, and at the same time so hard done by, I almost wept. But that would have been game over.

NOVELS AND SHORT STORIES   **47**

1. On the lines below, identify the conflicts you found in the passage above.

Internal: _____

_____

_____

External: _____

_____

_____

Answers

Hopefully, you noticed that the passage contained evidence of more than one conflict. Here are the three major conflicts you should have found:

1. The main internal conflict is that main character struggles with her decision to get married. She does not necessarily love the man she is about to agree to marry.
2. On another level, there is an internal conflict that she feels to provide for herself and her sister, since her father's factories are closed and he is aging. This is a conflict because she is only nineteen and would probably rather live life than take on so much responsibility.
3. The external conflict in this passage is the fighting between the two sisters. They are obviously in disagreement over the marriage.

Types of Questions

Sometimes a question will ask you to pinpoint lines or times when a conflict is implied. The following question refers to the previous passage:

2. Which of the following quotes gives the reader the first clue that the marriage is not favorable to the main character?

(1) "Haven't you looked at Father? Haven't you *seen* him? He's like an old man."

(2) This annoyed me: What right had she to be doing the crying? It ought to have been me, if anyone.

(3) "We couldn't live on that. Waitresses make next to nothing."

(4) I felt so virtuous, and at the same time so hard done by, I almost wept.

(5) "How do you know that I don't?" I said, exasperated.

The correct answer is (2), This annoyed me: What right had she to be doing the crying? It ought to have been me, if anyone. This thought shows the reader that the main character feels she has a right to sadness and that she is upset that her sister is the one crying over the idea of the wedding. Choice (4) further shows us that the main character is not in favor in marriage, but the question asked for the *first* clue. Choice (4) is found at the end of the excerpt. The other three choices do not contribute to the idea of an unfavorable marriage.

Try a few more questions about the above passage. These will cover many of the types of questions we have reviewed so far in this chapter.

3. How old is the sister who is about to get married?

_____

4. What are her main reasons for getting married?

_____
_____
_____

5. Why does the main character state at the end that if she cried, it would be "game over"?

  (1) The sisters are playing a game where crying is against the rules.

  (2) The man she is about to marry hates crying.

  (3) Her sister feels that crying is a sign of childish weakness.

  (4) Crying would show that her previous words were meaningless.

  (5) She promised not to cry in front of her sister.

Answers

3. She is 18, almost 19.

4. They have no money because their father is old, the factories are closing, and the banks are seeking their money.

5. The correct answer is (4), Crying would show that her previous words were meaningless. They are having financial difficulties. The main character has spent the scene trying to convince her sister that marriage is the best way out of the situation. She is trying to be strong. If she cries, it will show her sister that she does have doubts and is not as strong and prepared as she pretends to be. Therefore, her previous argument would be meaningless. Choice (3), _Her sister feels that crying is a sign of childish weakness_, might be true, but the focus of the question is on the main character's feelings. There is nothing in the passage to indicate that choices (1), (2), or (5) would be the answer.

- **Compare** questions ask you to find how things are alike. **Contrast** questions ask you to find how things are different. Find details about the situation first, then compare. There are two types of conflict: **internal** and **external.**

- Characters are motivated by their **feelings**. Examine motivations to find **deeper, inner** conflict.

Drawing Conclusions and Predicting

Drawing conclusions and **predicting** are comprehension skills that good readers perform automatically. Think of the last movie you watched. Were you upset because the ending was too predictable? Did you figure parts of the movie out before they happened? If so, then you have acquired good skills in this area already—you will just need to apply those same skills to what you read.

The good news is that you practice these skills every day. If a coworker arrives late and flustered and you know that her car is constantly in the auto shop for repairs, you might draw a conclusion that she had car troubles again that morning. If your brother begins a relationship with a girl who is not "his type," you can predict that their relationship will not last very long. Humans are often predictable creatures of habit; fiction writers create characters as close to real life as possible so we can relate to them. This should make your job of drawing conclusions and predicting much easier.

> Keep the following tips in mind when a question asks you to draw conclusions or predict:
>
> - Gather information about the character(s) or item about which you are being asked. Details are key.
>
> - Make educated guesses **before** you read the answer choices. Sometimes a few answers will *sound* good, but they have an added detail or two that is NOT supported by details in the passage.
>
> - Make predictions based on character traits, situations, and previous events. They must be **realistic**.

Read the following passage, which is adapted from "The Gift of the Magi" by O. Henry. Then answer the questions that follow.

WHAT IS THIS COUPLE LIKE?

Line
Della finished her cry and attended to her cheeks with the powder rag. She stood by the window and looked out dully at a grey cat walking a grey fence in a grey backyard. Tomorrow would be Christmas Day, and she had only $1.87 with which to buy Jim a
(5) present. She had been saving every penny she could for months, with this result. Twenty dollars a week doesn't go far. Expenses had been greater than she had calculated. They always are. Only $1.87 to buy a present for Jim. Her Jim. Many a happy hour she had spent planning for something nice for him. Something fine
(10) and rare and sterling—something just a little bit near to being worthy of the honour of being owned by Jim.

There was a pier-glass between the windows of the room. Perhaps you have seen a pier-glass in an $8 flat. A very thin and very agile person may, by observing his reflection in a rapid sequence of longitudinal strips, obtain a fairly accurate conception of his looks. Della, being slender, had mastered the art.

Suddenly she whirled from the window and stood before the glass. Her eyes were shining brilliantly, but her face had lost its colour within 20 seconds. Rapidly she pulled down her hair and let it fall to its full length.

Now, there were two possessions of the James Dillingham Youngs in which they both took a mighty pride. One was Jim's gold watch that had been his father's and his grandfather's. The other was Della's hair. Had the Queen of Sheba lived in the flat across the airshaft, Della would have let her hair hang out the window some day to dry just to depreciate Her Majesty's jewels and gifts. Had King Solomon been the janitor, with all his treasures piled up in the basement, Jim would have pulled out his watch every time he passed, just to see him pluck at his beard from envy.

So now Della's beautiful hair fell about her, rippling and shining like a cascade of brown waters. It reached below her knee and made itself almost a garment for her. And then she did it up again nervously and quickly. Once she faltered for a minute and stood still while a tear or two splashed on the worn red carpet.

On went her old brown jacket; on went her old brown hat. With a whirl of skirts and with the brilliant sparkle still in her eyes, she fluttered out of the door and down the stairs to the street.

Where she stopped the sign read: "Mme. Sofronie. Hair Goods of All Kinds." One flight up Della ran, and collected herself, panting. Madame, large, too white, chilly, hardly looked the "Sofronie."

"Will you buy my hair?" asked Della.

"I buy hair," said Madame. "Take yer hat off and let's have a sight at the looks of it."

Down rippled the brown cascade.

"Twenty dollars," said Madame, lifting the mass with a practised hand.

"Give it to me quick," said Della.

Oh, and the next 2 hours tripped by on rosy wings. Forget the hashed metaphor. She was ransacking the stores for Jim's present.

She found it at last. It surely had been made for Jim and no one else. There was no other like it in any of the stores, and she had turned all of them inside out. It was a platinum fob chain simple and chaste in design, properly proclaiming its value by

(55) substance alone and not by meretricious ornamentation—as all good things should do. It was even worthy of The Watch. As soon as she saw it she knew that it must be Jim's. It was like him. Quietness and value—the description applied to both. Twenty-one dollars they took from her for it, and she hurried home with the
(60) 87 cents. With that chain on his watch Jim might be properly anxious about the time in any company. Grand as the watch was, he sometimes looked at it on the sly on account of the old leather strap that he used in place of a chain.

1. Based on the passage above, what conclusion can be drawn about the family's financial situation?

_____

2. Based on the passage above, what conclusion can be drawn about the relationship between Jim and Della?

_____

_____

_____

Continue reading the passage:

WHAT ARE THE POSSIBILITIES?

Jim stepped inside the door, as immovable as a setter at the
(65) scent of quail. His eyes were fixed upon Della, and there was an expression in them that she could not read, and it terrified her. It was not anger, nor surprise, nor disapproval, nor horror, nor any of the sentiments that she had been prepared for. He simply stared at her fixedly with that peculiar expression on his face.
(70) "You've cut off your hair?" asked Jim, laboriously, as if he had not arrived at that obvious fact yet, even after the hardest mental labor.

"Cut it off and sold it," said Della. "Don't you like me just as well, anyhow? I'm me without my hair, ain't I?"
(75) "Don't make any mistake, Dell," he said, "about me. I don't think there's anything in the way of a haircut or a shave or a shampoo that could make me like my girl any less. But if you'll unwrap that package, you may see why you had me going awhile at first."

3. Based on your conclusion above and the new information in the second part of the passage, make a prediction about the story's next events.

　

4. Now take it a step further. If your above prediction comes true, based on what you know already, how do you think Della and Jim will handle it?

　

Answers

1. If you figured out that the couple is poor, then you paid attention to the details and drew a valid conclusion. Notice how the author mentions that Della had "only $1.87 with which to buy Jim a present. She had been saving every penny she could for months, with this result. Twenty dollars a week doesn't go far. Expenses had been greater than she had calculated. They always are."

2. The passage indicates that Della and Jim are husband and wife, but to draw a conclusion you must look closer at the details. Della talks about the "honour of being owned by Jim." She is happy to be married to him. Della also talks about her strong desire to purchase a special Christmas gift for her husband. She is willing to sell her hair, her most prized possession, to make her husband happy.

3. Jim probably bought Della a gift for which she needed her hair. Because of his peculiar expression, you can guess that he no longer knows what to do with the gift he has purchased.

4. Based on your knowledge of Della and Jim's relationship, you might assume that they each had the same desire to make the other happy. This desire will lead to a dilemma because they will each possess an expensive gift that can no longer be used. However, the love they share surpasses material possessions. The sacrifices made by each character will enhance their relationship.

Vocabulary in Context

Since you cannot always carry a dictionary, thesaurus, or computer in your pocket (especially not during the GED Language Arts, Reading Test), you must use context clues to figure out the meaning of an unknown word. There are many types of context clues, and knowing what to look for will help you with these types of questions. Here are explanations of the five main types.

Definition Clues

This is perhaps the easiest of them all. The definition to the unknown word is actually *in* the sentence:

- The prisoner was in a state of *wrath*—a feeling of intense anger.
- He acted ill, but it was merely a *ruse*, a clever trick to deceive us.

Restatement Clues

These clues also have the definition of the unknown word in the sentence, but the definition is stated in easier language.

- The principal's decision was *punitive*; that is, it was meant to punish the student.
- The story was about a *pauper*, or a person without wealth, who dreamed of owning a house.

Example Clues

In an example clue, the meaning of the unknown word is suggested through examples in the sentence.

- My boyfriend bought me pearl earrings with some *flaws*, including a bumpy surface and uneven color.
- The sign said we should drive with extra *precaution* because the roads were icy.

Comparison and Contrast Clues

Sometimes you can tell the meaning of an unknown word when it is compared or contrasted to something more familiar.

- The coach treated his players with *empathy*, like that of a mother to her children.
- The show was held in the main house, but later the party would be held in the *annex*.

FICTION

Nearby Clues

Often the meaning of an unknown word can be determined from looking at sentences before or after the sentence with the unknown word.

- For ten years I had thought Guy was my friend. Now I realized that I was wrong as I listened to my friends tell me about the *derogatory* remarks he had been making.

- She used red paint very *liberally* in her landscape. It was almost as if the other colors were unnecessary to her vision.

Before you practice this type of GED Language Arts, Reading question, keep in mind these helpful hints for vocabulary-in-context questions:

- Grammatically speaking, all of the answer choices will *fit* into the sentence and make sense. Try to cover up the word in the sentence and think of your own word before plugging in the choices. Then use the process of elimination with the answer choices to see which one best matches *your* synonym.

- Some words have more than one definition. Be prepared.

- Remember, you are looking for the *best* synonym.

Ready to try some real questions? Read the passage below and answer the questions that follow.

WHAT HAPPENED ON HER BIRTHDAY?

Line

My thirtieth birthday was quite an *ordeal*. First, I was prepared for a surprise party since I had heard whispers around me for weeks beforehand. But it turns out that it was just gossip I was being spared, not big, secretive party plans as I had imagined. On
(5) the morning of my birthday, I was treated to an animated *diatribe* from a homeless person while walking to work. He apparently wanted to point out the flaws in society and felt that my ear was worthy of a speech on the subject for two blocks. Work was busy and full of deadlines; at least it went by quickly. After work, I took
(10) a different route home and walked through a very *affluent* neighborhood, much unlike the middle-class sameness I was used to. This made me slightly jealous instead of hopeful for a better future as I had intended.

Looking forward to a fun birthday dinner with family, I arrived
(15) home instead to an empty house and a dog begging to be walked. I grabbed his leash and cut another path through the newly fallen snow on the driveway. Instead of participating in *gregarious* conversation around the dinner table, I wondered at my fate of aloneness with the dog and hunger in our bellies. Where was ev-

NOVELS AND SHORT STORIES 55

(20) eryone, I thought? Soon my question was answered as the family car pulled up the street. They got out of the car with presents and apologies: the traffic, the lines at the mall, the sold-out items for which they had searched. I realized that turning 30 had its *trivial* problems like any other age, but what mattered most was the big
(25) picture.

1. Which of the following is the best meaning of the word *ordeal* (line 1), as it is used in this passage?

   (1) Long celebration

   (2) Difficult experience

   (3) Good bargain

   (4) Religious event

   (5) Unimportant happening

2. Which of the following is the best meaning of the word *diatribe* (line 5), as it is used in this passage?

   (1) Speech with harsh words

   (2) Political agenda

   (3) Ancient view of the world

   (4) Present

   (5) Fallen building

3. Which of the following is the best meaning of the word *affluent* (line 10), as it is used in this passage?

   (1) Broken-down

   (2) Large

   (3) Rich

   (4) Well known

   (5) Populated

4. Which of the following is the best meaning of the word *gregarious* (line 17), as it is used in this passage?

   (1) Rude and obnoxious

   (2) Friendly and sociable

   (3) Soft-spoken

   (4) Argumentative

   (5) Occurring once

5. Which of the following is the best meaning of the word *trivial* (line 23), as it is used in this passage?

   (1) Of a game-like nature

   (2) Hard-working

   (3) Having three parts

   (4) Hazardous, dangerous

   (5) Small, unimportant

Answers

1. **The correct answer is (2), Difficult experience.** The whole passage describes an experience that was painful to the speaker: Turning 30 and the immediate events surrounding the day. There was no *long celebration* or *religious event*, so choices (1) and (4) can be eliminated. Nor was the birthday *unimportant*, choice (5). Choice (3) is completely unrelated to any context clues from the passage.

2. **The correct answer is (1), Speech with harsh words.** The homeless man is described as staying with the speaker of the passage for two blocks. This tells the reader that there was a long speech about society and that it was not just a passing comment. He was also described as animated, which indicates feelings and emotion. The homeless man probably did not have a *political agenda*, choice (2), since he is homeless and not likely to be running for office. There was no mention of *an ancient view of the world*, *presents* given to anyone, or *fallen buildings*, choices (3), (4), and (5).

3. **The correct answer is (3), Rich.** Since the speaker of the passage is taking a different route, which is not the middle-class sameness he or she is used to, you can determine that this word describes a neighborhood with a different financial status than his or her own. The speaker is also described as jealous; this indicates that choice (1), *broken-down*, is probably not the correct definition. That leaves you with *large*, *rich*, *well known*, or *populated*. Only one choice, *rich*, continues to give a financial description.

4. **The correct answer is (2), Friendly and sociable.** The idea of gregarious conversation around a dinner table is contrasted to the speaker's aloneness and hunger. Therefore the word gregarious must indicate some sort of social sharing and is definitely a positive, happy term.

5. **The correct answer is (5), Small, unimportant.** Since the speaker contrasted trivial problems to not meaning as much as the "big picture," the context clues point you to a word that means *small* or *not as important*. The big picture is that the speaker's family was home for his or her birthday at the end, despite a long day of hassles and disappointments. No other choice would leave you with the positive ending that is supposed to be grasped at this time.

> A strong vocabulary is one of the best tools for success on any standardized test. Unknown words can come from anywhere—books, cartoons, television, conversations—but the only way to learn from them is to keep track of them. As you study for your GED Language Arts, Reading test, keep a list of all unknown words you encounter. Look them up in a dictionary and write their definitions on the list. Keep reviewing the list until you have learned all of the words.

Putting It All Together

You have finished all the topics in the fiction chapter of this book. Now you are ready to take a final look at fiction skills with some real practice. First, take a look at what you have learned:

- A good reader does not just *read* a book; he or she also plays a continuous movie in his or her head while reading every word.
- The **main idea** of a paragraph or passage is the most important idea.
- A main idea in **fiction** is often not *stated* but *suggested* or *implied*.
- Be careful of **EXTREME** words in answer choices.
- It is always important in a detail question to **prove your answer.**
- Use **guiding questions** wisely.
- **Sequence** clue words include *first, second, later, then, while, before, during, after,* and *last*.
- The **point of view** of the story lets the reader know the perspective from which the story is told.
- **Setting** is very important to the message of a story. It tells when and where a story takes place.
- The **mood** of a piece of fiction comes from how the author makes the reader feel.
- **Tone** can be formal, informal, playful, serious, hopeful, or somber. It can also be positive, negative, or neutral. This is where the author shows his attitude toward his subject.
- Questions might require you to **compare** or **contrast**. Find details first.
- There are two types of **conflict**: internal and external. Conflict can be found by reading carefully. Keep track of character traits and events.
- Characters are motivated by their feelings. Examine motivations to find deeper inner conflict.
- To **draw conclusions** or **predict,** gather information about the character(s) or item about which you are being asked. Details are key. Make educated guesses **before** you read the answer choices.

- Make predictions based on character traits, situations, and previous events. They must be **realistic.**
- There are five types of context clues to use to attack unknown vocabulary words: Definition Clues, Restatement Clues, Example Clues, Compare/Contrast Clues, and Nearby Clues. Find your OWN synonym before looking at the answer choices, which may ALL sound good.

The following passages appear as they would on a GED Language Arts, Reading Test, and the questions are similar to what you will find on the test. Answers are found at the end of the chapter. If you have trouble with a particular skill, go back and review before moving on to Nonfiction.

Read the following passage from "The Tell-Tale Heart" by Edgar Allan Poe.

WHAT IS HE AFRAID OF?

Line

I kept quite still and said nothing. For a whole hour I did not move a muscle, and in the meantime I did not hear him lie down. He was still sitting up in the bed, listening; just as I have done night after night hearkening to the death watches in the wall.

(5) Presently, I heard a slight groan, and I knew it was the groan of mortal terror. It was not a groan of pain or of grief—oh, no! It was the low stifled sound that arises from the bottom of the soul when over-charged with awe. I knew the sound well. Many a night, just at midnight, when all the world slept, it has welled up from my

(10) own bosom, deepening, with its dreadful echo, the terrors that distracted me. I say I knew it well. I knew what the old man felt, and pitied him although I chuckled at heart. I knew that he had been lying awake ever since the first slight noise when he had turned in the bed. His fears had been ever since growing upon him. He had

(15) been trying to fancy them causeless, but could not. He had been saying to himself, "It is nothing but the wind in the chimney, it is only a mouse crossing the floor," or, "It is merely a cricket which has made a single chirp." Yes, he has been trying to comfort himself with these suppositions; but he had found all in vain. ALL IN

(20) VAIN, because Death in approaching him had stalked with his black shadow before him and enveloped the victim. And it was the mournful influence of the unperceived shadow that caused him to feel, although he neither saw nor heard, to feel the presence of my head within the room.

(25) When I had waited a long time very patiently without hearing him lie down, I resolved to open a little—a very, very little crevice in the lantern. So I opened it—you cannot imagine how stealthily, stealthily—until at length a single dim ray like the thread of the spider shot out from the crevice and fell upon the vulture eye.

(30)   It was open, wide, wide open, and I grew furious as I gazed upon it. I saw it with perfect distinctness—all a dull blue with a hideous veil over it that chilled the very marrow in my bones, but I could see nothing else of the old man's face or person, for I had directed the ray as if by instinct precisely upon the damned spot.

(35)   And now have I not told you that what you mistake for madness is but overacuteness of the senses? Now, I say, there came to my ears a low, dull, quick sound, such as a watch makes when enveloped in cotton. I knew that sound well too. It was the beating of the old man's heart. It increased my fury as the beating of a

(40)   drum stimulates the soldier into courage.

    But even yet I refrained and kept still. I scarcely breathed. I held the lantern motionless. I tried how steadily I could maintain the ray upon the eye. Meantime the tattoo of the heart increased. It grew quicker and quicker, and louder and louder, every instant.

(45)   The old man's terror must have been extreme! It grew louder, I say, louder every moment!—do you mark me well? I have told you that I am nervous: so I am. And now at the dead hour of the night, amid the dreadful silence of that old house, so strange a noise as this excited me to uncontrollable terror. Yet, for some

(50)   minutes longer I refrained and stood still. But the beating grew louder, louder! I thought the heart must burst.

    And now a new anxiety seized me—the sound would be heard by a neighbor! The old man's hour had come! With a loud yell, I threw open the lantern and leaped into the room. He shrieked

(55)   once—once only. In an instant I dragged him to the floor, and pulled the heavy bed over him. I then smiled gaily, to find the deed so far done. But for many minutes the heart beat on with a muffled sound. This, however, did not vex me; it would not be heard through the wall. At length it ceased. The old man was

(60)   dead. I removed the bed and examined the corpse. Yes, he was stone, stone dead. I placed my hand upon the heart and held it there many minutes. There was no pulsation. He was stone dead. His eye would trouble me no more.

1. What can you conclude about how the main character feels about the death of the man? The main character feels

    (1) uninterested.
    (2) scared.
    (3) sad.
    (4) guilty.
    (5) satisfied.

2. What conclusion can you draw from the statement, "I knew what the old man felt, and pitied him although I chuckled at heart"?

    (1) The main character is afraid for the old man.
    (2) The main character cares about the old man's feelings.
    (3) The old man feels relieved that the main character is watching over him.
    (4) The main character not only understands the old man's fear but also takes pleasure in causing it.
    (5) The old man's fears are silly and therefore make the main character laugh.

3. How does the main character know that the old man is indeed dead?

    (1) He places his hands over the old man's heart and feels that it has stopped beating.
    (2) He places a mirror under the old man's nose to check his breathing.
    (3) He puts a pillow over the old man's face.
    (4) He crushes the old man with the bed.
    (5) He is never really sure that the old man is dead.

4. Which of the following is the best meaning of the word *tattoo* as it is used in this passage?

    (1) Entertaining music
    (2) A call or signal
    (3) A pony
    (4) Mark on the body
    (5) Rapid beating

Read the following passage from the novel *Plainsong* by Kent Haruf.

WILL THE BOYS EVER GET THEIR MOTHER BACK?

Line   Upstairs in the bathroom they combed their wet hair, drawing it up into waves and fluffing it with their cupped hands so it stood up stiffly over their foreheads. Water trickled down their cheeks and dribbled behind their ears. They toweled off and went out
(5)   into the hallway and stood hesitant before the door until Ike turned the knob and then they entered the hushed half-lit room.

   She lay in the guest bed on her back now with her arm still folded across her face like someone in great distress. A thin woman, caught as though in some inescapable thought or atti-
(10) tude, motionless, almost as if she were not even breathing. They stopped inside the door. There were the brief lines of light at the edges of the drawn window shades and from across the room they could smell the dead flowers in the vase on the tall chest of drawers.

(15) "Yes?" she said. She did not stir or move. Her voice was nearly a whisper.

   "Mother?"

   "Yes."

   "Are you all right?"

(20) "You can come over here," she said.

   They approached the bed. She removed her arm from over her face and looked at them, one boy then the other. In the dim light their wet hair appeared very dark and their blue eyes were almost black. They stood beside the bed looking at her.

(25) "Do you feel any better?" Ike said.

   "Do you feel like getting up?" said Bobby.

   Her eyes looked glassy, as if she were suffering from fever. "Are you ready for school now?" she said.

   "Yes."

(30) "What time is it?"

   They looked at the clock on the dresser. "Quarter of eight," Ike said.

   "You better go. You don't want to be late." She smiled a little and reached a hand toward them. "Will you each give me a kiss
(35) first?"

   They leaned forward and kissed her on the cheek, one after the other, the quick embarrassed kisses of little boys. Her cheek felt cool and she smelled like herself. She took up their hands and held them for a moment against her cool cheeks while she looked
(40) at their faces and their dark wet hair. They could just bear to glance at her eyes. They stood waiting uncomfortable, leaning

over the bed. At last she released their hands and they stood up. "You'd better go on," she said.

"Goodbye, Mother," Ike said.

(45) "I hope you get better," Bobby said.

They went out of the room and closed the door. Outside the house in the bright sunlight they crossed the drive and went across Railroad Street and walked down in the path through the ditch weeds and across the railroad tracks and through the park
(50) toward school. When they arrived at the playground they separated to join their own friends and stood talking with the other boys in their own grades until the first bell rang and called them into class.

5. According to the passage, what did the boys do before they went to visit their mother?

(1) They ate breakfast.
(2) They rode their bikes.
(3) They picked new flowers.
(4) They washed and combed their hair.
(5) They walked their dog.

6. Which of the following words best describes the mood in this passage?

(1) Uncomfortable
(2) Excited
(3) Dreary
(4) Imaginative
(5) Rapid

7. Why do the boys hesitate outside their mother's door?

(1) She is not dressed yet.
(2) She has not yet called them in.
(3) They are scared to see their mom still in bed and unwell.
(4) They are late for school and debate leaving the house.
(5) Their father calls them from downstairs.

8. What can you infer about the boys' feelings toward their mother?

(1) They love her very much and are respectful and hopeful.
(2) They love her very much but know there is no hope for her illness.
(3) They love her more than they love their father.
(4) They are resentful of her illness and act poorly because of it.
(5) They do not feel much for their mother.

Answers

1. **The correct answer is (5), satisfied.** The main character is content with the knowledge that the old man is terrified. He takes pleasure in the old man's misery. There is no evidence in the story to support the other answer choices.

2. **The correct answer is (4), The main character not only understands the old man's fear but also takes pleasure in causing it.** None of the other choices is proved by evidence in the passage.

3. **The correct answer is (1), He places his hands over the old man's heart and feels that it has stopped beating.** This answer is explicitly stated at the end of the selection.

4. **The correct answer is (5), Rapid beating.** The main character is describing the beating of the old man's heart. He states that he can hear the sound of the old man's heart, and it is getting louder and faster as the tension increases in the story. One of the other answer choices is a definition of the word *tattoo*, but choice (5) is the only answer that fits the context of the story.

5. **The correct answer is (4), They washed and combed their hair.** In the first paragraph, the boys comb their wet hair and shape it before toweling it off. This indicates a washing. The passage does not mention eating breakfast, picking flowers, or a dog. And they ride their bikes to school after they leave their mother's room.

6. **The correct answer is (1), Uncomfortable.** Since the boys are hesitant outside the door, give embarrassed kisses, and stand uncomfortably before she lets them go, you can infer that the boys are not *excited* or *imaginative*. There is no basis for choice (5) in the passage at all; on the contrary, time seems to move slowly here. You might be tempted to choose *dreary* because of the illness and dead flowers, but the focus of the passage is on the boys and how they feel toward their mother. This creates an uncomfortable mood, not a dreary one.

7. **The correct answer is (3), They are scared to see their mom still in bed and unwell.** This question asks you to draw a conclusion about the boy's behavior based on the information in the passage. Since they ask their mom if she feels better or feels like getting up, you know they are upset about her staying in bed all day.

8. **The correct answer is (1), They love her very much and are respectful and hopeful.** Again, you are asked to make an inference about the boys' feelings based on their actions and descriptions. The boys obviously love their mother and show no signs of resentment, so choices (4) and (5) cannot be correct. There is no evidence of who they love more, their mother or father, so choice (3) cannot be correct. And her illness and impossibility of a cure are not discussed, so choice (2) cannot be the answer.

SECTION III

Nonfiction

Essays and Articles 2

Nonfiction surrounds us every day. It is writing about real people, places, things, or events. Examples of common nonfiction you might see are:

- Cookbooks
- Train schedules
- Magazine articles
- Newspaper articles
- Textbooks
- Instruction guides
- Interviews
- Assembly manuals
- Self-help books
- Advertisements

If you regularly read a magazine or newspaper, then you have had a lot of practice with understanding nonfiction. Make a point of reading for information as well as pleasure, especially while studying for the GED Language Arts, Reading Test. Many of the skills you will learn in this section are similar to the skills tested in fiction, but here they are applied to nonfiction text. In this chapter, we are going to explore the kinds of nonfiction you will see on the test.

Biographical Text

A **biography** is the story of a person's life. It is told by someone else. The writer, or biographer, researches the subject through interviews, letters, books, diaries, and any other information he or she can find. A good biographer will find information that provides the reader with an accurate description of the subject's life, both the good and the bad.

An **autobiography** is the story of a person's life as told by that person. Autobiographies are usually written in first person point of view. Therefore, they tell the story of a life from the person's perspective. Both biographies and autobiographies have elements common to fiction—character, setting, and plot—but remember, these are written about **real** people and events.

Let us try some questions that test your biographical and autobiographical skills. The following is a paragraph about Charles Dickens, an English author from the midnineteenth century. Notice how the questions that follow are different and similar to the questions on fiction passages.

WHO WAS CHARLES DICKENS?

Line
Charles Dickens is one of the *titans* of English literature. Unlike so many other writers, he was immensely popular in his own time. Dickens began his writing career as a newspaper reporter when he was quite young. His first book was made up of articles
(5) written for the London *Evening Chronicle*. He was an *astute* observer of London life and later based some of his most memorable characters on his early experiences as a reporter. Fame came with *The Pickwick Papers*, a humorous novel published in monthly *segments* during 1836–37. *A Christmas Carol* and *Oliver Twist*
(10) are among other popular Dickens stories still widely read.

1. Which word is the best synonym for the word *titans* as it is used in the passage?

    (1) Giants

    (2) Monsters

    (3) Writers

    (4) Readers

    (5) Workers

2. Which word is the best synonym for the word *astute* as it is used in the passage?

    (1) Hard-working

    (2) Multitalented

    (3) Being responsible

    (4) Having keen judgment

    (5) Unaware

3. Which word is the best synonym for the word *segments* as it is used in the passage?

    (1) Magazines

    (2) Plots

    (3) Offices

    (4) Parts

    (5) Extras

4. Which sentence could logically be inserted in this paragraph?

   (1) *Oliver Twist* became a successful musical play.

   (2) He had much sympathy for the poor and great understanding of people.

   (3) Chaucer and Shakespeare are two other literary giants.

   (4) Charles Dickens' mother was named Mary.

   (5) In Dickens' day, newspapers were printed with hand cranks.

5. What would be the best title for this paragraph?

   (1) "Popular Novels by Dickens"

   (2) "A Great English Writer"

   (3) "Giants of English Literature"

   (4) "The Childhood of Dickens"

   (5) "Living in London"

Answers

1. **The correct answer is (1), Giants.** Use the context clues from the entire passage to see that the word means large and very accomplished. No other answer choice has the idea of "largeness."

2. **The correct answer is (4), Having keen judgment.** The words "observer" and "reporter" show that Dickens watched what was going on around him. Since he was successful, you can assume that his judgments were keen and sharp.

3. **The correct answer is (4), Parts.** Since the passage mentions "monthly" segments, you know they continued each month. This is closest to saying monthly pieces or *parts*.

4. **The correct answer is (2), He had much sympathy for the poor and great understanding of people.** Paragraphs should have unity, and only choice (2) continues to explain Dickens' influences and works. Choice (1) is too specific for such a general paragraph. Choices (4) and (5) do not relate directly to the main idea, and choice (3) is completely unrelated.

5. **The correct answer is (2), "A Great English Writer."** The paragraph only talks about one writer and mentions a few of his works, so choices (1) and (3) cannot be the answer. The topics of choices (4) and (5) are not even explored in the paragraph.

The passages on the GED Language Arts, Reading Test will be longer in length than the one you just read. They will be between 250 and 500 words, just like in the fiction section. Let us try two more biographical passages that are closer in length to the passages on the test. Read the following biography of Colin Powell.

WHAT MAKES THIS MAN SUCCESSFUL?

Line   Colin Powell was born in New York City on April 5, 1937, and was raised in the South Bronx. His parents, Luther and Maud Ariel Powell, *immigrated* to the United States from the island of Jamaica. Colin was educated in the New York City public schools
(5) and graduated from the City College of New York, where he earned a bachelor's degree in geology.

  While in college he joined a training program for the U.S. Army, called ROTC. When he graduated in 1958, he was commissioned as a second lieutenant in the infantry. Colin trained as
(10) both a paratrooper and an Army Ranger. Later, he went back to college to get more education, including a Master of Business Administration degree from George Washington University in Washington, D.C.

  Colin was in the Army for thirty-five years and served through-
(15) out the world in various posts and jobs. He rose to a four-star General. He earned many military awards and decorations from the United States as well as from foreign countries. He was also knighted by Queen Elizabeth of England as the Knight Commander of the Bath.

(20)   In 1989, he was *appointed* to the highest military position in the U.S. Department of Defense at the Pentagon as Chairman of the Joint Chiefs of Staff. He was the youngest person and the first African American to hold this post. After he retired from the Army in 1993, Secretary Powell spent two years writing a book
(25) about his life. It was called *My American Journey* and became a best-selling book when it was published in 1995. He was also a very popular public speaker and traveled around the world to talk to many audiences.

  President George W. Bush asked Colin to serve as America's
(30) sixty-fifth Secretary of State in January of 2001. Thanks to all of his long years of service to the country, Colin was overwhelmingly approved by the U.S. Congress. Today, he works as President Bush's chief foreign policy adviser. He is the first African American in the history of the United States to serve in this important job.

1. Which word is the best synonym for the word *immigrated* (line 3)?
    (1) Moved
    (2) Left
    (3) Continued
    (4) Graduated
    (5) Lived

2. Which is NOT a position that was held by Colin Powell?

   (1) Second Lieutenant in the infantry
   (2) Paratrooper
   (3) Chairman of the Joint Chiefs of Staff
   (4) New York City public school teacher
   (5) Author

3. Which word is the best synonym for the word *appointed* (line 20)?

   (1) Assigned
   (2) Authorized
   (3) Furnished
   (4) Settled
   (5) Arranged

4. Colin Powell was the first African American to hold which position?

   (1) Second Lieutenant in the infantry
   (2) Paratrooper
   (3) Four-star general
   (4) Author
   (5) Chairman of the Joint Chiefs of Staff

5. Why is Colin Powell's appointment as Secretary of State significant?

   (1) Colin Powell was overwhelmingly confirmed and the first African American to hold the position.
   (2) Colin Powell was nearly rejected for the job by the U.S. Congress.
   (3) Colin Powell was popular with many people.
   (4) George W. Bush initially was thinking about selecting another candidate.
   (5) Colin Powell never wanted to be Secretary of State.

Answers

1. **The correct answer is (1), Moved.** Colin Powell's parents immigrated to the United States from Jamaica. They moved from one place to another. The Powells did not leave the United States, so choice (2) is incorrect. The other answer choices have nothing to do with immigration.

2. **The correct answer is (4), New York City public school teacher.** Colin Powell was educated in the New York City public schools. He did not work there. All of the other choices are mentioned in the passage.

3. **The correct answer is (1), Assigned.** Colin Powell was assigned to, or given, his position based on his accomplishments. Although the other answer choices are also synonyms for *appointed*, they do not support the use of the word in the passage.

4. The correct answer is (5), Chairman of the Joint Chiefs of Staff. Colin Powell was also the first African American to serve as Secretary of State, but this is not one of the answer choices. Although Powell held each of the other positions, he was not the first African American to accomplish these goals.

5. The correct answer is (1), Colin Powell was overwhelmingly confirmed and the first African American to hold the position. These facts are stated in the last paragraph of the passage. None of the other choices is supported by the information presented in the selection.

Now read about another famous American, Frederick Douglass. In the following passage, which is adapted from his autobiography, Douglass wrote what he saw when he first escaped slavery and moved to the northern United States.

WHAT IS IT LIKE TO BE FREE?

Line

In the afternoon, I visited the wharves of New Bedford. Here I found myself surrounded with the strongest proofs of wealth. Lying at the wharves, and riding in the stream, I saw many ships of the finest model, in the best order, and of the largest size. Upon
(5) the right and left, I was walled in by granite warehouses, filled with the necessaries and comforts of life. Added to this, almost everybody seemed to be at work, but noiselessly so, compared with what I had been accustomed to in Baltimore. There were no loud songs heard from those engaged in loading and unloading
(10) ships. I saw no whipping of men; but all seemed to go smoothly on. Every man appeared to understand his work, and went at it with a sober, yet cheerful earnestness. To me this looked exceedingly strange. From the wharves I strolled around the town, gazing with wonder and admiration at the splendid churches,
(15) beautiful houses, and fine gardens. Everything *evinced* an amount of wealth, comfort, taste, and refinement that I had never seen in any part of slaveholding Maryland.

Every thing looked clean, new, and beautiful. I saw few or no dilapidated houses, with poverty-stricken inmates; no half-naked
(20) children and bare-footed women, such as I had been accustomed to see in Baltimore. The people looked more able, stronger, healthier, and happier, than those of Maryland. I was for once made glad by a view of extreme wealth, without being saddened by seeing extreme poverty. But the most astonishing as well as
(25) the most interesting thing to me was the condition of the colored people, a great many of whom, like myself, had escaped here as a refuge from the hunters of men. I found many, who had not been seven years out of their chains, living in finer houses, and evidently enjoying more of the comforts of life, than the average of
(30) slaveholders in Maryland. I will venture to assert that my friend

ESSAYS AND ARTICLES   73

(35) Mr. Nathan Johnson lived in a neater house; dined at a better table; took, paid for, and read more newspapers; better understood the moral, religious, and political character of the nation,—than nine tenths of the slaveholders in Talbot County, Maryland. Yet Mr. Johnson was a working man. His hands were hardened by toil, and not his alone, but those also of Mrs. Johnson.

1. In the passage, the word *evinced* (line 15) most nearly means to

(1) cover up.

(2) make flavorful.

(3) display clearly.

(4) make comfortable.

(5) cultivate.

2. Which of the following is NOT used by Douglass to describe life in New Bedford?

(1) Clean, new, and beautiful

(2) Poverty stricken

(3) A refuge from hunters of men

(4) Wealthy

(5) Cheerfully earnest

3. The author's main point in this passage is

(1) slavery has good points as well as bad points.

(2) loading and unloading ships is lucrative work.

(3) slavery is not necessary to create an economically stable society.

(4) slavery causes poverty.

(5) slavery is necessary for a strong economy.

4. A good title for this passage might be

(1) "The Cost of Slavery."

(2) "A Life of Chains."

(3) "A View of Freedom."

(4) "A Hard Road to Freedom."

(5) "A Search for Jobs."

5. What of the following does Douglass experience while watching the men work?

(1) Loud songs sung by workers

(2) Curses directed at workers

(3) Whipping of men

(4) Unemployed men wandering on the wharves

(5) Men working with dignity

Answers

1. **The correct answer is (3), display clearly.** In the passage, Douglass notes that everything he sees demonstrates the comfortable lifestyle of the people in the town. This comfort is clearly displayed in the construction of the buildings and the care with which the gardens are tended. *Evincing* is therefore closest in meaning to choice (3).

2. **The correct answer is (1), Clean, new, and beautiful.** Although Douglass uses these words in the passage, he is contrasting slave-holding Maryland and the town in which he is currently describing. All of the other answer choices are descriptions of a slave community. Because the question asks for the choice that does NOT describe such a community, none of these choices is correct.

3. **The correct answer is (3), slavery is not necessary to create an economically stable society.** Douglass writes about how well former slaves and other members of the community are doing in comparison to people who live in a slave-holding community. In his description, the free community is wealthier and happier than the slave community. Douglass never states that there is anything good about slavery, so choice (1) is incorrect. There is no indication that the wharf workers make a lot of money, so choice (2) can be eliminated. There is no evidence to support choices (4) and (5).

4. **The correct answer is (3), "A View of Freedom."** This passage is about the joys and advantages of freedom. Although Douglass touches on the disadvantages and cruelty of slavery, choices (1) and (2), it is not the focus of the paper. The road to freedom may in fact be difficult (4), but there is no discussion of this in the selection. Choice (5) is incorrect because no one in the passage is looking for a job.

5. **The correct answer is (5), Men working with dignity.** All of the other choices are things Douglass has seen in the past. His experiences in this town are exactly the opposite.

Essays

A short work of nonfiction that deals with a single subject is called an essay. In an essay, the author appeals to the readers' common sense and emotions. Essays can be formal or informal in tone. Formal essays explore topics in a serious manner, like seatbelt safety or teen drinking. They are organized and researched. Informal essays are lighter in tone and language and can be written about almost any topic. Usually the informal essay is a reflection of the author's feelings, experiences, and personality.

On the GED Language Arts, Reading Test, you will be expected to understand an essay from the author's point of view. You must watch for the author's tone to see how the author feels about the subject. This means you must pay attention to the *way* the author writes. Does the author use humor or exaggeration to get his or her point across? Does he or she mention statistics to make a more convincing case?

Read the following passage, which describes the role the National Zoo plays in animal conservation.

WHY IS THE NATIONAL ZOO IMPORTANT?

Line

The Smithsonian's National Zoo was created by an Act of Congress in 1889 for "the advancement of science and the instruction and recreation of the people." Plans for the Zoo were drawn up by three extraordinary people: Samuel Langley, third Secretary of the
(5) Smithsonian Institution; William Temple Hornaday, noted conservationist and head of the Smithsonian's vertebrate division; and Frederick Law Olmstead, the premier landscape architect of his day. Together they designed a new zoo to exhibit animals for the public and to serve as a refuge for wildlife, such as bison and beaver, which
(10) were rapidly vanishing from the North American continent.

In its first half century, the National Zoo, like most zoos around the world, exhibited as many exotic species as possible. Animals were easy to capture in the wild, and just as easy to replace when they died. However, the number of many species in the wild be-
(15) gan to decline drastically, largely due to human activities. The fate of the earth's animals and plants became a pressing concern. Many of these species were favorite zoo animals, such as elephants and tigers.

In the early 1960s, the Zoo turned its attention to breeding and
(20) studying threatened and endangered species. Although some zoo animals had been breeding and raising young, no one knew why some species did so successfully and others didn't. In 1965 the zoological research division was created to study the reproduction, behavior, and ecology of zoo species, and learn how best to meet the
(25) needs of the animals. Later, in 1975, the Zoo established the Conservation and Research Center (CRC), thus renewing its original commitment to serve as a "refuge for vanishing wildlife." On 3,200 acres of Virginia countryside, rare species, such as Mongolian wild horses, scimitar-horned oryx, maned wolves, cranes, and other spe-
(30) cies live and breed in peaceful, spacious surroundings.

New knowledge about the needs of zoo animals and commitment to their well-being has changed the look of the National Zoo. Today, the animals live in natural groupings rather than alone and in cages. Rare and endangered species, such as golden lion
(35) tamarins, Sumatran tigers, and sarus cranes, breed and raise their young. Most notably, the National Zoo has been the home to giant pandas for thirty years. First Hsing Hsing and Ling Ling in 1972, and, since 2000, Mei Xiang and Tian Tian, have symbolized the Zoo's efforts to celebrate, study, and protect endangered spe-

(40) cies and their habitats. As the National Zoo nears its 115th anniversary, its mission to study, celebrate, and protect animals and their habitats is as vital as ever if humankind is to save what remains of the earth's biological diversity.

1. Which of the following is NOT part of the mission of the National Zoo?

    (1) Study animals
    (2) Protect the diversity of animals
    (3) Protect the habitats of animals
    (4) Celebrate animals
    (5) Create educational programs

2. The zoo was created by an Act of Congress to

    (1) give animals a place to live.
    (2) become a part of the Smithsonian Institute.
    (3) advance science and to teach people and give them a place to relax.
    (4) exhibit as many exotic species as possible.
    (5) study the impact of human activities on wildlife.

3. Based on the passage, the author likely believes that the National Zoo

    (1) is misguided in its mission and cannot make a difference for wildlife.
    (2) fails to address the needs of the community.
    (3) is a vital resource for the survival of many species.
    (4) must hire more qualified people if it is going to help wildlife.
    (5) is the best zoo in the world.

4. Why did the zoo begin focusing on threatened and endangered species?

    (1) The zoo wanted to renew its commitment to serve as a refuge for vanishing wildlife.
    (2) The zoo wanted to study why some species were unsuccessful at raising young in captivity.
    (3) President Nixon felt it was important to conserve wildlife and asked the zoo to help.
    (4) The community needed more educational programs for its citizens.
    (5) The zoo had 3,200 acres of land to use for these species.

5. Why are the giant pandas symbolic of the zoo's efforts?

    (1) The giant pandas are an endangered species that has desperately needed the services and protection of the National Zoo.
    (2) The giant pandas are an endangered species that everyone likes.
    (3) The giant pandas enjoy living at the zoo.
    (4) The giant pandas bring more visitors, and thus more revenue, to the zoo than any other species.
    (5) The giant pandas are a celebrated species in China.

Answers

1. **The correct answer is (5), Create educational programs.** Although the zoo does provide educational programs, there is no mention of this item in the mission statement of the zoo. See the second sentence of the first paragraph for the mission statement.

2. **The correct answer is (3), advance science and to teach people and give them a place to relax.** Each of the answer choices represents a goal for the zoo. However, only choice (3) is given as the reason Congress created the zoo. See the first sentence of the first paragraph to review the answer to this question.

3. **The correct answer is (3), is a vital resource for the survival of many species.** The author's tone throughout this passage is one of admiration for the National Zoo and its contribution to the survival of threatened and endangered species. Choices (1), (2), and (4) suggest that there are shortcomings with the current mission and function of the zoo. The author of this piece is never critical of the zoo's performance. Choice (5) may be true, but the author does not compare the National Zoo to other zoos in this article. None of the information in this passage supports this choice.

4. **The correct answer is (2), The zoo wanted to study why some species were unsuccessful at raising young in captivity.** The answer to this question is addressed in the third paragraph of the selection. The passage does mention that the zoo renewed its commitment to serving as a refuge for vanishing wildlife (1), but this renewal occurs with the establishment of the CRC in 1975. The zoo began to focus on threatened and endangered species in the early 1960s, fifteen years before the CRC. There is no mention of Nixon, choice (3), in the passage. Although the zoo has an abundance of land, choice (5), and educational programs, choice (4), these are not the reasons for the focus on specific species.

5. **The correct answer is (1), The giant pandas are an endangered species that has desperately needed the services and protection of the National Zoo.** There is no evidence in the passage to support any of the other answer choices. Since the information about the pandas is included in the same paragraph as endangered species like golden lion tamarins, Sumatran tigers, and sarus cranes, you can infer that pandas, also, are endangered.

Fact vs. Opinion

Some essays are meant to persuade the reader to feel a certain way or to take a certain action. A **persuasive essay** presents an argument and attempts to convince readers of a certain opinion. When reading an essay, just like other nonfiction text, you must separate the facts from the opinions. Readers sometimes assume that an idea in a nonfiction work is a fact when it is really just the writer's opinion. To figure out if a sentence is fact or opinion, ask yourself the following questions:

- Can this statement be proven true?
- Is this statement someone's personal belief?
- Can this statement be supported by factual evidence?

Read the following excerpt from a famous essay by Thomas Paine called "The Crisis, No. 1." Paine wrote many essays during the Revolutionary War that encouraged Americans to support the fight for independence, even during difficult times.

HOW CAN THIS MAN MAKE A CHANGE?

Line These are the times that try men's souls. The summer soldier and the sunshine patriot will, in this crisis, shrink from the service of his country. But he who stands NOW deserves the love and thanks of man and woman. Tyranny is not easily conquered. Yet
(5)   the harder the conflict, the more glorious the triumph. It would be strange indeed, if so *celestial* an article as FREEDOM should not be highly rated. Britain, with an army to enforce her tyranny, has declared that she has a right, not only to tax, but "to bind us in all cases whatsoever." If being bound in that manner is not sla-
(10) very, then there is no such thing as slavery upon Earth.

Before answering the questions on page 79, try to identify the areas where the author presents his *persuasive* points. How does he show you that this is an example of a *persuasive* essay?

_____
_____
_____

Answer

There are two (2) main places where the author shows his persuasive methods:

1. First of all, he opens the essay with an appeal to his readers' emotions:

   "These are the times that try men's souls. The summer soldier and the sunshine patriot will, in this crisis, shrink from the service of his country. But he who stands NOW deserves the love and thanks of man and woman."

   This shows the readers that the essay will be **asking** them to take a stand.

2. Then he provides history and facts, followed by an answer or comment:

   Britain, with an army to enforce her tyranny, has declared that she has a right, not only to tax, but "to bind us in all cases whatsoever." If being bound in that manner is not slavery, then there is no such thing as slavery upon Earth.

These are both elements of persuasion. He is trying to get his audience and readers to come to his way of thinking on the issue of British control of the colonies.

To persuade readers, authors must include **facts and examples** to support their opinions. As a reader, your job is to distinguish between fact and opinion in order to form your own opinions and ideas. Look at the following pair of quotes from the essay. Decide which is fact and which is Paine's opinion.

A. "These are the times that try men's souls."

B. "Britain, with an army to enforce her tyranny, has declared that she has a right, not only to tax, but 'to bind us in all cases whatsoever.'"

   Fact: _____   Opinion: _____

Answers

In this set of statements, **B** is the *fact* and **A** is the *opinion*. A fact is based on knowledge, statements that anyone can look up to be true. An opinion may be true to a majority of the population, but it is not a documented fact. In the above statements, it is documented and true that Britain attempted to tax and exert control over the American colonies.

Now it is time for some more GED practice questions. Answer the following questions based on the previous passage. Look back at the passage and reread it as necessary.

1. The word *celestial* most nearly means

    (1) difficult.

    (2) true.

    (3) free.

    (4) distant.

    (5) divine.

2. How does Paine summarize the relationship between the American colonies and Britain?

    (1) Britain has tried to enslave the people of the colonies by forcing them to pay unfair taxes.

    (2) The colonies have acted too quickly in declaring independence.

    (3) Britain has always been benevolent in its dealings with the colonies.

    (4) Britain's laws have always been fair and Godly.

    (5) The colonies want Britain to take care of them but Britain refuses.

3. What does Paine mean by the quote "The summer soldier and the sunshine patriot will, in this crisis, shrink from the service of his country."

    (1) Soldiers and patriots can only fight in the summer.

    (2) Soldiers and patriots who fight for the country only when things are good will run when things are difficult.

    (3) Soldiers and patriots who support the country when things are good will be proud to serve the country when things are difficult.

    (4) Sunshine is important to soldiers and patriots who serve the country.

    (5) The number of soldiers and patriots is getting smaller each day.

Answers

1. **The correct answer is (5), divine.** The context clue in the sentence is heaven. The word *celestial* means divine or perfect. Paine believes that freedom is a right given to all men by God.

2. **The correct answer is (1), Britain has tried to enslave the people of the colonies by forcing them to pay unfair taxes.** This is a direct summary.

3. **The correct answer is (2), Soldiers and patriots who fight for the country only when things are good will run when things are difficult.** A summer or sunshine friend is a person who is only your friend when things are going your way. These people often disappear when you are going through a rough time. Paine is comparing some soldiers and patriots to these so-called fair-weather friends. Choices (1) and (4) are incorrect because Paine is not making any real references to the weather. He is making a metaphorical statement. Choice (3) is exactly the opposite of what Paine states. Choice (5) is not at all supported by the passage.

- Biographies and autobiographies are two types of nonfiction that tell about a person's life.

- Essays are great tools for writers to reach people on an emotional level, to get the public to really connect to a topic. They use persuasion.

- To determine whether a statement is fact or opinion, look for what can be proven—if it can't be proven, it is opinion.

Magazine Articles

Magazine articles are an entertaining form of nonfiction because a magazine article must include information that will interest the reader. No matter what your interests are, there is a magazine out there for you: from tennis to car mechanics and from collecting dolls to raising ferrets.

Read the following passage, "From Our National Parks" by John Muir.

HOW DOES THIS MAN FEEL ABOUT THE GREAT OUTDOORS?

Line

Thousands of tired, nerve-shaken, over-civilized people are beginning to find out that going to the mountains is going home. Wildness is a necessity. Mountain parks and reservations are useful not only as fountains of timber and irrigating rivers, but as foun-

(5) tains of life. Awakening from the *stupefying* effects of the vice of over-industry and the deadly apathy of luxury, they are trying as best they can to mix and enrich their own little on goings with those of Nature, and to get rid of rust and disease. Briskly venturing and roaming, some are washing off sins and cares in all-day

(10) storms on mountains; sauntering in meadows; tracing rivers to their sources; jumping from rock to rock; and rejoicing in deep, long-drawn breaths of pure wildness. This is fine and natural and full of promise.

1. What does the author mean when he says that mountain parks and reservations are "fountains of life" (lines 4–5)?

   (1) They are full of places to get cool drinks of water.

   (2) They are places where people can go to relax and reflect on life.

   (3) They have a wide variety of wildlife for people to see.

   (4) They offer over-industry and luxury.

   (5) They are places where people are able to live.

2. According to the author, which of the following is NOT something people do in the wilderness parks?

   (1) Wash off their sins

   (2) Walk through meadows

   (3) Jump on rocks

   (4) Rid themselves of rust and disease

   (5) Hunt for wild game

3. According to the passage, the best synonym for the word *stupefying* (line 5) is

   (1) astonishing.
   (2) annoying.
   (3) lazy.
   (4) numbing.
   (5) irreversible.

4. Based on the information in the passage, there is a growing interest in

   (1) creating more industry near rivers.
   (2) creating pictures of scenery.
   (3) climbing rocks and trees.
   (4) preserving forests and wild parks.
   (5) living a life of luxury.

Answers

1. **The correct answer is (2), They are places where people can go to relax and reflect on life.** This answer is a conclusion you can draw from the facts that are presented in the passage. The author states that people are taking vacations to forests and parks to get away from the pressures of daily life. Nature rejuvenates the people and restores their sense of purpose and tranquility.

2. **The correct answer is (5), Hunt for wild game.** You must look at the details in the passage where the author refers to wilderness activities. He writes about all of the things that people can do when they visit forests and national parks. All of the other answer choices are listed in the passage. Although many people hunt in the forest, hunting in national parks is often prohibited. In addition, there is no support for choice (5) in the passage. Since the question asks you to find the answer that is NOT addressed in the passage, choice (5) is correct.

3. **The correct answer is (4), numbing.** Although *astonishing* is a synonym for *stupefying*, it is not the best answer. The author states that the visitors are "awakening" when they come to the forests and parks. In order for someone to awaken, he or she must have been asleep in some way. The author implies that the visitors are numb because of their experiences in the industrial world, which is why choice (4) is the best answer.

4. **The correct answer is (4), preserving forests and wild parks.** This answer can be inferred by all of the things that people are now doing in nature areas.

Did you notice that the same skills you learned in the fiction section help you on the nonfiction passages as well? For example, the passage above contains questions about detail, tone, vocabulary, and prediction. These skills were all taught in the fiction chapter. If at any time you feel that you are lost, go back and reread the fiction chapter to polish up your skills.

Media Review Articles

In today's world, time is valuable. Most people do not set out each morning planning to waste their time. This is one reason why there is such a huge market for media reviews. Almost every television show, movie, CD, or book ever created has been critiqued in magazines, newspapers, entertainment news shows, and the Internet.

As a reader, you need certain skills to maneuver through a review article. You must have the skills to summarize, separate facts from opinions, and recognize bias and tone. These are the skills you will focus on in this section while you read the following review.

Read the article and answer the questions that follow.

WHAT DID THESE STUDENTS DO DURING SUMMER VACATION?

Line   The annual Peru, Indiana, circus is under way, and it is well worth a visit if you find yourself in the northern part of the state. Since 1959, each July this small farming town transforms itself into a three-ring big top.

(5)   Prepare to be amazed by the nimble performers—and especially by the acrobats—as they combine athletics with artistic beauty. Their brightly colored costumes, covered in sequins and rhinestones, glitter and shine as the performers fly through the air with the greatest of ease. They balance on tightropes, swing (10) from trapezes, and build human pyramids of dizzying heights— more than three death-defying stories above the ground!

Sounds impressive, right? Well, consider this: There are no professional performers in this circus. They are all *amateurs*. In fact, the performers are all local teenagers who are putting their (15) summer vacation to good use. From the time the school year ends until the circus begins, you will be hard-pressed to find any of these Indiana children playing video games or watching TV. With the help of the adults in town (most of whom appeared in the circus when they were adolescents), more than two hundred kids (20) learn how to tumble, flip, and soar like the acrobats of the world-famous Ringling Brothers. The *culmination* of weeks of long, hard work is the annual circus, which is open to the public.

We've no doubt that you'll be inspired by these talented young people. But hurry! The circus is only in town for three more days, (25) and it won't return until next year!

1. Which of the following is the best synonym for the word *amateurs* in line 13?

    (1) Paid performer

    (2) One who performs as a hobby

    (3) One who admires professional performers

    (4) Unpaid performer

    (5) One who dislikes circuses

2. Why are the young people who are taking part in the circus unable to play video games?

    (1) They are busy practicing their skills for the circus.

    (2) They do not like playing video games as much as tumbling.

    (3) They are not allowed to play video games until the circus is over.

    (4) They do not own any video games.

    (5) They believe that playing video games decreases their skills as performers.

3. What type of community is Peru, Indiana?

    (1) Industrial

    (2) Farming

    (3) Suburban

    (4) Urban

    (5) Unknown

4. Which word is the best synonym for the word *culmination* in line 21?

    (1) Lowest point

    (2) Climax

    (3) Body

    (4) Heart

    (5) Brilliance

5. Why do people who wish to see the circus need to hurry?

    (1) Many of the performers are going back to school.

    (2) Many of the performers have been injured.

    (3) The circus is only in town for a short time.

    (4) The circus shows sell out quickly.

    (5) The weather is becoming too hot for the performers.

Answers

1. **The correct answer is (4), unpaid performer.** Paid performers, choice (1), are professionals, and the passage states that there are no professionals in the circus. Although the performers may be hobbyists who perform for fun, choice (2), or because they admire professional performers, choice (3), there is nothing in the passage to support these answers. It is obvious that the young people enjoy what they are doing, so, choice (5), is incorrect.

2. **The correct answer is (1), They are busy practicing their skills for the circus.** Playing video games may, in fact, result in a decrease of skills, choice (5), simply because the young people must practice in order to improve their skills, and playing video games would take away from their practice time. There is nothing in the passage to support any of the remaining choices.

3. **The correct answer is (2), Farming.** This answer is specifically stated in the second sentence of the passage.

4. **The correct answer is (2), Climax.** The culmination of the youths' hard work is the circus. The circus is the highest point, or peak, of the entire experience. Climax is another word for highest point.

5. **The correct answer is (3), The circus is only in town for a short time.** The passage indicates that the circus is in town only for three more days. There is no support for any of the other answer choices.

Recognizing Bias

Bias is a strong preference for one side or point of view. Bias can either be **for** or **against** something. A reviewer shows bias by using words that emphasize a positive or negative image of what is being reviewed. For example, at the beginning of the review, the author says that the circus is "well worth a visit." This shows that the author likes the circus and wants other people to see it.

Here are three phrases from the review. Which two phrases help show the reviewer's bias in favor of the Peru circus?

1. We've no doubt that you'll be inspired by these talented young people.
2. They balance on tightropes, swing from trapezes, and build human pyramids of dizzying heights—more than three death-defying stories above the ground!
3. This small farming town transforms itself into a three-ring big top.

Answer

(1) "We've no doubt" shows that the author believes anyone who sees this circus will be as inspired as she by the performers' skills.

(2) Instead of merely writing "more than three stories above the ground," the reviewer writes "death-defying." This is an example of excitement and positive bias.

(3) The third phrase shows no bias. It is pure fact.

Book Review

A book review usually discusses the plot and characters of a book along with how well the book is written. Reviewers want to create buzz about a book. They do this by critiquing the story as well as its author's styles and techniques. The reviewer must also be careful not to give away too much of the story. Otherwise, there would be no point in a customer buying the book! The reviewer's purpose is to give enough facts for the reader to make a decision about whether or not the book is worth a read.

Read the following book review about Jane Austen. Then answer the questions that follow.

HOW WAS SHE A PIONEER?

Line

Jane Austen lived a quiet and uneventful life in the English countryside. She didn't go to college, she wasn't a great traveler, and she didn't live among the great thinkers of her time. Like so many other early nineteenth-century women, she should have

(5) gone unnoticed by the world. However, Jane Austen wasn't like other women. Despite her limited view of the world, she managed to write six well-known novels: *Sense and Sensibility*, *Pride and Prejudice*, *Mansfield Park*, *Emma*, *Northanger Abbey*, and *Persuasion*.

(10) Austen once said, "I think I may boast to be, with all possible vanity, the most unlearned and uninformed female who ever dared to be an authoress." Her works prove just the opposite. She had a clear understanding of what makes people "tick." In her heroines, Jane Austen created literature's first realistic female

(15) characters. Yes, they all find love and live happily ever after, but Austen's characters are hardly the stuff of silly schoolgirl romances. These women are also human, with flaws, fears, and unrealized dreams. Who can forget Emma Woodhouse's flashes of cruelty when she makes fun of poor Miss Bates or snubs Jane

(20) Fairfax, or Elizabeth Bennett's uncivil behavior to Mr. Darcy? And let's not forget Anne Elliot, who caves to the pressure of her family and friends, and rejects Captain Wentworth's proposal of marriage because he has no fortune.

(25) Male writers had certainly created female characters prior to Austen, but none were able to do so as convincingly as Austen because they did not know what it meant to be a woman. With her groundbreaking novels, Austen paved the way for future generations of women to express themselves. Women like Toni Morrison, Flannery O'Connor, and Virginia Woolf stand on equal footings
(30) with the greatest male writers. Had a talented young woman not emerged onto the literary scene in 1811, their voices might never have been heard.

1. How does the author feel about Jane Austen and her works?

   (1) She believes Austen's contribution to literature is insignificant and does little to promote women's abilities.
   (2) She appreciates Austen's writing but does not really like it.
   (3) She dislikes her writing and cannot understand why Austen's works are celebrated.
   (4) She thinks men contributed more to female characters than Austen ever could have with her limited experience.
   (5) She believes that Austen's work is invaluable and created an environment in which other women authors could thrive.

2. What makes Jane Austen's female characters more realistic than other female characters of the time?

   (1) They are involved in schoolgirl romances.
   (2) They have flaws, fears, and unrealized dreams.
   (3) They do not allow the men in their lives to control their actions.
   (4) They all live happily ever after with the men of their dreams.
   (5) They do not submit to the pressure of their friends and family.

3. Which of the following is not listed as a character flaw demonstrated by one of Austen's characters?

   (1) Failing to learn from their mistakes
   (2) Flashes of cruelty
   (3) Making fun of others
   (4) Caving in to the pressure of family and friends
   (5) Rejecting proposals of marriage for materialistic reasons.

4. According to the author, why were female characters previously unconvincing?

   (1) The characters did not have compassion.
   (2) The characters were written by men.
   (3) The characters were all cruel.
   (4) The characters were uneducated and superficial.
   (5) The characters fell in love and lived happily ever after.

5. According to the passage, what was Jane Austen's opinion of her own writing?

   (1) She was proud of all of her works.
   (2) She was insecure and afraid to allow others to read her work.
   (3) She did not think she had enough education or experience to write well.
   (4) She thought that she could write as well as any man of her time.
   (5) She did not enjoy writing.

Answers

1. **The correct answer is (5), She believes that Austen's work is invaluable and created an environment in which other women authors could thrive.** The focus of this article is the author's belief that Jane Austen's work contributed to the evolution of female characters and allowed other women to express themselves through their writing. Because the author of this passage is praising Austen's work and her contribution to the literary world, the other answer choices do not make sense.

2. **The correct answer is (2), They have flaws, fears, and unrealized dreams.** The answer to this question is stated in second paragraph of the passage.

3. **The correct answer is (1), Failing to learn from their mistakes.** All of the other answer choices are mentioned in the second paragraph of the passage. The author writes, "Who can forget Emma Woodhouse's flashes of cruelty when she makes fun of poor Miss Bates or snubs Jane Fairfax, or Elizabeth Bennett's uncivil behavior to Mr. Darcy? And let's not forget Anne Elliot, who caves to the pressure of her family and friends, and rejects Captain Wentworth's proposal of marriage because he has no fortune."

4. **The correct answer is (2), The characters were written by men.** There is no evidence in the passage to support the idea that all of the characters lack compassion (1) or are cruel (3). There is also no support in the selection for the statement that the female characters were uneducated and superficial (4). The author of the passage does say that the female characters fall in love and live happily ever after; however, she does not say that this is what makes the characters unconvincing.

5. The correct answer is (3), She did not think she had enough education or experience to write well. The answer to this question is evident in the quote from Jane Austen that the author incorporates into the passage. "Austen once said, 'I think I may boast to be, with all possible vanity, the most unlearned and uninformed female who ever dared to be an authoress.'" This quote indicates that Austen did not have a great deal of confidence in her ability because she felt she lacked experience.

In the Workplace 3

Business-Related Documents

In the workplace, you are required to fill out forms and documents, read instructions, and understand material related to your job. Forms and documents provide ways to gather, organize, and communicate information. This section will focus on these two areas of nonfiction text.

Job Application

Most forms and documents contain small boxes for specific information. Take a careful look at a common workplace document on the following page: the job application.

Notice its organization: Section 1 collects information about the job the applicant is seeking; section 2 is for general information; section 3 is for work experience, and section 4 explains the company's Equal Opportunity policy.

XYZ, Inc.   Application for Employment

1 Position applied for: _____

Application for: Full-Time ☐   Part-Time ☐   Temporary ☐

How did you learn about XYZ?   Relative ☐   Friend ☐   Advertisement ☐   Other ☐

2

_____   _____   _____   _____
Last Name   First   Middle   Social Security Number

_____   _____   _____   _____   _____   _____
Address #   Street   City   State   Zip Code   Phone #

Date available for work: _____   Preferred shift: Day ☐   Evening ☐   Night ☐

Have you previously worked at XYZ?   Yes ☐   No ☐   If yes, when? _____

3 Work Experience   Start with most recent employer

Employer name _____   Dates: from _____ to _____

Address _____

Supervisor Name _____   Title _____   Phone # _____

Position held _____

Reason for leaving _____   Final Salary _____

Employer name _____   Dates: from _____ to _____

Address _____

Supervisor Name _____   Title _____   Phone # _____

Position held _____

Reason for leaving _____   Final Salary _____

4

Equal Opportunity Employer

XYZ is an employer committed to the principles of fair and equal employment opportunity. It is our policy to abide by and support all federal and state laws prohibiting employment discrimination based on race, color, creed, religion, sex, sexual orientation, marital status, national origin, age, or the mental or physical disability of an otherwise qualified applicant.

Read the section titles, headings, and instructions carefully and then answer the following questions.

1. In what section do you write whether you've worked for XYZ, Inc., before?

   _____

   _____

2. In what section do you write in the job position for which you're applying?

   _____

3. What box(es) would you check under "Date Available for Work" if your schedule allowed you to only work from 9 a.m. to 5 p.m.?

   _____

4. Name 3 ways in which XYZ, Inc., is prohibited from denying employment.

   _____

   _____

   _____

Answers

1. Look at the bottom of section 2. There are two boxes for you to mark whether you've worked at XYZ before.
2. You write your desired position in section 1 under "Position applied for."
3. You would need to check "Day" under the "Preferred shift" portion of section 2.
4. Section 5 states that the company will not discriminate against people based on their race, color, creed, religion, sex, sexual orientation, marital status, national origin, age, or mental or physical disability.

Fine Print

"Reading the fine print" is always important. Sometimes you sign up for a product over the phone or through the mail, and then you're sent items that you did not realize you even ordered. This might be a result of neglecting the fine print. It is important to read all terms, clauses, and conditions before signing up for anything. Look at the following example:

Apply for an internship with George III Clothing and you could be sent to New York where you'll spend 3 weeks learning from the fashion experts. Some students will even go on to work with the top designers in Milan and Paris for the Spring Fashion Event 2005.

No purchase necessary. 15 entrants win a summer study program. 3 of these winners receive a 1-week internship. Contest open to graduate students only between the ages of 21 and 30. Must be U.S. resident to win. You are not eligible if you are a relative of an employee of George III Clothing or a resident of Delaware. Contest ends 5/30/03. Restrictions apply. See www.KinggeorgeclothingIII.com for more details and rules.

IN THE WORKPLACE

1. What must you apply for in order to be eligible to win prizes?

2. Do you have to buy George III merchandise to be eligible?

3. Which of the following people is eligible to actually win the summer study program?

    (1) A 54-year old struggling designer from Florida
    (2) An 18-year old scholarship winner from New York
    (3) A 22-year old graduate student from Delaware
    (4) A 24-year old graduate student from Kentucky

4. Why can't the daughter of a sales associate win the contest?

5. Where can you go for further details?

6. How many people will actually win a trip to Milan or Paris?

Answers

1. You must apply for an internship with the company to win.
2. No, it says no purchase necessary to win.
3. Only choice (4) can win because of the criteria in small print. Choice (1) is too old. Choice (2) is too young. Choice (3) is from Delaware.
4. The rules in small print state that you cannot be related to any employee of the company.
5. The company's Web site will provide further information.
6. The fine print does not say that anyone will win this trip to Milan or Paris, just that "some people" will go on to work there. This is a deceptive tactic that gets people interested in the company, so make sure you always read the fine print!

NONFICTION

Amendments to Company Policy

Sometimes it is important to be aware of changes in a company's policies. Usually, the changes will be specified in a blurb at the top. Look at the following document and answer the questions that follow.

Effective January 1, 2005

(Changes are indicated in *italics*)

Days observed as holidays

XYZ, Inc., shall observe the following 12 paid holidays, as well as any other days designated as holidays by the Governor or by the President of the United States:

1. New Year's Day—January 1
2. *Martin Luther King Jr. Day*—Third Monday in January
3. George Washington Day—Third Monday in February
4. Memorial Day—Last Monday in May
5. Independence Day—July 4
6. Labor Day—First Monday in September
7. *Patriot's Day*—September 11
8. Columbus Day—Second Monday in October
9. Veteran's Day—November 11
10. Thanksgiving Day—Fourth Thursday in November
11. The day after Thanksgiving
12. Christmas Day—December 25

---

1. What is the date that these changes go into effect?

_____

2. What are the two new holidays?

_____

3. Are these holidays paid or unpaid?

4. What holiday is observed on the fourth Thursday in November?

5. How many holidays were previously observed in the year 2004?

Answers

1. The changes go into effect on January 1, 2005.
2. The two new holidays are Patriot's Day and Martin Luther King, Jr. Day.
3. They are all paid holidays.
4. Thanksgiving Day is observed then.
5. There were ten before the two new additions.

Brochures

Just as the internship advertisement from the last section attempts to persuade people to do something, a brochure is made to persuade people to accept an idea. Obviously, you should not believe everything you read, especially in a brochure. Use good judgment to decipher the messages they project.

Brochures can be useful, however, as sources of information. To get the best use out of them, read the titles, look through the headings, and make your decision about their issue after understanding their information.

The following brochure might be found sent home from a child's school to help parents help their children in reading.

SPEED READING

- **Comprehension**
- **Study Skills**

Program 5: For entering 6th–8th graders
Program 6: For entering 9th–11th graders

In these programs, your child will double her reading speed while improving reading comprehension from one to two whole grade levels.

She will learn the best way to study textbooks, take notes, prepare for tests, and develop her vocabulary. As a result, she will finish her school assignments in less time and get better grades.

This is your child's chance to learn the same speed-reading skills that we teach in our college-level program. Small classes allow us to individualize instruction to your child's needs.

Program 7: For entering 12th graders, college students, and adults

In this program, you will double your reading speed in textbooks and triple your speed in easy reading materials. In addition, you will learn comprehension, concentration, and retention techniques that will help you remember more.

You will learn the best way to study textbooks, take notes, prepare for tests, and develop your vocabulary. As a result, you will be able to finish school assignments in less time and get better grades.

Includes Lifetime Instruction Privilege: You may repeat Program 7 at any time in the future—for free!

For more information or to register:

Call 800-555-1234

7 a.m.–7 p.m. Mon.–Thurs., 7 a.m.–6 p.m. Fri, and 7 a.m.–1 p.m. Sat.

1. What is the main idea of the above brochure?
   _____
   _____
   _____

2. If your child is an 11th grader this year, what speed-reading program would she take over the summer?
   _____

3. How many grade levels do programs 5 and 6 claim to raise your child's abilities?
   _____

4. If you are an adult, which program will help you to better remember what you learn?
   _____

5. Which of the following would be the most useful time to call for more information?

   (1) Sunday at 1 p.m.
   (2) Monday at 9 a.m.
   (3) Friday at 7 p.m.
   (4) Saturday at 2 p.m.
   (5) Wednesday at 9 p.m.

6. Name three claims made about Programs 5 and 6.
   _____
   _____
   _____

Answers

1. Learning speed-reading will help you in other areas. Once you learn how to read quickly, skills like comprehension, studying, note taking, test preparation, vocabulary, concentration, and memory will improve.

2. An 11th grader would take Program 7 over the summer because she would be entering 12th grade at the end of the summer.

3. Programs 5 and 6 claim to improve your reading comprehension 1 to 2 grade levels.

4. An adult would take Program 7 in order to improve memory.

5. The phones are only open certain hours of certain days. Calling on Monday at 9 a.m. is the only choice that is included in the times on the brochure.

6. Programs 5 and 6 claim to double reading speed, improve comprehension 1 to 2 grade levels, and teach the best way to study, take notes, prepare for tests, and develop vocabulary. They also claim better grades and a faster completion time for schoolwork.

SECTION IV

Poetry and Drama

Poetry 4

Like other forms of writing, poetry (also known as verse) can be about anything. A poem packs all kinds of ideas, feelings, sounds, beats, and images into a few carefully chosen words. When reading a poem, you need to think about the themes as well as the poetic devices used to get its message across. Take a look at the following poem, which is known as a limerick.

> There once was a teacher in school,
> Who never obeyed any rules.
> She'd forgotten one day,
> To show up for her play,
> And now she is stuck serving gruel*.

---

*Gruel is made by boiling grain in milk or water, like porridge or oatmeal. It is usually served for breakfast and does not taste very good.

What is the main idea of the limerick above? A rebellious teacher forgot to show up at her play and now she has been demoted to serving horrible food instead of teaching.

Rhyme and Rhythm

Think of your favorite song. Did you know that a song is a poem set to music? Poems are also like music because they can **rhyme** and have a **rhythm**, or a beat. It is not necessary for a poem to have rhyme or rhythm, but you should be able to find patterns for both.

Read the following poem, "To My Dear and Loving Husband," by Anne Bradstreet, an early American poet. Listen for the poem's musical quality.

HOW MUCH DID SHE LOVE HER HUSBAND?

Line If ever two were one, then surely we.
　　　　If ever man were lov'd by wife, then thee.
　　　　If ever wife was happy in a man,
　　　　Compare with me, ye women, if you can.
(5)　　 I prize thy love more than whole Mines of gold
　　　　Or all the riches that the East* doth hold.
　　　　My love is such that Rivers cannot quench,
　　　　Nor ought but love from thee give recompence.
　　　　Thy love is such I can no way repay.
(10)　　The heavens reward thee manifold**, I pray.
　　　　Then while we live, in love let's so persevere
　　　　That when we live no more, we may live ever.

During the seventeenth century, when this poem was written, the East* (known today as Asia) was famous for luxurious products like silk and spices. Manifold** means many times.

Can you find a pattern of rhyme? Rhythm? To put it in another way, do you think that this poem could be made into a rap, chant, or song? Absolutely! This poem is made up of **couplets**, or pairs of lines. In each couplet, the last word in each line rhymes. The rhyme and rhythm contribute to the spirit of the poem and the spirit of Anne Bradstreet and her husband.

Another factor that contributes to the appeal of the poem is the rhythm. If you clapped your hands to each beat in a line, you would clap ten or eleven times. This means there are ten or eleven **syllables** in each line. There is also a pattern of stressed and unstressed syllables (they are loud, soft, loud, soft, loud, soft) in each line. Both the syllables and the stresses give the poem a beat, or rhythm.

The GED Language Arts, Reading test will contain poems that are rhythmic, like the one above, as well as poems that have no rhyme or rhythm. Your understanding of poetry will be deeper if you are aware of the techniques used by poets of both types of poems.

A **stanza** is a group of lines put together in a poem. They are like **paragraphs** in fiction. They are separated from each other by spaces in between them. When there are two lines only in a stanza, it is also called a **couplet**.

Now answer the following questions about "To My Dear and Loving Husband."

1. Which of the following best describes the way Anne Bradstreet feels about her husband?

    (1) She loves him but cannot live with him.

    (2) Her love is so strong that she will continue to love him, even after death.

    (3) Her love for her husband is unrequited, which causes her pain.

    (4) She wishes her husband would go away because she does not love him at all.

    (5) She would love her husband more if they had mines of gold.

2. According to the poem, what two personal qualities does Bradstreet's husband bring to her?

    (1) Worth and death

    (2) Love and companionship

    (3) Support and dreams

    (4) Freedom and value

    (5) Love and laughter

3. What is the best synonym for the word *recompetence* in line 8?

    (1) Compensate

    (2) Owe

    (3) Insult

    (4) Understood

    (5) Explained

4. Which of the following best summarizes the phrases in lines 1–4 that describe Bradstreet's love?

    (1) Bradstreet has found others who are in as much love as she.

    (2) Bradstreet is not as happy with her husband as she should be.

    (3) Bradstreet believes that the love in her marriage is one sided.

    (4) Bradstreet feels that her love for her husband surpasses the love all other people have.

    (5) Bradstreet wants a prize for staying with her husband for so long.

Answers

1. **The correct answer is (2), Her love is so strong that she will continue to love him, even after death.** The poet says, "I prize thy love more than whole Mines of gold" and "That when we live no more, we may live ever." She says that her husband's love means everything to her and that she hopes their love will continue even after they die. Choices (1), (3), and (4) are not supported by the poem. Choice (5) is expressly contradicted in the poem.

2. **The correct answer is (2), Love and companionship.** The poem describes the husband's love and attention toward his wife.

3. **The correct answer is (1), Compensate.** The word recompense means "to give an equivalent for; to compensate." The other answers do not explain this image of being covered in grief and rage.

4. **The correct answer is (4), Bradstreet feels that her love for her husband surpasses the love all other people have.** You can find this answer in three lines: "If ever two were one, then surely we" and "If ever wife was happy in a man/Compare with me, ye women, if you can." These two phrases refer to Bradstreet's belief that she is the happiest woman alive. The other answer choices do not appear in the poem.

Look at the following poem by William Shakespeare. Shakespeare was a British playwright and poet who lived in England from 1564 to 1616. His language is slightly different from what you are probably used to. But it is important for you to study this style of English because you might see a similar, old poem on the GED Language Arts, Reading Test.

WHERE IS THE FATHER?

"Full Fathom Five"

Line   Full fathom* five thy father lies,
        Of his bones are coral made,
        Those are pearls that were his eyes.
        Nothing of him doth fade
(5)   But doth suffer a sea change
        Into something rich and strange.
        Sea nymphs hourly ring his knell.**
        Ding-dong.
        "Hark! Now I hear them—ding-dong, bell."

---

*A fathom is a length of six feet, which is used to measure water depth.
**A knell is a funeral bell.

1. Can you detect a pattern of rhyme? Rhythm? Write what you know on the lines below:

___

> **The speaker is the voice of the poem.**

2. What do you think the speaker of "Full Fathom Five" is trying to say? What is the main idea?

___

Answers

1. **The correct answer is that there is one stanza to this poem.** The poem is written in a pattern of stressed and unstressed syllables that give it a beat. Lines 1 and 3 rhyme, lines 2 and 4 rhyme, lines 5 and 6 rhyme, and lines 7 and 9 rhyme.

2. **The correct answer is that the poem is about a man who has died at sea.** His body has decayed into something "rich and strange." The speaker is remembering the deceased.

Did you notice that Shakespeare used a different language than the one you are used to? There are two reasons for this. One, the poem was written 400 years ago, when words like "thy" and "doth" were used instead of "your" and "do." (Words like this also appear in Anne Bradstreet's poem, which was written a few decades after Shakespeare's poem, in the 1600s.) Also, it was written in a very poetic language, complete with metaphors, onomatopoeia, and alliteration. (We'll talk about these special kinds of language in a little while.) It is not important to know the specific names of these poetic devices for the GED Language Arts, Reading Test, but you must at least be aware that the language used in poems is different from everyday language.

- Poems are written in groups of lines called **stanzas**.
- The **speaker** is the voice of the person telling the poem.
- Poems are sometimes written with language that has **rhythm**, or beat, and **rhyming** words.

Poetic Devices

Now it is time to learn more about the language used in poems. Poets use techniques to make their message more interesting than it might be in a regular paragraph of prose writing. We call these techniques **poetic devices**. When done right, they make a strong point with their strange and unusual word choice.

Now look at the poem "Full Fathom Five" again.

"Full Fathom Five"

Line
Full fathom five thy father lies,
Of his bones are coral made,
Those are pearls that were his eyes.
Nothing of him doth fade
(5) But doth suffer a sea change
Into something rich and strange.
Sea nymphs hourly ring his knell.
Ding-dong.
"Hark! Now I hear them—ding-dong, bell."

Look at the first line. What letter repeats itself four times in one line? If you answered "F," you are correct. This is a form of expression that contributes to the beautiful language of the poem. It is called **alliteration**.

Now look again at the last two lines. What word is written twice? If you noticed that the word "ding-dong" repeats, then you are on your way to becoming a much better reader of poetry. Not only is the poet using **repetition**, which is a common device for making a strong point, but he also uses a strange word to represent a sound. When a word represents a sound, it is called **onomatopoeia**.

Look at the poem below by Edgar Allan Poe, a nineteenth-century American writer, for more examples of alliteration and onomatopoeia.

WHAT CAN BE HEARD?

"The Bells"

Line   Hear the sledges* with the bells—
        Silver bells!
        What a world of merriment their melody foretells!
        How they tinkle, tinkle, tinkle,
(5)   In the icy air of night!
        While the stars that oversprinkle
        All the heavens, seem to twinkle
        With a crystalline** delight;
        Keeping time, time, time,
(10)   In a sort of Runic rhyme, ***
        To the tintinnabulation**** that so musically wells
        From the bells, bells, bells, bells,
        Bells, bells, bells—
        From the jingling and the tinkling of the bells.

A sledge* is a sled that travels over ice and snow.
Crystalline** means clear or transparent.
A Runic rhyme*** is a poem that is mystical and obscure.
And tintinnabulation**** means the ringing of bells.

1. Many of the words in this poem represent sounds. Find three verbs that sound like bells:

   _____

2. Look at the length of the lines in the poem above. How do the lengths of the lines contribute to the effect of the poem on the reader?

   _____

   _____

Answers

1. Poe repeats many of the same words throughout the poem to represent sounds! Any of the following are correct: tinkle, oversprinkle, twinkle, and jingling.

2. Hopefully, you saw that the short lines give the poem momentum, or speed it up, and that the longer lines drag out the moment a bit longer. This makes it seem like the bells are playing a song.

Comparisons

Sometimes a poet makes his point by using words in unusual ways. You have already learned two examples of this, **alliteration** and **onomatopoeia**. What about the following lines by William Shakespeare:

Of his bones are coral made,

Those are pearls that were his eyes.

In those two lines, the poet is comparing bones to coral and eyes to pearls. These body parts are described in terms of items found in the water, since that is where the dead body lies. By using figurative language, Shakespeare makes a clear point that the body is lying dead in the ocean, but it can still be beautiful in the way it has adapted to its environment. The words "coral" and "pearl" paint a different picture of a dead body than what we usually think of.

Be on the lookout for poetic devices such as alliteration, onomatopoeia, and comparisons. Poets choose their words carefully for a reason. It is up to you, the reader, to figure out their messages.

Theme and Main Idea

Since a poem is a way for a poet to express himself or herself using words, then there must be a theme or main idea to every poem. That theme or main idea is the point of the poem. It answers the question, *Why was this written?* For the following poems, you will be asked to find the same poetic devices you have just learned, but now you must also find the main ideas.

Take a look at the poem "Dreams," by Paul Laurence Dunbar, a nineteenth-century poet. Then answer the questions that follow.

WHERE DO OUR DREAMS GO?

Line What dreams we have and how they fly
Like rosy clouds across the sky;
Of wealth, of fame, of sure success,
Of love that comes to cheer and bless;
(5) And how they wither, how they fade,
The waning wealth, the jilting jade—
The fame that for a moment gleams,
Then flies forever,—dreams, ah—dreams!

O burning doubt and long regret
(10) O tears with which our eyes are wet,
Heart-throbs, heart-aches, the glut of pain,
The somber cloud, the bitter rain,
You were not of those dreams—ah! well,
Your full fruition who can tell?
(15) Wealth, fame, and love, ah! love that beams
Upon our souls, all dreams—ah! dreams.

1. How does the first stanza of the poem differ from the second?

___

___

___

2. What is the speaker of the poem saying about dreams?

   (1) Dreams can never be taken away from a person.

   (2) Dreams of wealth and fame are the best dreams.

   (3) Unrealized dreams are a main cause of heartache and unhappiness in people.

   (4) Unrealized dreams are part of life; people must learn to accept disappointment.

   (5) Dreams never change.

3. What are some of the phrases that the poet uses to create a sad tone?

_____

_____

_____

4. What is the main goal of the speaker in this poem?

   (1) To create a fear of dreaming

   (2) To show respect for those who have dreamed and failed

   (3) To persuade others to dream

   (4) To show the importance of dreaming

   (5) To show that unrealized dreams are a main cause of heartache and unhappiness in people

Answers

1. The first stanza addresses the hopefulness and happiness associated with dreams. The second stanza addresses the pain of having an unrealized or destroyed dream.

2. **The correct answer is (3), Unrealized dreams are a main cause of heartache and unhappiness in people.** The speaker of the poem describes the pain created by dreams in the second stanza. He refers to tears, doubt, and regret. The speaker emphasizes this pain by using such words as *somber* and *bitter*.

3. The poem describes bitter rain, burning doubt, jilting jade, and glut of pain, all of which give it a sad tone.

4. **The correct answer is (5), Unrealized dreams are a main cause of heartache and unhappiness in people.** The speaker knows that once a dream has been lost, the dreamer is disappointed, sad, and frustrated. The goal of the speaker is to show how important dreams are in the creation of unhappiness.

Next we will use some classical poetry to discuss the main ideas in poems. Some themes remain true through all time: love, children, death, happiness, and hardships. These are all aspects of life in today's world, just as they were 100, 200, or even 1,000 years ago. Read the following poem by seventeenth-century English poet Andrew Marvell and answer the questions that follow.

WHAT WILL SHE SAY?
"To His Coy Mistress"

Line   Had we but world enough, and time,
          This coyness, lady, were no crime.
          We would sit down, and think which way
          To walk, and pass our long love's day.
(5)   Thou by the Indian Ganges* side
          Shouldst rubies find: I by the tide
          Of Humber** would complain. I would
          Love you ten years before the Flood,
          And you should, if you please, refuse
(10)   Till the conversion of the Jews.
          My vegetable love should grow
          Vaster than empires, and more slow.
          An hundred years should go to praise
          Thine eyes, and on thy forehead gaze:
(15)   Two hundred to adore each breast;
          But thirty thousand to the rest;
          An age at least to every part,
          And the last age should show your heart.
          For, lady, you deserve this state,
(20)   Nor would I love at lower rate.
            But at my back I always hear
          Time's winged chariot hurrying near:
          And yonder all before us lie
          Deserts of vast eternity.
(25)   Thy beauty shall no more be found;
          Nor, in thy marble vault, shall sound
          My echoing song: then worms shall try
          That long-preserved virginity,
          And your quaint honour turn to dust,
(30)   And into ashes all my lust.
          The grave's a fine and private place,
          But none, I think, do there embrace.
            Now therefore, while the youthful hue
          Sits on thy skin like morning dew,
(35)   And while thy willing soul transpires
          At every pore with instant fires,
          Now let us sport us while we may;
          And now, like amorous birds of prey,
          Rather at once our Time devour,

---

*The Ganges is a river in India that is considered sacred by Hindus.
**The Humber is a river in England.

(40) Than languish in his slow-chapt power.
Let us roll all out strength and all
Out sweetness up into one ball,
And tear our pleasures with rough strife
Through the iron gates of life.
(45) Thus, though we cannot make our sun
Stand still, yet we will make him run.

1. Look at the words used in the poem above. Since it was written nearly 350 years ago, some of the words might be unfamiliar. Write the unfamiliar words on the lines below.

   _____
   _____
   _____

2. Try to figure out the meaning of the unfamiliar words in question 1 by using context clues. Write your guesses on the lines below.

   _____
   _____
   _____

3. One easy way to find the **main idea** is to summarize a poem **stanza by stanza**. What is the main point in each of the three stanzas above? (Hint: You want to find one sentence that basically says it all for the entire 46 lines)

   Stanza 1 (20 lines):
   _____
   _____

   Stanza 2 (12 lines):
   _____
   _____

   Stanza 3 (14 lines):
   _____
   _____

4. Based on what you wrote above, what is the theme, or main message, of this poem?

   (1) Life goes on, even when you feel it will not.

   (2) Live for today; seize all opportunities.

   (3) Death is cruel.

   (4) Life is worth living if you are young.

   (5) There is always enough time for love.

Answers

1. and 2. Some example words and their translations include:

thou: you

shouldst: should

thine: your

yonder: somewhere away in the distance or future

honour: British spelling of honor

slow-chapt: a fancy way to say "slowly happening"

If you found any other words that you did not know, look them up in a dictionary to check your answers.

3. The speaker in this poem is a man talking to his girlfriend. In each stanza, he speaks directly to her.

Stanza 1: *You are worth waiting all the time in the world for to love.*

Stanza 2: *But we don't have all the time in the world.*

Stanza 3: *So let's enjoy our love and our lives while we're young and live them to the fullest.*

4. The correct answer is (2), Live for today; seize all opportunities. The Latin translation for "seize the day" is "*carpe diem*," a phrase often used to describe the message in this famous poem. The young man says to the woman that he would love to be able to have the time to wait for her and court her and spend thousands of years worshipping her, but they will not live forever. It would be a waste, he says, to let the worms be the only ones allowed to explore her body (after she dies and is buried in the ground, of course). This is his plea to gain physical intimacy from his coy mistress. (*Coy* means shy.)

After all that explanation and questioning, does the poem make more sense now? We hope so. Just study poems in pieces. When looking for the main idea, sum up each stanza first. That way you can keep track of where the theme is heading, and hopefully you will end up in the same place at the end!

Do not forget these important points about poetry:

- Poems are sometimes written in a language that has **rhythm**, or beat, and **rhyming** words.
- A **stanza** is a group of lines put together in a poem.
- When there are two lines only in a stanza, it is also called a **couplet**.
- The **speaker** is the **voice** of the poem.
- **Alliteration** is the repetition of a letter.
- When a sound is represented by a word, it is called **onomatopoeia**.
- There is a **theme**, or main idea, to every poem.

Drama 5

In drama, characters and plot are developed through dialogue and action. Dramas, also known as plays, are meant to be acted out in front of an audience, so they are written in **script** form. This looks very different from a story because it includes stage directions, narration, and dialogue between characters. The action in plays is written in the format of **scenes**. These scenes are sometimes grouped together into bigger **acts**. When a play is filled with humor, it is called a **comedy**. When it is more serious, it is referred to as either a **drama** or a **tragedy**.

Take a look at the following scene.

Line   **Annabel:** "But darling, can't we just agree to disagree?"
Thomas: "Not about something this big, Annabel." (*Thomas walks toward the front door, takes his coat off the rack and looks back at* Annabel.)
(5)   **Annabel:** (*Crying.*) "Thomas! Just let me . . ."
Thomas: (*Cutting her off.*) "I've let you, a thousand times I've let you. Goodbye Annabel." (*Thomas exits stage left. Annabel is left on the living room bench, sobbing.*)

This excerpt tells the reader a lot about the play. For example, is it most likely a comedy or a drama? Who are two of the characters? What is their history? Who makes the decision to leave? Where are they? All these questions can be answered from a mere six lines of dialogue and stage direction:

- The play is probably a drama.
- Two of the characters are named Annabel and Thomas.
- They have known each other for a long time.
- Thomas makes the decision to leave.
- They're in a house.

It is just as interesting as a story; the only difference is that a drama is told in a completely different way!

Understanding a Drama

A play is a story, just like the fiction we read in Part II of this book. But plays are written to be acted out among the characters. They use dialogue and stage direction to show the action. When you read a play, you must pay attention to where the characters are and what they are doing as much as what they say.

Plays come in different forms. There are comedies that make you laugh, dramas and tragedies that make you cry, classics that teach you about history, and social dramas that make you think about the world in which you live.

Before reading a play, think about the following points:

- What are the names of the characters?
- Where are they and what are they doing at the beginning of the play?
- What is the setting? (This means **where** does it take place and **when** does it take place.)

Since a play does not have a lot of setup and build-up (what we call **exposition** in a story), you will need to get yourself organized *while* you are reading a play. Don't be afraid to make notes in the margins of your test booklet. One major difficulty in answering questions about plays comes from when the reader skims over the stage directions or narration. These are very important!

Comedy

While reading a comedic play (or any play for that matter), keep in mind that plays are meant to be acted on a stage. Pay close attention to where the characters are when they are speaking. Turn it into a movie in your head. Often the comedy comes from what a character is *doing*, not *saying*. Also pay attention to the dialogue. This is especially necessary with playwrights who use **puns**, which means they sometimes play with words. For example:

> *After the car got a flat tire on our trip, dad said that we would have to retire.*

The family had to retire (or take a break) from their trip, at least for a little while, because of the flat tire. They would also have to replace the tire, or "retire" the car to get it fixed. This is a play on words.

Usually the main characters in a comedy are also involved in a serious issue. They deal with the seriousness of the situation with humor. Sometimes people prefer comedies to the more serious tones of everyday life.

Read the following play, which is based on an old English story, *King John and the Abbot of Canterbury*. Then answer the questions that follow.

WILL HE GET THE QUESTIONS RIGHT?

Scene IV

Throne room in KING JOHN'S *palace. Appropriate lavish furnishings, with throne in conspicuous position, placed obliquely to the audience. King John sits on the throne. The First Nobleman and Second Nobleman stand behind him. The Shepherd, disguised as Abbot stands facing the king.*

King John: (*Sneering.*)"Welcome, Sir Abbot, welcome. Just two weeks to the day since your last visit."(*Shepherd bows.*)

First Nobleman: (*With sarcasm.*)"The Abbot has, no doubt, spent the full two weeks studying His Majesty's questions."

(5) **Shepherd:** (*Bowing.*)"Yes. With most careful consideration."

Second Nobleman: (*With derision.*)"And, no doubt, with his careful consideration, the Abbot has found answers to all the questions."

Shepherd: (*Bowing.*)"Yes. Answers to all three questions."

(10) **King John:** (*Nettled.*)"Indeed. Indeed. And you know that failure to answer will cost you your life? You must ask no more leniency of me. A bargain's a bargain and should be kept fair and square. All the world may bear witness that I'm always fair."

Shepherd: (*Bowing.*)"Thank you, your Majesty, for so proper a
(15) suggestion."

King John: (*Astonished.*)"Suggestion? What *suggestion* did I make?"

Shepherd: (*Bowing.*)"But we need hardly call on all the world to bear witness in this case. It is sufficient to have present the three
(20) friends who came with me. May they be summoned here, your Majesty?"

King John: (*In anger.*)"What, sir? Did you bring witnesses?"

First Nobleman: (*Drawing close to the king.*)"Your Majesty's title to the Abbey will be the better established. And the justice of the
(25) sentence more plainly proved."

King John: (*Dubiously.*)"True. Entirely true. Let the Abbot's friends be summoned." (*First Nobleman goes out left.*)
(*Nodding.*)"Your three friends—all the world—it matters not to me who bears witness."

(30) **First Nobleman:** (*Entering from left, followed by the Regent of Cambridge, the Regent of Oxford, and the Abbot, disguised in the Shepherd's cloak and hood.*)"Your Majesty, the Regent of Cambridge."(*Who bows.*)"The Regent of Oxford."(*Who bows.*)"And the simple Shepherd you once saw before."(*Who bows.*)

(35) **King John:** (*Leaning forward.*) "Ah ha, the Shepherd. Well, no more ado. Our business must proceed. Now, then, Sir Abbot, it is understood. If you fail to answer my three questions, you shall lose your head, your wealth shall be mine."
Shepherd: (*Nodding assent.*) "And if, your Majesty, I give you an-
(40) swers, then my life is to be spared, and my estate remain my own."
King John: (*Turning to look at the witnesses.*) "Yes, that is the bargain as it stands." (*To Shepherd.*) "Now, then, the questions. Tell me, Sir Abbot, to the day, *How Long Shall I Live?*"
(45) **Shepherd:** (*Slowly, with great solemnity.*) "You shall live until the day that you die, and not one day longer. And you shall die when you take your last breath, and not one moment before."
King John: (*Baffled and uncertain.*) "You are witty, indeed. But we will let that pass, and say that your answer is right. And now
(50) tell me this: *How Soon May I Ride Round the Whole World?*"
Shepherd: (*Profoundly.*) "You must rise with the sun, and you must ride with the sun until it rises again the next morning. As soon as you do that, you will find that you have ridden round the whole world in twenty-four hours."
(55) **King John:** (*Smiling with reluctance.*) "Indeed, Sir Abbot, you are not only witty, you are wise. I had not myself thought that so long a journey could take so little time." (*Then leaning forward, sternly.*) "But enough. As you value your life, no more jesting. Tell me this if you can. *What Do I Think?*"
(60) **Shepherd:** (*Pauses, as if lost in thought; then stepping forward.*) "You *think*, your Majesty, you *think*—that I am the Abbot of Canterbury."
King John: (*In triumph.*) "Ha, I *know* it. Knowing is not the same as thinking. You've not told me what I *think*."
(65) **Shepherd:** (*Interrupting.*) "But, your Majesty, look." (*Throws off gown and pulls the beard away.*) "Not the Abbot am I. But only his shepherd." (*King John laughs in spite of himself, then laughs more loudly, and all present join in.*) (*Stepping nearer the throne.*) "Forgive me, your Majesty. I came in the hope that the Ab-
(70) bot would be saved. A bargain's a bargain."
King John: (*Breaking in.*) "Which I'll keep fair and square as all can bear witness. Your wit has served both you and the Abbot. Four pieces of silver each week shall be yours life long."
Shepherd: (*Bowing.*) "My thanks, your Majesty. But the Abbot?
(75) Do you pardon the Abbot?"
King John: (*Turns and looks at the witnesses; then turns to look at each Nobleman; then nods slowly.*) "For the Abbot, a free pardon from the King." (*Curtain falls.*)

1. What are the three questions the King has given to Sir Abbot?

   _____
   _____
   _____

2. What are the consequences of getting the questions wrong? What are the rewards to getting the questions correct?

   _____
   _____
   _____

3. How does the Abbot outwit King John?

   (1) He answers his first two questions with logic and tricks King John on the third question.
   (2) He makes a fast getaway and leaves his shepherd to suffer the consequences.
   (3) He convinces King John that his questions are unanswerable.
   (4) He uses mathematicians and scholars to answer the questions scientifically.
   (5) He quickly leaves when the King isn't looking.

4. At first, what is the attitude of the Noblemen toward the Shepherd (who they think is Sir Abbot)?

   (1) Condescending
   (2) Fearful
   (3) Considerate
   (4) Gracious
   (5) Intimidated

Answers

1. The three questions are:

   How long shall I live?

   How soon may I ride round the whole world?

   What do I think?

2. If Sir Abbot gets a question wrong, he will be put to death and his land and riches will become the property of the King. If Sir Abbot gets the three questions right, he will get to keep his land, his riches, and his life.

3. **The correct answer is (1), He answers his first two questions with logic and tricks King John on the third question.** He does not do any of the four other answer choices.

4. **The correct answer is (1), Condescending.** The play states that the Noblemen speak to the Shepherd with "derision," which means they are laughing at his expense. They do not think he will be successful in answering the questions. Therefore, they think the Shepherd is a lesser person than themselves. This feeling can be summarized by the feeling of condescension.

Tragedy

One of the most famous playwrights in history is William Shakespeare. Shakespeare wrote in England, as you learned earlier. Besides poems, he wrote comedies, dramas, and histories. Shakespeare wrote some tragedies that you might be familiar with: *Romeo and Juliet*, *Hamlet*, and *Macbeth* are three of his most famous. To understand what a tragedy is, think about what all these plays have in common. Each play ends with the death of the main character or characters, and each death is the result of a misunderstanding, a miscommunication, or a tragic character flaw. Some tragedies contain all three disastrous elements. Here, for example, is a quick summary of *Romeo and Juliet*:

> *Romeo and Juliet fall in love, but their families hate each other so they cannot tell anyone. Juliet's cousin accidentally kills Romeo's friend, Mercutio, while trying to kill Romeo. Romeo kills Juliet's cousin because he has to avenge Mercutio's death. Romeo is sent into exile. Romeo kills himself when he believes Juliet is dead. He does not know that she isn't really dead. When Juliet finds Romeo's body, she kills herself.*

When dealing with tragedies, you must look for examples of tragedy. In other words, look for ways that the main character or characters cannot succeed because of circumstances beyond their control. You will need to draw conclusions, make inferences, and pay attention to detail, just as you would if you were reading a piece of fiction.

Read the following excerpt from the play *The Diary of Anne Frank* and answer the questions that follow. This tragedy takes place during World War II and is based on the real-life story of Anne Frank and her family, who hid from the Nazis because they were Jewish. This is from the beginning of the play.

HOW HAS ANNE'S LIFE CHANGED?

Line   **Mr. Frank:** Annele, there's a box there. Will you open it? (*He indicates a carton on the couch. Anne brings it to the center table. In the street below there is the sound of children playing.*)

Anne: (*As she opens the carton.*) "You know the way I'm going to
(5) think of it here? I'm going to think of it as a boardinghouse. A very peculiar summer boardinghouse, like the one that we—"(*She breaks off as she pulls out some photographs.*) "Father! My movie stars! I was wondering where they were! I was looking for them this morning . . . and Queen Wilhelmina! How wonderful!"

(10) **Mr. Frank:** "There's something more. Go on. Look further."(*He goes over to the sink, pouring a glass of milk from a thermos bottle.*)

Anne: (*Pulling out a pasteboard-bound book.*) "A diary!"(*She throws her arms around her father.*) "I've never had a diary. And I've always
(15) longed for one."(*She looks around the room.*)"Pencil, pencil, pencil, pencil."(*She starts down the stairs.*)"I'm going down to the office to get a pencil."

Mr. Frank: "Anne! No!"(*He goes after her, catching her by the arm and pulling her back.*)

(20) **Anne:** (*Startled.*)"But there's no one in the building now."

Mr. Frank: "It doesn't matter. I don't want you ever to go beyond that door."

Anne: (*Sobered.*) "Never . . . ? Not even at nighttime, when everyone is gone? Or on Sundays? Can't I go down and listen to the ra-
(25) dio?"

Mr. Frank: "Never. I am sorry, Anneke. It isn't safe. No, you must never go beyond that door."(*For the first time Anne realizes what "going into hiding" means.*)

Anne: "I see."

(30) **Mr. Frank:** "It'll be hard, I know. But always remember this, Anneke. There are no walls, there are no bolts, no locks that anyone can put on your mind. Miep will bring us books. We will read history, poetry, mythology."(*He gives her the glass of milk.*)"Here's your milk."(*With his arm about her, they go over to the couch, sit-
(35) ting down side by side.*)"As a matter of fact, between us, Anne, being here has certain advantages for you. For instance, you remember the battle you had with your mother the other day on the subject of overshoes? But in the end you had to wear them?

(40) Well now, you see, for as long as we are here you will never have to wear overshoes! Isn't that good? And the coat you inherited from Margo, you won't have to wear that anymore. And the piano! You won't have to practice on the piano. I tell you, this is going to be a fine life for you!"

(45) *(Anne's panic is gone. Peter appears in the doorway of his room, with a saucer in his hand. He is carrying his cat.)*

Peter: "I . . . I . . . I thought I'd better get some water for Mouschi before . . ."

Mr. Frank: "Of course."

1. How does Anne trick herself at first about "going into hiding"?

   (1) She pretends she is on vacation.

   (2) She pretends she is at a boardinghouse.

   (3) She brings her friends with her.

   (4) She brings her cat.

   (5) She tells herself it is only for one week.

2. Anne loves and trusts her father. How does he help her feel less afraid?

   (1) He lets her play downstairs.

   (2) He stays up with her late at night.

   (3) He brings Anne her movie star pictures and a diary.

   (4) He cooks Anne her favorite meal.

   (5) He makes her bedroom look exactly like her room at home.

3. Which of the following events from the excerpt supports the idea that Anne is happy to receive a diary?

   (1) Anne is pretending that she is in a boardinghouse.

   (2) Anne is a hard worker and receives A's in English class.

   (3) Anne has kept a diary previously.

   (4) Anne is sad that she can't go downstairs.

   (5) Anne immediately looks for a pencil.

4. What does Mr. Frank mean by "there are no walls, there are no bolts . . ."

   (1) The door to the hiding place will be left open.

   (2) No one will be able to hold them inside because there are no bolts.

   (3) No one is able to put a stop to their learning while in hiding.

   (4) No one can stop them from building while in hiding.

   (5) The library has no lock on its door.

Answers

1. **The correct answer is (2), She pretends she is at a boardinghouse.** Anne tells herself in the beginning that she is going to pretend like she is at a strange summer boardinghouse. Choice (1) is not specific enough because she actually states that it is a boardinghouse she will pretend to be at. Choices (3) and (5) are not in the excerpt. Choice (4) is not the answer because the cat does not belong to Anne.

2. **The correct answer is (3), He brings Anne her movie star pictures and a diary.** You can clearly see that she is unpacking items her dad brought for her. He does not imply or state that he is going to do any of the other answer choices.

3. **The correct answer is (5), Anne immediately looks for a pencil.** Anne states that she's never had a diary, so choice (3) is incorrect. She is sad that she cannot go downstairs, so choice (4) is true. However, it does not directly show her fondness for her new diary. Choice (1) is also not relevant to her diary. Choice (2) is not stated in the excerpt. Only choice (5) makes sense as support of Anne's excitement over the diary.

4. **The correct answer is (3), No one is able to put a stop to their learning while in hiding.** Mr. Frank states, "There are no walls, there are no bolts, no locks that anyone can put on your mind. Miep will bring us books. We will read history, poetry, mythology." He is trying to show Anne that although they are locked up and cannot leave their hiding place, there is no limit to what they can read and learn. There is no restriction to their learning. The other choices are not supported by the excerpt.

Social Drama

Some plays deal with major social issues. Plays of this type have central conflicts such as prejudice, big corporate morals, class laws, peace, or just about any other topic that you might hear about on the nightly news. The problems are not always solved in the play. Instead, the playwright makes a comment to society about the issue. Social dramas might be humorous or serious in their approach to the conflict, or they might be a combination of the two styles.

Do not forget to take notes on these important points when you are working with a play:

- What are the names of the characters?
- Where are they and what are they doing at the beginning of the play?
- What is the setting? (This means **where** does it take place and **when** does it take place.)
- What motivates the characters?

Read the following excerpt from *A Doll's House* by Henrik Ibsen, a late nineteenth-century writer. Pay attention to the dialogue, actions, and character motivations. Then answer the questions that follow.

WHAT DOES THIS MAN WANT?

Line

Krogstad: (*Controlling himself.*) "Listen to me, Mrs. Helmer. If necessary, I am prepared to fight for my small post in the Bank as if I were fighting for my life."

Nora: "So it seems."

(5) **Krogstad:** "It is not only for the sake of the money; indeed, that weighs least with me in the matter. There is another reason—well, I may as well tell you. My position is this. I daresay you know, like everybody else, that once, many years ago, I was guilty of an indiscretion."

(10) **Nora:** "I think I have heard something of the kind."

Krogstad: "The matter never came into court; but every way seemed to be closed to me after that. So I took to the business that you know of. I had to do something; and, honestly, I don't think I've been one of the worst. But now I must cut myself free

(15) from all that. My sons are growing up; for their sake I must try and win back as much respect as I can in the town. This post in the Bank was like the first step up for me—and now your husband is going to kick me downstairs again into the mud."

Nora: "But you must believe me, Mr. Krogstad; it is not in my

(20) power to help you at all."

Krogstad: "Then it is because you haven't the will; but I have means to compel you."

Nora: "You don't mean that you will tell my husband that I owe you money?"

(25) **Krogstad:** "Hm!—suppose I were to tell him?"

Nora: "It would be perfectly infamous of you. (*Sobbing*.) To think of his learning my secret, which has been my joy and pride, in such an ugly, clumsy way—that he should learn it from you! And it would put me in a horribly disagreeable position."

(30) **Krogstad:** "Only disagreeable?"

Nora: (*Impetuously*.)"Well, do it, then!—and it will be the worse for you. My husband will see for himself what a blackguard you are, and you certainly won't keep your post then."

Krogstad: "I asked you if it was only a disagreeable scene at (35) home that you were afraid of?"

Nora: "If my husband does get to know of it, of course he will at once pay you what is still owing, and we shall have nothing more to do with you."

Krogstad: (*Coming a step nearer*.)"Listen to me, Mrs. Helmer. Ei-
(40) ther you have a very bad memory or you know very little of business. I shall be obliged to remind you of a few details."

Nora: "What do you mean?"

Krogstad: "When your husband was ill, you came to me to borrow two hundred and fifty pounds."

(45) **Nora:** "I didn't know anyone else to go to."

Krogstad: "I promised to get you that amount."

Nora: "Yes, and you did so."

Krogstad: "I promised to get you that amount, on certain conditions. Your mind was so taken up with your husband's illness, and
(50) you were so anxious to get the money for your journey, that you seem to have paid no attention to the conditions of our bargain. Therefore it will not be amiss if I remind you of them. Now, I promised to get the money on the security of a bond which I drew up."

(55) **Nora:** "Yes, and which I signed."

Krogstad: "Good. But below your signature there were a few lines constituting your father a surety for the money; those lines your father should have signed."

Nora: "Should? He did sign them."

(60) **Krogstad:** "I had left the date blank; that is to say, your father should himself have inserted the date on which he signed the paper. Do you remember that?"

Nora: "Yes, I think I remember . . ."

128 POETRY AND DRAMA

> Take a minute to think about what you have read. Summarize the previous action in a couple of sentences:
>
> _____
> _____
> _____
>
> Once you understand what is happening in the scene, answer the following questions.

1. Krogstad's real occupation is probably which of the following?

    (1) A banker

    (2) A loan shark

    (3) A doctor

    (4) A salesman

    (5) A con artist

2. Why is Nora indebted to Krogstad?

    (1) Her father needed the money for an operation.

    (2) She needed to buy some new furniture.

    (3) She needed money when her husband was sick.

    (4) She is greedy.

    (5) She likes to spend money without her husband's knowledge.

3. What does Krogstad want Nora to do for him?

    (1) Pay him the money she owes

    (2) Buy her husband an expensive gift

    (3) Kill her husband

    (4) Talk to her husband about allowing Krogstad to keep his job

    (5) Get her father's signature on some legal documents

4. Based on the information in the play, which of the following statements is true about Nora?

    (1) She is an evil woman who lies to her husband.

    (2) She is in love with Krogstad.

    (3) She wishes her husband would have died from his illness.

    (4) She allows her father to tell her what to do.

    (5) She is a generally nice woman whose good intentions place her in trouble.

Answers

1. **The correct answer is (2), A loan shark.** From the conversation, you should have been able to deduce that Krogstad has lent Nora money illegally and dishonestly.

2. **The correct answer is (3), She needed money when her husband was sick.** Krogstad states this almost exactly. None of the other answer choices are supported by the play.

3. **The correct answer is (4), Talk to her husband about allowing Krogstad to keep his job.** Krogstad tells Nora that he is worried about keeping his "post at the Bank." Despite Krogstad's plea, Nora does not wish to speak with her husband about allowing Krogstad to keep his job. Her refusal to intervene on his behalf angers Krogstad, and he resorts to blackmail.

4. **The correct answer is (5), She is a generally nice woman whose good intentions place her in trouble.** You can tell that Nora's original intentions were good because she borrows money in order to help her sick husband. It is obvious that her desperation to help her husband has caused her to do something she normally would not. As a result she is in great trouble with Krogstad, who seems to be a desperate and dangerous man. This play can be seen as social commentary because it attacks the values of a society and it exposes flaws such as greed and deception. Plays like this are popular because society likes to debate its issues in interesting formats. A social drama is one such forum for exposing the social conflicts of the times.

SECTION V

Reevaluating Your Skills

Posttest 1

The time has come to test the skills you have learned. When you are finished and have checked your answers, go back and review any areas in which you need more help. The following test is structured just like a real GED Language Arts, Reading Test. The only difference, though, between a real test and this one is that here, the answers are provided. Good luck!

Questions 1–5 refer to the following passage from the short story "Paul's Case," by Willa Cather.

WHY IS THIS BOY IN TROUBLE?

Line   It was Paul's afternoon to appear before the faculty of the Pittsburgh High School to account for his various misdemeanors. He had been suspended a week ago, and his father had called at the Principal's office and confessed his perplexity about his son. Paul
(5)   entered the faculty room suave and smiling. When questioned by the Principal as to why he was there, Paul stated, politely enough that he wanted to come back to school. This was a lie, but Paul was quite accustomed to lying; found it, indeed, indispensable for overcoming friction.
(10)   His teachers were asked to state their respective charges against him. Disorder and *impertinence* were among the offenses named, yet each of his instructors felt that it was scarcely possible to put into words the real cause of the trouble, which lay in a sort of defiant manner of the boy's; in the contempt which they all knew he
(15)   felt for them, and which he made not the least effort to conceal. Once, when he had been making a synopsis of a paragraph at the blackboard, his English teacher had stepped to his side and attempted to guide his hand. Paul had started back with a shudder and thrust his hands violently behind him. The astonished woman
(20)   could scarcely have been more hurt and embarrassed had he struck at her. The insult was so involuntary and definitely personal as to be unforgettable. In one way and another he had made all his teachers, men and women alike, conscious of the same feeling of physical aversion. In one class he habitually sat with his hand

(25) shading his eyes; in another he always looked out of the window; in another he made a running commentary on the lecture, with humorous intention.

His teachers felt this afternoon that his whole attitude was symbolized by his shrug and his flippantly red carnation flower,
(30) and they fell upon him without mercy, his English teacher leading the pack. He stood through it smiling, his pale lips parted over his white teeth. (His lips were continually twitching, and he had a habit of raising his eyebrows that was contemptuous and irritating to the last degree.) Older boys than Paul had broken down
(35) and shed tears under that baptism of fire, but his set smile did not once desert him, and his only sign of discomfort was the nervous trembling of the fingers that toyed with the buttons of his overcoat, and an occasional jerking of the other hand that held his hat. Paul was always smiling, always glancing about him,
(40) seeming to feel that people might be watching him and trying to detect something. This was usually attributed to insolence or "smartness."

1. What is the main idea of the passage?
   (1) People who are disrespectful toward their teachers should be expelled from school.
   (2) People who do not perform as others expect are often disliked and misunderstood.
   (3) When parents cannot handle their children, the children should be sent away to school.
   (4) Processes for dealing with discipline problems at school must be changed.
   (5) Society often expects its members to conform to certain behaviors.

2. Why was Paul suspended?
   (1) He struck a teacher.
   (2) He stole an opal pin from his roommate.
   (3) He disobeyed his teachers and failed to conceal his hatred of them.
   (4) He made jokes throughout one of his teacher's lectures.
   (5) He personally insulted his teachers and refused to work.

3. Why does Paul lie about wanting to come back to school?
   (1) He wants to please his father.
   (2) He genuinely wants to stay in school.
   (3) Although he does not like school, he likes his teachers and friends
   (4) He wants to overcome the conflict in this situation.
   (5) He wanted to prove to the older boys that he could win this case.

4. Which of the following is the best synonym for the word *impertinence* as it is used in the passage?

   (1) Disrespect

   (2) Imperfection

   (3) Disregard

   (4) Violence

   (5) Impatience

5. The main conflict in the passage is between Paul and

   (1) his father.

   (2) his English teacher.

   (3) the principal.

   (4) himself.

   (5) the entire school community.

Questions 6–10 are based on the following excerpt from a biographical article on George Gershwin, a famous American composer.

WHY IS THIS MAN SO POPULAR?

Line

The American composer, George Gershwin, was born in 1898 in Brooklyn, New York, the son of Russian-Jewish immigrants. He began playing music at age 11, when his family bought a second-hand piano for his older brother, Ira. However, George surprised every-

(5) one when he played a popular song, which he had taught himself by following the keys on a neighbor's player piano. His parents decided that George should receive lessons, too. He studied with a famous music teacher, Charles Hambitzer. He was so impressed with Gershwin's talent that he gave him lessons for free.

(10) Gershwin dropped out of school at age 15 and earned a living by making piano rolls for player pianos and by playing in New York nightclubs. His most important job in this period was his work as a song plugger. Song pluggers advertised sheet music of popular songs by playing and singing those songs in stores. At that time,

(15) sheet-music sales were the measure of a song's popularity. Song pluggers had to work long hours for the music publishers who employed them. As a result of his hard work, Gershwin's piano technique improved greatly. While still in his teens, Gershwin became known as one of the most talented pianists in New York City. As a

(20) result, he worked as an *accompanist* for popular singers and as a rehearsal pianist for Broadway musicals.

His knowledge of jazz and popular music grew quickly, and one of his songs was included in the Broadway musical *The Passing Show of 1916*. George became friends with many promi-

(25) nent Broadway composers. He particularly admired the music of Irving Berlin. In 1919, entertainer Al Jolson performed Gershwin's song *Swanee* in the musical *Sinbad*. The song became a hit, and Gershwin became an overnight celebrity. His song sold more than 2 million recordings and a million copies of
(30) sheet music.

6. According to the article, how was the popularity of songs measured?

    (1) Billboard Top 20
    (2) Record sales
    (3) Radio play
    (4) Sheet-music sales
    (5) Gallop Poll

7. Which of the following does the article say is part of Gershwin's success?

    (1) His wife is very supportive.
    (2) He is able to show the world through a kid's eyes.
    (3) His father was able to help him get a job with a friend.
    (4) His music is based on popular music of the time.
    (5) His music was included in Broadway musicals.

8. Based on this passage, which of the following types of music would Gershwin find most interesting?

    (1) Pop music
    (2) Rock music
    (3) Rhythm and blues music
    (4) Rap music
    (5) Show tunes

9. Which of the following statements from the passage is an opinion?

    (1) "George Gershwin was born in 1898 in Brooklyn, New York."
    (2) "George surprised everyone when he played a popular song, which he had taught himself by following the keys on a neighbor's player piano."
    (3) "Gershwin dropped out of school at age 15 and earned a living by making piano rolls for player pianos."
    (4) "His most important job in this period was his work as a song plugger."
    (5) "As a result of his hard work, Gershwin's piano technique improved greatly."

10. The word *accompanist,* as used in line 20, most nearly means someone who

    (1) plays music for a singer.

    (2) sings with another

    (3) creates musical scores.

    (4) directs Broadway plays.

    (5) lives in New York City.

Questions 11–15 refer to the following excerpt, which is adapted from Shakespeare's play, *Romeo and Juliet*.

WHAT MOTIVATES THESE CHARACTERS?

Friar Laurence enters the churchyard with a lantern, a crow, and a spade.

Friar Laurence: "Many times this evening
My old feet have stumbled on graves! Who's there?"
Balthasar: "A friend who knows you well."
Friar Laurence: "Tell me, good my friend,
(5) What torch is over there that casts its light
Upon grubs and eyeless skulls?
It seems to burn in the Capel's monument.*"
Balthasar: "It does, holy sir. And there's my master,
Someone who you love."
(10) **Friar Laurence:** "Who is it?"
Balthasar: "Romeo."
Friar Laurence: "How long has he been there?"
Balthasar: "Half an hour."
Friar Laurence: (*Anxiously.*) "Come with me to the vault."
(15) **Balthasar:** "I dare not, sir.
My master does not know that I am still here.
He threatened me with death if I stayed to watch."
Friar Laurence: "Stay, then; I'll go alone. Fear comes upon me:
O, I am much afraid of some ill, unlucky thing."
(20) **Balthasar:** "As I slept under this tree,
I dreamed that my master and another fought,
And that my master killed him."
Friar Laurence: "Romeo!"
(*Advances.*)
(25) "What blood is this that stains
The stony entrance of this sepulchre?**
Why are these swords lying bloody in this place of peace?"

---

*Capel's monument and **sepulcher refer to Juliet's family's tomb.

(*Enters the tomb, where the bodies of Romeo and Paris lie, dead.*)

(30) "Romeo! O, no! Who else? What, Paris too?
And soaked in blood? The lady stirs."
(*Juliet, who has been sleeping in the tomb, wakes.*)
Juliet: "O friar! Where is my Romeo?"
(*Noise within.*)

(35) **Friar Laurence:** "I hear some noise. Lady, come away.
Your husband lies there dead; And Paris too.
Come, I'll take you to a convent of holy nuns:
Do not stay to look, for the guards are coming;
Come, Juliet!"

(40) (*Noise again.*)
"I dare not stay any longer."
Juliet: "Go then, for I will not leave."
(*Exit Friar Laurence. Juliet approaches Romeo's body.*)
"What's here? A cup, closed in my true love's hand?

(45) Poison, I see, has been his timeless end:
He has drunk it all, and left none for me? I will kiss your lips;
Perhaps some poison does still hang on them."
(*Kisses him.*)
"Your lips are warm."

(50) **First Watchman:** (*Within.*) "Lead, boy: Which way?"
Juliet: "Someone comes. Then I'll be quick. O happy dagger!"
She stabs herself with Romeo's dagger, falls on his body, and dies.

11. Why is Friar Laurence afraid when he finds out Romeo has been in the cemetery for so long?

   (1) He fears that Romeo will be angry because he has had to wait too long.
   (2) He fears that Balthasar is lying.
   (3) He is in a cemetery and is afraid of death.
   (4) He fears that Romeo has done something to harm himself.
   (5) He fears that the guards will find Romeo and arrest him.

12. What does Friar Laurence find when he reaches Juliet's tomb?

   (1) He finds Romeo and Paris dead.
   (2) He finds Juliet dead.
   (3) He finds nothing unusual.
   (4) He finds Balthasar hiding in the tomb.
   (5) He finds Juliet's body has been stolen.

13. What does Juliet mean when she says, "Your lips are warm"?

  (1) Friar Laurence has told her a lie.

  (2) Balthasar has been a good friend to Romeo.

  (3) Romeo has been dead for only a little while, so his body is not yet cold.

  (4) Juliet does not expect her lips to be warm on so cold a night.

  (5) Juliet is upset over Romeo's death and refuses to believe he is gone.

14. Why does Friar Laurence leave Juliet alone?

  (1) He wants to find Balthasar to tell him what has happened.

  (2) He wants to call the guards for help.

  (3) He is afraid of looking into the faces of the dead men in the tomb.

  (4) He knows the guards are coming and is afraid of being caught in the tomb.

  (5) He thinks Juliet should have some time to say goodbye to Romeo.

15. What happens to Juliet at the end of the scene?

  (1) She leaves the tomb with Friar Laurence.

  (2) She kills herself with Romeo's dagger.

  (3) She waits for the guards to arrive so she can explain what happened to Romeo.

  (4) She goes crazy at the sight of Romeo's body.

  (5) She goes home with her parents.

Questions 16–18 are based on this article from a travel magazine.

WHAT MAKES THIS CITY UNIQUE?

Line   The Forbidden City is a palace in the center of Beijing, China. Construction began in 1406, and the emperor's court officially moved in by 1420. The Forbidden City got its name because most people were barred from entering. Even government officials and the imperial
(5)   family were permitted only limited access. Only the emperor could enter any section at will. Today, visitors from all over the world can walk about this palace, which is now a museum. The 1987 film *The Last Emperor* was even filmed here.

   The architecture of the Forbidden City conforms rigidly to tra-
(10)   ditional Chinese principles. All buildings within the walls follow a north-south line. The most important buildings face south to honor the sun. The designers arranged the other buildings to impress all visitors with the great power of the Emperor. This architectural concept was carried out to the smallest detail. For
(15)   example, the importance of a building was determined not only by its height or width but also by the style of its roof and the number of statues placed along the roof's ridges.

   One of the most impressive landmarks of the Forbidden City is the Meridian Gate, the formal entrance to the southern side of

(20) the Forbidden City. The gate is 38 meters high at its roof ridge. When you stand in front of this majestic structure, you understand how *awed* people felt when they stood there listening to imperial proclamations. As you walk through the gate, you come into a large courtyard. Running through the courtyard is the
(25) Golden River, which is crossed by five white marble bridges. These bridges lead to the Gate of Supreme Harmony. This leads to the heart of the Forbidden City. Its three main halls stand atop a three-tiered marble terrace overlooking an immense plaza. The plaza has enough space to hold tens of thousands of people.

16. What is the main purpose of the passage?

(1) To prevent people from visiting the Forbidden City
(2) To discuss the architecture of the Forbidden City
(3) To provide potential travelers with information about the Forbidden City
(4) To show how the Forbidden City has changed over the years
(5) To promote the movie, *The Last Emperor*

17. The word *awed,* as used in line 22, most nearly means

(1) horrified.
(2) amazed.
(3) appalled.
(4) alarmed.
(5) afraid.

18. Today, when visitors from around the world go to the Forbidden City they

(1) must wait in line for hours.
(2) must receive an imperial invitation to walk around the palace.
(3) are able to walk about the palace freely.
(4) must avoid the Gate of Supreme Harmony.
(5) cannot stand in front of the Meridian Gate.

Questions 19–24 are based on the following excerpt from the poem "The Raven," by Edgar Allan Poe.

HOW IS THIS MAN AFFECTED?

Line Once upon a midnight dreary, while I pondered, weak and weary,
Over many a quaint and curious volume of forgotten lore,
While I nodded, nearly napping, suddenly there came a tapping,
As of some one gently rapping, rapping at my chamber door.
(5) "'Tis some visitor," I muttered, "tapping at my chamber door—
Only this, and nothing more."

Ah, distinctly I remember it was in the bleak December,
And each separate dying ember wrought its ghost upon the floor.
Eagerly I wished the morrow;—vainly I had sought to borrow
(10) From my books surcease of sorrow—sorrow for the lost Lenore—
For the rare and radiant maiden whom the angels name Lenore—
Nameless here for evermore.

And the silken sad uncertain rustling of each purple curtain
Thrilled me—filled me with fantastic terrors never felt before;
(15) So that now, to still the beating of my heart, I stood repeating,
"'Tis some visitor entreating entrance at my chamber door—
Some late visitor entreating entrance at my chamber door;—
This it is, and nothing more."

Presently my soul grew stronger; hesitating then no longer,
(20) "Sir," said I, "or Madam, truly your forgiveness I implore;
But the fact is I was napping, and so gently you came rapping,
And so faintly you came tapping, tapping at my chamber door,
That I scarce was sure I heard you"—here I opened wide the door;—
(25) Darkness there, and nothing more.

19. What is the speaker doing at the beginning of the poem?

(1) Sleeping

(2) Eating

(3) Reading

(4) Singing

(5) Walking

20. When do the events of the poem take place?

- **(1)** Early morning in the summer
- **(2)** Late afternoon in autumn
- **(3)** Midnight on Christmas Day
- **(4)** Late at night in winter
- **(5)** Early evening in spring

21. Why is the speaker in need of a distraction?

- **(1)** He is thinking about a lost love.
- **(2)** He is having a nightmare.
- **(3)** He is disinterested in the book he is reading.
- **(4)** His wife is angry with him.
- **(5)** He is depressed and cold.

22. Which of the following is closest in meaning to the word *entreating* in stanza 3?

- **(1)** Begging
- **(2)** Leaving
- **(3)** Knocking
- **(4)** Hanging
- **(5)** Tapping

23. The actions of the speaker indicate that he is

- **(1)** happy that he has a visitor.
- **(2)** too depressed to answer the door.
- **(3)** oblivious to the knocking at his door.
- **(4)** afraid of the sounds he hears at his door.
- **(5)** interested in ghosts.

24. What does the speaker imply in the last line of the poem?

- **(1)** He is trying to forget about his past.
- **(2)** He is begging his love for forgiveness.
- **(3)** There never was any knocking at the door.
- **(4)** The knocking that he heard was just a dream.
- **(5)** Although he distinctly heard knocking, he is surprised to find no one at the door.

Questions 25–28 refer to the following newspaper article.

IS THE EXHIBIT WORTH SEEING?

Line The traveling art exhibition "Italian Renaissance Masters" recently made a stop at the local university and gave local art enthusiasts an opportunity to witness some of the masterpieces of the Italian Renaissance without having to travel abroad. While
(5)   many of the works of art took my breath away, the one work that stood out was the "David" by Michelangelo. The polished marble hero stood glistening in the lights of the museum hall as passersby stopped in awe. The colossal athletic figure spoke to all who stared in amazement. The gentle slopes and curves of his body,
(10) the incredible detail on his hands and feet, and the perfectly proportioned torso told a story of a craftsman who toiled for countless hours in search of perfection. The master had created a work of art that looked like it might step down from the pedestal at any moment. The figure looked like a Roman god. Every detail had
(15) been artfully considered. The hero's hair, cloak, and facial features all looked lightly delicate though they were made of solid marble. As I examined every detail of the masterpiece, I couldn't help but think that God himself must have created this perfect figure. I enjoyed all of the art and highly recommend the exhibit
(20) to everyone. However, I must suggest that you save the "David" for last, as all other works of art simply pale in comparison.

25. The passage is most likely which of the following?

    (1) A work of fiction
    (2) A commentary
    (3) An inter-office memo
    (4) A persuasive essay
    (5) A movie review

26. The figure referred to in the passage is most likely which of the following?

    (1) A figure in a painting
    (2) A model
    (3) A character in a movie
    (4) An actor
    (5) A sculpture

27. The overall mood or tone of the passage could best be described as which of the following?

- **(1)** Apprehensive
- **(2)** Reserved and stoic
- **(3)** Negative and condescending
- **(4)** Positive and complimentary
- **(5)** Sad

28. Which of the following best describes the author's feelings about what he saw at the exhibition?

- **(1)** The author was amazed at what he saw.
- **(2)** The author liked what he saw but was not too impressed.
- **(3)** The author would not recommend the exhibit to anyone else.
- **(4)** The author did not like any one thing more than another at the exhibit.
- **(5)** The author was bored by what he saw at the exhibit.

Questions 29–33 refer to the following passage, an excerpt from "The Story of the Bad Little Boy" by Mark Twain.

HOW IS THIS BOY DIFFERENT?

Line

Once there was a bad little boy whose name was Jim—though, if you will notice, you will find that bad little boys are nearly always called James in your Sunday-school books. It was strange, but still it was true, that this one was called Jim.

(5) He didn't have any sick mother, either—a sick mother who was pious and had the consumption, and would be glad to lie down in the grave and be at rest but for the strong love she bore her boy, and the anxiety she felt that the world might be harsh and cold towards him when she was gone. Most bad boys in the Sunday-

(10) books are named James, and have sick mothers, who teach them to say their prayers, and sing them to sleep with sweet, plaintive voices, and then kiss them good-night, and kneel down by the bedside and weep. But it was different with this fellow. He was named Jim, and there wasn't anything the matter with his

(15) mother—no consumption, nor anything of that kind. She was rather stout than otherwise, and she was not pious. Moreover, she was not anxious on Jim's account. She said if he were to break his neck it wouldn't be much loss. She always spanked Jim to sleep, and she never kissed him good-night. On the contrary, she boxed*

(20) his ears when she was ready to leave him.

When Jim's mother *boxes his ears, she is hitting him on the ears.

(25) Once this little bad boy stole the key of the pantry, and slipped in there and helped himself to some jam, and filled up the vessel with tar, so that his mother would never know the difference. But all at once a terrible feeling didn't come over him, and something didn't seem to whisper to him, "Is it right to disobey my mother? Isn't it sinful to do this? Where do bad little boys go who gobble up their good kind mother's jam?" and then he didn't kneel down all alone and promise never to be wicked any more, and rise up with a light, happy heart, and go and tell his mother all about it, (30) and beg her forgiveness, and be blessed by her with tears of pride and thankfulness in her eyes. No; that is the way with all other bad boys in the books; but it happened otherwise with this Jim, strangely enough. He ate that jam, and said it was bully in his sinful, vulgar way; and he put in the tar, and said that was bully (35) also, and laughed, and observed "that the old woman would get up and snort" when she found it out. When she did find it out, he denied knowing anything about it, and she whipped him severely, and he did the crying himself. Everything about this boy was curious—everything turned out differently with him from the way it (40) does to the bad James in the books.

29. Which word best describes Jim's personality?

(1) Timid

(2) Warm

(3) Charming

(4) Peculiar

(5) Rebellious

30. In the line "He ate that jam, and said it was bully," (line 33) the word *bully* most nearly means

(1) troublesome.

(2) bullish.

(3) good.

(4) having the texture of a bull.

(5) sticky.

31. How is Jim's mother different from the mothers in the church stories?

(1) She is poorer than those ladies in the stories.

(2) She does not belong to a church.

(3) She is not dying and does not kiss her son goodnight.

(4) She has no other children.

(5) She does not have a sweet, plaintive voice.

32. In which of the following activities would Jim most likely participate?

(1) Joining a study group at school

(2) Choir practice at the local church

(3) Sneaking out of the house after bedtime

(4) Volunteer park cleanup

(5) Jam-making classes on the weekends

33. Based on the last line in the passage, predict how the rest of this story will unfold.

(1) Jim becomes the model son when he graduates high school.

(2) Jim continues to avoid punishment for his sins while living a charmed life.

(3) Jim gets caught and spends ten years in jail for attempted murder.

(4) Jim's mother dies from consumption and forgives him on her deathbed.

(5) Jim accidentally falls out of a tree while stealing apples and decides to turn his life around.

Questions 34–36 refer to the following advertisement for a miniature golf course.

CRANBURY BOG MINIATURE GOLF

Cranbury Bog offers four spacious 18-hole miniature golf courses over acres and acres of countryside.

It's challenging . . . and fun! Cranbury Bog is like no other miniature golf course in the world!

After your games, you can relax in the state-of-the-art clubhouse or out on the deck.

We guarantee you'll enjoy yourself. Check us out!

Two-for-one on Fridays. Bring the kids. Available for parties.

Fees:

Adults (18+) $15
Students (12–17) $10
Children (3–11) $5
Seniors (55+) $2.50

Children under 3 years are not permitted in the clubhouse.

34. According to the advertisement, why is Cranbury Bog unlike any other miniature golf course?

  (1) Cranbury Bog does not allow children.
  (2) Cranbury Bog is available for parties.
  (3) Cranbury Bog sits on more acreage than any other golf course.
  (4) The advertisement does not specify the reason.
  (5) Cranbury Bog offers more holes of miniature golf than any other golf course.

35. It can be inferred that "Two-for-one on Fridays" means

  (1) Two people can play for the price of one only on Fridays.
  (2) It only costs $1 to play on Fridays.
  (3) Friday is the only day that two people can play.
  (4) Kids can only play on Fridays.
  (5) All scores are doubled on Fridays.

36. According to the fee chart, how much does it cost for someone who is 54 years old?

  (1) $15
  (2) $10
  (3) $5
  (4) $2.50
  (5) There is no charge.

Questions 37–40 refer to the following biography.

HOW DID THIS MAN DEDICATE HIS LIFE TO LAW ENFORCEMENT?

Line   Eliot Ness was born in Chicago in 1902. After graduating from the University of Chicago, he worked as an investigator for the Retail Credit Co., of Atlanta. He was assigned to the Chicago territory, where he *conducted* background investigations for the pur-
(5)   pose of credit information.
    In 1926, his sister's husband, an FBI agent, suggested that he try law enforcement. Ness took a job with the U.S. Treasury Department's Prohibition Bureau during a time when bootlegging (the illegal sale of alcohol) was rampant throughout the nation.
(10) He headed a federal enforcement unit that covered Illinois, Indiana, and Wisconsin. This unit was very successful in developing cases and obtaining prosecutions against people engaged in illegal activities, including the notorious mobster Al Capone. Many years later, this unit's achievements were portrayed in a novel, a
(15) TV series, and a movie, all of which were called *The Untouchables*. In 1933, after the Prohibition Act was repealed, Ness's unit

of special agents was disbanded, and Ness was transferred, first to Cincinnati, and then to Cleveland.

(20) Ness left the FBI in 1935, but continued to work in public service. He served as Cleveland's Director of Public Safety, running the city's Police and Fire Departments. With the onset of World War Two, he took a position with the federal government's Defense, Health and Welfare Service in 1942. The responsibilities of his new position, Director of Social Protection, were immense.

(25) Ness had to combat social problems that existed on military bases throughout the nation. For his outstanding leadership in this job, he received the Navy's Meritorious Service Citation.

37. Which word is the best synonym for the word *conducted* (line 4)?

(1) Escorted

(2) Directed

(3) Controlled

(4) Behaved

(5) Ignored

38. Who encouraged Ness to consider law enforcement as a career?

(1) His sister

(2) His wife

(3) His mother

(4) His brother-in-law

(5) His sister-in-law

39. Why was Ness's unit of special agents disbanded?

(1) The Prohibition Act was repealed, making the unit unnecessary.

(2) Al Capone was arrested, so Ness and his unit no longer had any work to do.

(3) World War II began, requiring all FBI agents to join the Armed Forces.

(4) Ness was so successful as an FBI agent that organized crime came to an end.

(5) Ness was transferred to Cincinnati.

40. Which of the following is NOT a job held by Ness?

(1) Director of Public Safety

(2) Director of Social Protection

(3) Writer for television and movies

(4) Investigator for the Retail Credit Company

(5) FBI agent with the Treasury Department

Answers

1. **The correct answer is (2), People who do not perform as others expect are often disliked and misunderstood.** Much of this passage is about Paul's inability to do what his teachers expect of him. He is not a typical student, and they do not know what to do with him. Paul's teachers may feel he is disrespectful, but the focus of the passage is not really Paul's suspension from school, choice (1); it is his interaction with others. There is only one brief mention of Paul's father in the passage, choice (3), so his relationship with his father is not important. We also do not know why Paul attends this particular school. The school's discipline procedures, choice (4), are not in question in this passage. Although this passage is making a social statement about conformity, choice (5) is not the best answer. This passage focuses on the inability of Paul's teachers to see beyond his behavior. Although they might like Paul to act like all of the other students in their classes, the real issue of the passage is their feelings toward Paul.

2. **The correct answer is (3), He disobeyed his teachers and failed to conceal his hatred of them.** The teachers justify Paul's suspension because he is "defiant" and openly shows "the contempt which they all knew he felt for them." Paul never hit a teacher, choice (1), and there is nothing in the passage to support choice (2). Choices (4) and (5) are simply examples of the behaviors that Paul demonstrates in class.

3. **The correct answer is (4), He wants to overcome the conflict in this situation.** In the first paragraph, the author writes, "Paul was quite accustomed to lying; found it, indeed, indispensable for overcoming friction." Paul has learned that lying is the best way to solve his problems and avoid further conflict.

4. **The correct answer is (1), Disrespect.** By definition, impertinence means lack of respect for others.

5. **The correct answer is (5), between Paul and the entire school community.** Although all of the other answer choices are a source of conflict (or potential conflict), they are not the focus of this passage. Paul is at odds with the entire school, and the author shows this by setting up a scene where Paul must defend himself against the authority of his school (all of his teachers and the principal).

6. **The correct answer is (4), Sheet-music sales.** The details are in the fourth sentence of the second paragraph of the passage.

7. **The correct answer is (5), His music was included in Broadway musicals.** This comes from the first sentence of the last paragraph. There is no evidence in the excerpt to show that he has a supportive wife, choice (1), or that his music is based on popular music of his time, choice (4). There is no indication that he tries to show the world through the eyes of children, so choice (2) cannot be correct. The excerpt does not say his father got him a job with a friend, choice (3).

8. **The correct answer is (5), Show tunes.** Since we know Gershwin played and wrote music for Broadway musicals, we can assume that this type of music appealed to him. We can rule out choices (2), (3) and (4) because these types of music were not popular in Gershwin's time. Choice (1) is incorrect because the passage states that Gershwin was taught how popular music was inferior to material in Broadway shows.

9. **The correct answer is (4), "His most important job in this period was his work as a song plugger."** All the other answer choices can be proven by outside information, but this statement is the author's assessment of Gershwin's occupation. Those words are the author's opinion.

10. **The correct answer is (1), someone who plays music for a singer.** The context clues show that Gershwin plays music for singers on the stage, and the passage states that he plays the piano. The word *accompanist* means a person who plays an instrumental part for a vocalist or instrumentalist.

11. **The correct answer is (4), He fears that Romeo has done something to harm himself.** After Balthasar tells the Friar that Romeo threatened to kill him if he went back to the tomb, the Friar says, "Fear comes upon me:/O, much I fear some ill unlucky thing." The unlucky thing he fears is Romeo's death, which is confirmed when the Friar reaches the tomb. Romeo was not expecting the Friar, so he would not be angry at his tardiness, choice (1). The Friar never indicates that he has a reason to believe Balthasar is lying, choice (2) or that he is afraid of death, choice (3). Friar Laurence does not consider the watchmen, choice (5), until he hears a noise while speaking to Juliet. By this time, his fears have been realized.

12. **The correct answer is (1), He finds Romeo and Paris dead.** When Friar Laurence enters the tomb, he talks about the blood he sees on the floor. He then sees a pale Romeo and a bloody Paris on the floor and announces their deaths.

13. **The correct answer is (3), Romeo has recently died and his body is not yet cold.** Right before Juliet speaks this line, she kisses Romeo on the lips. She is anguished to discover that his lips are warm because she realizes Romeo has just died. Had she awakened a moment sooner, she would have seen him alive.

14. **The correct answer is (4), He knows the guards are coming and is afraid of being caught in the tomb.** Friar Laurence says to Juliet, "I hear some noise. Stay not to question, for the watch is coming; Come, go, good Juliet, I dare no longer stay."

15. **The correct answer is (2), She kills herself with Romeo's dagger.** You can find this in the last set of stage directions: "She stabs herself with Romeo's dagger, falls on his body, and dies."

16. **The correct answer is (3), To provide potential travelers with information about the Forbidden City.** Because this article was written for a travel magazine, we can assume that readers would be interested in visiting the city. There is no indication that the article is trying to keep people from visiting the city, choice (1). Although each of the other choices is addressed in some way in the passage, none is the focus of the article.

17. **The correct answer is (2), amazed.** Although all of the answer choices represent definitions of the word *awe*, there is no indication that people are afraid of or disgusted by the appearance of the gates. In fact, the suggestion that many people stood in the place listening to proclamations indicates that people wanted to see the gates. Therefore all of the other answer choices are incorrect.

18. **The correct answer is (3), are able to walk about the palace freely.** This is stated in the text. In addition, there is evidence in the passage to contradict all of the other answer choices. No other choice has support from the passage.

19. **The correct answer is (3), Reading.** The speaker of the poem states that he "pondered . . . over many a quaint and curious volume of forgotten lore." He refers to books (volumes) and states that he has been reviewing them with great thought and care (pondered). Although the speaker mentions the word "napping," he adds the word "nearly." This means that he is not yet asleep. The other choices are not mentioned in the poem.

20. **The correct answer is (4), Late at night in winter.** The speaker tells us the setting of the story. In the first sentence of the poem, the speaker tells us the time ("Once upon a midnight dreary"). It is midnight, or 12 a.m. The first sentence of the second stanza tells us the month (". . . it was in the bleak December"). December is a winter month. The other answer choices are not supported by the passage.

21. **The correct answer is (1), He is thinking about a lost love.** The speaker tells us that he is reading books to take his mind off of "the lost Lenore." Even if we do not know who Lenore is, it is obvious that she was important to the speaker. Choice (5) may be true, but there is no evidence to support that the speaker is cold. The other answer choices are not supported by the passage.

22. **The correct answer is (1), Begging.** The word *entreat* means to beg or plead.

23. **The correct answer is (4), afraid of the sounds he hears at his door.** It is stated in the poem that the noises "filled me with fantastic terrors." The speaker tries to tell himself that his imagination is running wild. The speaker clearly hears the knocking, so choice (3) is incorrect. He cannot be too depressed to answer the door, choice (2), because the last lines of the poem contradict this. Although the word *ghost* is used in the poem, there is no evidence to support that the speaker is interested in ghosts, choice (5). There is also no evidence to support that the speaker is pleased with the prospect of having a guest, choice (1).

24. **The correct answer is (5), Although he distinctly heard knocking, the speaker is surprised to find no one at the door.** The poem ends with the line, "Darkness there, and nothing more." When the speaker opens the door to see who has been knocking, no one is on his doorstep. All the speaker sees is the dark of night. There is no evidence to support any other answer choice.

25. **The correct answer is (4), A persuasive essay.** The passage is a critique of an art exhibition and of a specific work of art in the exhibition.

26. **The correct answer is (5), A sculpture.** The figure described by the author is a very famous sculpture by the Renaissance artist Michelangelo. The sculpture is called "David."

27. **The correct answer is (4), Positive and complimentary.** The author's language praises the exhibit throughout the passage.

28. **The correct answer is (1), The author was amazed at what he saw.** The author expresses his wonder and amazement, especially about the statue, "David."

29. **The correct answer is (5), Rebellious.** The boy does not listen to his mother or adhere to any rules that a boy should follow. This is the best answer to describe his bad behavior.

30. **The correct answer is (3), good.** He says the word as if the word itself is describing something that shouldn't be; the jam is not only forbidden, it tastes good. Jim laughs after eating it, feeling no remorse. Clearly the jam must have been tasty, which rules out the other answer choices.

31. **The correct answer is (3), She is not dying and does not kiss her son goodnight.** Unlike the mothers in the church stories who are all dying of consumption and who kiss their bad sons goodnight and sing to them with sweet voices, Jim's mother is healthy and boxes her son's ears rather than kiss him. The story does not say that she is *poorer than those ladies in the stories* or *without a sweet, plaintive voice*. The story also does not tell about her church habits, only that she is not pious or religious. We also do not know if Jim has any brothers or sisters. Therefore, choice (4) is irrelevant.

32. **The correct answer is (3), Sneaking out of the house after dark.** Since Jim is a boy who likes to get into trouble, it is doubtful that he would participate in any of the other activities. They are all activities that "good" boys do and which Jim would consider boring.

33. **The correct answer is (2), Jim continues to avoid punishment for his sins while living a charmed life.** The last line states that nothing in his life would turn out the same way as the bad James in the bible stories. In keeping with this theme, Jim will probably continue to get into trouble and continue getting away with his wrongdoings. There is no evidence in the last lines to point to a positive ending or any of the other endings suggested in the other choices.

34. **The correct answer is (4), The advertisement does not specify the reason.** The advertisement makes the claim that Cranbury Bog is not like any other miniature golf course, but it doesn't offer the reasons why. There is no indication that Cranbury Bog has more acreage or more holes of golf than other courses or that other courses are unavailable for parties. Cranbury Bog *does* allow children.

35. **The correct answer is (1), Two people can play for the price of one only on Fridays.** Of the choices given, there is only one possible correct answer. The advertisement does not mention that there are limits to how many people or how many times a person can play. It also does not mention that the fees change on particular days.

36. **The correct answer is (1), $15.** According to the fee chart, a senior citizen is a person who is 55 years old or older. The $15 fee applies to an adult who is not yet 55 years old.

37. **The correct answer is (2), Directed.** Choices (1), (3), and (4) are synonyms for the verb *conducted*, but they do not make sense in the passage. Choice (5) has nothing to do with the word *conducted*.

38. **The correct answer is (4), His brother-in-law.** The passage states that Ness's "sister's husband" suggested he enter law enforcement. His sister's husband would be his brother-in-law. None of the other choices is mentioned in the passage.

39. **The correct answer is (1), The Prohibition Act was repealed, making the unit unnecessary.** The answer to this question is stated in the second paragraph of the passage. Ness was transferred to Cincinnati, choice (5), but this did not happen until after the unit of special agents was disbanded. Ness took an active role in the arrest of Al Capone, choice (2), but other people committed crimes that Ness would have investigated. Ness's job was not dependent on Al Capone. The special agent unit was disbanded in 1933. World War II did not even begin until 1939 and Ness's involvement in the war did not begin until after 1942, so choice (3) is incorrect. Choice (4) is not supported in any way.

40. **The correct answer is (3), Writer for television and movies.** Although Ness's life is the basis of television shows and movies, such as *The Untouchables*, he was not a writer. All of the other choices are addressed in the passage.

Posttest 2

You will probably find the questions in the following posttest to be more difficult than the questions that you have already seen in this book. There's a good reason for that: these questions are just as tough as the ones you'll find on the real GED. So just take your time, and do your best. We think you're ready for the challenge!

Questions 1–6 refer to the following poem by William Shakespeare.

WHAT IS THE AUTHOR TRYING TO SAY?

Line   Tired with all these, for restful death I cry,
        As, to behold desert a beggar born,
        And needy nothing trimm'd in jollity,
        And purest faith unhappily forsworn,
(5)   And gilded honour shamefully misplac'd,
        And maiden virtue rudely strumpeted,
        And right perfection wrongfully disgrac'd,
        And strength by limping sway disabled,
        And art made tongue-tied by authority,
(10) And folly, doctor-like, controlling skill,
        And simple truth miscall'd simplicity,
        And captive good attending captain ill:
            Tir'd with all these, from these would I be gone,
            Save that, to die, I leave my love alone.

1. Which of the following best describes the mood of this poem?

(1) Cheery

(2) Thankful

(3) Dark

(4) Optimistic

(5) Light

2. Which of the following states a reason for which the author does not desire to die?

    (1) Art

    (2) Truth

    (3) Virtue

    (4) Faith

    (5) Love

3. The line, "And art made tongue-tied by authority," most likely means what?

    (1) The author does not like art.

    (2) The author is frustrated because no one will buy his art.

    (3) The author believes that expression through art is limited by bureaucracy.

    (4) The author was deaf.

    (5) The author was mute.

4. Which of the following best describes the main idea of the poem?

    (1) The author is complaining about life.

    (2) The author is reminiscing about his life.

    (3) The author is dreaming of a future life.

    (4) The author is wishing for a better life.

    (5) The author is describing someone else's life.

5. Which of the following best characterizes the symbolism of the line, "And captive good attending captain ill"?

    (1) "Captive good" describes doctors, and "captain ill" describes sick people.

    (2) "Captive good" represents the idea that universal good is enslaved, and "captain ill" represents the evil that has enslaved it.

    (3) "Captain ill" represents the captain of a ship.

    (4) "Captive good" represents the common man.

    (5) "Captain ill" describes the government.

6. Which of the following would be the best title for this poem?

    (1) "Wishing for a Better Life"

    (2) "How I Mourn for My Lost Love"

    (3) "Without These Things, Life Would Be without Meaning"

    (4) "Tired With All These, for Restful Death I Cry"

    (5) "For Art, Truth, and Faith Do I Live"

Questions 7–12 refer to the following excerpts of *Don Quixote* by Cervantes.

WHAT KIND OF MAN IS THE MAIN CHARACTER?

Line

In a village of La Mancha, the name of which I have no desire to call to mind, there lived not long since one of those gentlemen that keep a lance in the lance-rack, an old buckler, a lean hack, and a greyhound for coursing . . .

(5) You must know, then, that the above-named gentleman whenever he was at leisure (which was mostly all the year round) gave himself up to reading books of chivalry with such ardor and avidity that he almost entirely neglected the pursuit of his field-sports, and even the management of his property; and to such a
(10) pitch did his eagerness and infatuation go that he sold many an acre of tillage-land to buy books of chivalry to read, and brought home as many of them as he could get . . .

. . . His fancy grew full of what he used to read about in his books, enchantments, quarrels, battles, challenges, wounds,
(15) wooings, loves, agonies, and all sorts of impossible nonsense; and it so possessed his mind that the whole fabric of invention and fancy he read of was true, that to him no history in the world had more reality in it.

In short, his wits being quite gone, he hit upon the strangest
(20) notion that ever madman in this world hit upon, and that was that he fancied it was right and requisite, as well for the support of his own honor as for the service of his country, that he should make a knight-errant of himself, roaming the world over in full armor and on horseback in quest of adventures, and putting in
(25) practice himself all that he had read of as being the usual practice of knights-errant; righting every kind of wrong, and exposing himself to peril and danger from which, in the issue, he was to reap eternal renown and fame.

7. In the passage, the line "one of those gentlemen that keep a lance in the lance-rack" refers to which of the following?

(1) A doctor
(2) A lawyer
(3) A knight
(4) A musician
(5) A king

8. Which of the following is a true statement about the man described in the passage?

    (1) The man liked books, but he could not read.

    (2) The man owned a bookstore.

    (3) The man borrowed books whenever he could.

    (4) The man loved books, and he loved to read about chivalry.

    (5) The man taught others in the village to read.

9. Which of the following can be said about the man's mental state based on the information in the passage?

    (1) The man had gone crazy.

    (2) The man was a genius.

    (3) The man had the intelligence of a child.

    (4) The man was mad at someone.

    (5) The man was mad because he couldn't get books.

10. Based on the context of the passage, which of the following is the best definition for "knight-errant"?

    (1) A knight who reads

    (2) A knight who performs tasks

    (3) A knight who fights dragons

    (4) A knight who is a knight by mistake

    (5) A knight who makes mistakes

11. Based on the passage, which of the following is most likely to be the plot of the story?

    (1) The man becomes a bookseller and sells all the books he's collected.

    (2) The man becomes famous for his book collection.

    (3) The man becomes a knight and has many adventures.

    (4) The man becomes an author and writes about knights.

    (5) The man becomes a farmer and tills his land.

12. Which of the following is the main idea of the passage?

    (1) The main character is so obsessed with reading about knights that fantasy becomes reality for him.

    (2) The main character is a knight who loves to read about other knights.

    (3) Books have such power that they can drive a man mad.

    (4) Knights are one of the most popular topics for books.

    (5) It is important for knights to read so that they are prepared for whatever tasks they face.

Questions 13–16 refer to the following document.

WHY WAS THIS MEMO SENT TO EMPLOYEES?

From: J.R. Smith, Manager, Smith and Smith Service Company

To: Smith and Smith Service Company Employees

In light of recent time card punching practices of some Smith and Smith Service Company employees, management has instituted a new time card punching procedure for all employees. This new procedure will take effect on March 1, 2002 for all non-salaried employees. The new procedure is as follows:

1. Each employee should arrive at the Smith and Smith building no more than 15 minutes before and no later than 5 minutes before shift begins. Upon arrival, each employee should avoid loitering. Each employee should report to the floor manager's office as soon as possible after arriving at the Smith and Smith building.
2. Each employee must punch his or her time card no more than 5 minutes before shift begins and no later than 2 minutes after shift begins.
3. Each employee must punch his or her time card no more than 2 minutes before or 5 minutes after shift ends.
4. If an employee is discovered punching another employee's time card, both employees may be subject to suspension.
5. If an employee punches in before the permitted punch-in time or punches out after the permitted punch-out time more than twice in a 30-day period or more than four times in a 90-day period, the employee may be subject to suspension.
6. An employee's failure to punch a time card for a shift may result in a punitive reduction of wages for that shift.
7. Any actions concerning the time clock by an employee that may be considered by management as fraudulent or malicious may be grounds for termination and/or prosecution.

13. Which of the following can best sum up the main idea of the document?

    (1) The management is looking for an employee who has defrauded the company.

    (2) The management has tried many different things in the past to curb fraudulent behavior by its employees.

    (3) The management has a new policy for its employees, which is designed to guide its employees toward appropriate actions concerning the time clock.

    (4) The management wants to suspend employees so that it does not have to pay them.

    (5) The management is biased against non-salaried employees.

14. Which of the following best describe the tone of the document?

    (1) Irate and irrational

    (2) Emotionally charged

    (3) Matter of fact

    (4) Accusatory and suspicious

    (5) Malicious

15. Based on the information in the document, which of the following statements is most likely true?

    (1) Smith and Smith Company employees never misuse the time clock.

    (2) The Smith and Smith Company is notorious for abusing its employees.

    (3) The Smith and Smith Company has never had a time clock for employees to punch their time cards.

    (4) Employees of the Smith and Smith Company are notorious for abusing and breaking rules and regulations.

    (5) Some employees of the Smith and Smith Company have exercised poor judgment regarding the time clock and time card procedure, and this poor judgment has caused problems for the Smith and Smith Company.

16. To which of the following employees would this memo most probably NOT apply?

    (1) The assembly line workers

    (2) The janitorial staff

    (3) The maintenance staff

    (4) The receptionist

    (5) The accountant

Questions 17–20 refer to the following excerpts from "An Occurrence at Owl Creek Bridge," by Ambrose Bierce.

WHAT IS ACTUALLY HAPPENING IN THIS STORY?

Line   Doubtless, despite his suffering, he had fallen asleep while walking, for now he sees another scene—perhaps he has merely recovered from a delirium. He stands at the gate of his own home. All is as he left it, and all bright and beautiful in the morning sun-
(5) shine. He must have traveled the entire night. As he pushes open the gate and passes up the wide white walk, he sees a flutter of female garments; his wife, looking fresh and cool and sweet, steps down from the veranda to meet him. At the bottom of the steps she stands waiting, with a smile of ineffable joy, an attitude of
(10) matchless grace and dignity. Ah, how beautiful she is! He springs forwards with extended arms. As he is about to clasp her he feels a stunning blow upon the back of the neck; a blinding white light blazes all about him with a sound like the shock of a cannon—then all is darkness and silence!
(15)   Peyton Fahrquhar was dead; his body, with a broken neck, swung gently from side to side beneath the timbers of the Owl Creek Bridge.

17. Which of the following lines from the passage is an example of a simile?

(1) "a blinding white light"

(2) "bright and beautiful in the morning sunshine"

(3) "ineffable joy"

(4) "like the shock of a cannon"

(5) "a stunning blow"

18. Which of the following is the best summary of what actually happened to Peyton Fahrquhar?

(1) He was kidnapped from his home and then executed.

(2) He imagined seeing his home and wife as he was executed.

(3) He was delirious after a cannon fired.

(4) He imagined the scene after being struck by a cannon blow.

(5) Peyton Fahrquhar is not the person mentioned in the first paragraph.

19. Based on the information in the passage, which of the following most likely occurred before the action in the first paragraph?

    (1) Peyton Fahrquhar was injured somehow.
    (2) Peyton Fahrquhar died.
    (3) Peyton Fahrquhar fell asleep at his home.
    (4) Peyton Fahrquhar forgot how beautiful his wife was.
    (5) Peyton Fahrquhar robbed a bank.

20. Which of the following is true of the passage?

    (1) The passage is written in first person.
    (2) The passage is written in third person.
    (3) The author uses alliteration frequently throughout the passage.
    (4) The author uses onomatopoeia frequently throughout the passage.
    (5) The author uses a battlefield as the setting of the story.

Questions 21–26 refer to the following passage.

WHAT DOES THE AUTHOR THINK ABOUT THIS EXHIBIT?

Line The J. C. Smith Museum yesterday opened its latest exhibit, Art of the Midwest. The oil paintings of the exhibit showed little creativity and inspired but a yawn. The colors blended together like the shades of brown in a Midwestern corn field in the midst of a
(5) drought. The sketches resembled those of my 11-year-old nephew in his fifth-grade art class. The sculptures displayed in the museum showed some promise and potential. However, they lack the excellent vision necessary to highlight a major exhibition. The one bright spot of the show was the exquisite watercolors of Mid-
(10) western farm scenes. The watercolors portrayed the everyday life on Midwestern farms with the *grandeur* of the great artists or our time.

21. Which of the following can be said safely regarding the exhibit?

    (1) The author of the commentary dislikes the Midwest.
    (2) The art at the exhibit was bad art.
    (3) The art at the exhibit was good art.
    (4) The author of the commentary disliked most of the art at the exhibit.
    (5) The author of the commentary disliked all of the art at the exhibit.

22. The passage is most likely which of the following?

   (1) A work of fiction

   (2) A commentary

   (3) An interoffice memo

   (4) A persuasive essay

   (5) A movie review

23. Which of the following is NOT a type of art mentioned in the passage?

   (1) Oil paintings

   (2) Sculptures

   (3) Watercolor paintings

   (4) Pottery

   (5) Landscapes

24. "The colors blended together like the shades of brown in a Midwestern corn field in the midst of a drought," is an example of which literary device?

   (1) Metaphor

   (2) Personification

   (3) Simile

   (4) Onomatopoeia

   (5) Alliteration

25. The overall mood or tome of the passage could best be described as which of the following?

   (1) Apprehensive

   (2) Reserved and stoic

   (3) Negative and condescending

   (4) Positive and complimentary

   (5) Sad

26. The word *grandeur* is closest in meaning to which of the following?

   (1) Majesty

   (2) Greatness

   (3) Insignificance

   (4) Immoral

   (5) Splendid

Questions 27–30 refer to the following excerpt of *Pride and Prejudice*, by Jane Austen.

WHAT ARE MR. BINGLEY AND MR. DARCY LIKE?

Line

Mr. Bingley was good-looking and gentlemanlike; he had a pleasant countenance, and easy, unaffected manners. His sisters were fine women, with an air of decided fashion. His brother-in-law, Mr. Hurst, merely looked the gentleman; but his friend Mr. Darcy
(5) soon drew the attention of the room by his fine, tall person, handsome features, noble mien, and the report which was in general circulation within five minutes after his entrance, of his having ten thousand a year. The gentlemen pronounced him to be a fine figure of a man, the ladies declared he was much handsomer than
(10) Mr. Bingley, and he was looked at with great admiration for about half the evening, till his manners gave a disgust which turned the tide of his popularity; for he was discovered to be proud; to be above his company, and above being pleased; and not all his large estate in Derbyshire could then save him from having a most for-
(15) bidding, disagreeable countenance, and being unworthy to be compared with his friend.

Mr. Bingley had soon made himself acquainted with all the principal people in the room; he was lively and unreserved, danced every dance, was angry that the ball closed so early, and
(20) talked of giving one himself at Netherfield. Such amiable qualities must speak for themselves. What a contrast between him and his friend! Mr. Darcy danced only once with Mrs. Hurst and once with Miss Bingley, declined being introduced to any other lady, and spent the rest of the evening in walking about the room,
(25) speaking occasionally to one of his own party. His character was decided. He was the proudest, most disagreeable man in the world, and everybody hoped that he would never come there again. Amongst the most violent against him was Mrs. Bennet, whose dislike of his general behaviour was sharpened into par-
(30) ticular resentment by his having slighted one of her daughters.

27. Which of the following caused Mr. Darcy's unpopularity?

 (1) His poor hygiene
 (2) His pride
 (3) His lack of money
 (4) His appearance
 (5) His shoddy clothes

28. Which of the following best describes the tone of the passage?

   (1) Harsh

   (2) Unbiased

   (3) Open-minded

   (4) Favorable

   (5) Positive

29. Which of the following is the setting of the passage?

   (1) A party

   (2) A sporting event

   (3) A funeral

   (4) A restaurant

   (5) A church

30. The line "He was the proudest, most disagreeable man in the world" is an example of which of the following?

   (1) Personification

   (2) Simile

   (3) Metaphor

   (4) Alliteration

   (5) Hyperbole

Questions 31–36 refer to the following excerpt from *Romeo and Juliet*, by William Shakespeare.

WHAT IS ABOUT TO HAPPEN?

THE PROLOGUE (*Enter Chorus.*)

Line   **Chorus:** "Two households, both alike in dignity,
In fair Verona, where we lay our scene,
From ancient grudge break to new mutiny,
Where civil blood makes civil hands unclean.
(5)   From forth the fatal loins of these two foes
A pair of star-cross'd lovers take their life;
Whose misadventur'd piteous overthrows
Doth with their death bury their parents' strife.
The fearful passage of their death-mark'd love,
(10)   And the continuance of their parents' rage,
Which but their children's end naught could remove,
Is now the two hours' traffic of our stage;
The which, if you with patient ears attend,
What here shall miss, our toil shall strive to mend."

ACT I. Scene I. A public place. (*Enter Sampson and Gregory armed with swords and bucklers.*)

(15) **Sampson:** "Gregory, o' my word, we'll not carry coals."
Gregory: "No, for then we should be colliers."
Sampson: "I mean, an we be in choler we'll draw."
Gregory: "Ay, while you live, draw your neck out o' the collar."
Sampson: "I strike quickly, being moved."
(20) **Gregory:** "But thou art not quickly moved to strike."
Sampson: "A dog of the house of Montague moves me."
Gregory: "To move is to stir; and to be valiant is to stand: therefore, if thou art moved, thou runn'st away."
Sampson: "A dog of that house shall move me to stand: I will
(25) take the wall of any man or maid of Montague's."
Gregory: "That shows thee a weak slave; for the weakest goes to the wall."
Sampson: "True; and therefore women, being the weaker vessels, are ever thrust to the wall: therefore I will push Montague's men
(30) from the wall and thrust his maids to the wall."
Gregory: "The quarrel is between our masters and us their men."
Sampson: "'Tis all one, I will show myself a tyrant: when I have fought with the men I will be cruel with the maids, I will cut off their heads."
(35) **Gregory:** "The heads of the maids?"
Sampson: "Ay, the heads of the maids, or their maidenheads; take it in what sense thou wilt."
Gregory: "They must take it in sense that feel it."
Sampson: "Me they shall feel while I am able to stand: and 'tis
(40) known I am a pretty piece of flesh."
Gregory: "'Tis well thou art not fish; if thou hadst, thou hadst been poor-John.—Draw thy tool; Here comes two of the house of Montagues."
Sampson: "My naked weapon is out: quarrel! I will back thee."
(45) **Gregory:** "How! turn thy back and run?"
Sampson: "Fear me not."
Gregory: "No, marry; I fear thee!"
Sampson: "Let us take the law of our sides; let them begin."
Gregory: "I will frown as I pass by; and let them take it as they
(50) list."
Sampson: "Nay, as they dare. I will bite my thumb at them; which is disgrace to them if they bear it."

31. Which of the following is the setting of the passage?

   (1) A private residence in Verona

   (2) A public place in Padua

   (3) A church

   (4) A public place in Verona

   (5) A back room in the Montagues' home

32. Based on the passage, which of the following is the most likely purpose of the Chorus?

   (1) To sing a song before the play begins

   (2) To provide musical accompaniment

   (3) To inform the audience about things such as the setting

   (4) To interpret the play for the audience

   (5) To sing during intermission

33. In the line "Draw thy tool; Here comes two of the house of Montagues," the word *tool* means which of the following?

   (1) Hammer

   (2) Saw

   (3) Pen

   (4) Sword

   (5) Hand

34. In the line "Nay, as they dare. I will bite my thumb at them; which is disgrace to them if they bear it," which of the following is the best interpretation of the action of Sampson?

   (1) Sampson accidentally bit his own thumb.

   (2) Sampson will bite the thumbs of his enemies.

   (3) Sampson has made a disrespectful gesture.

   (4) Sampson is daring someone to bite his thumb.

   (5) Sampson has disgraced a bear.

35. Based on the information in the passage, which of the following is most likely to happen next in the play?

   (1) The two characters fight with one another.

   (2) The two characters have a confrontation with other characters from the house of Montague.

   (3) The two characters run away and hide.

   (4) The two characters befriend someone from the house of Montague.

   (5) The two characters continue to talk to each other.

36. Which of the following is the purpose of the prologue?
   (1) To briefly tell the story by telling the plot and giving away the ending
   (2) To allow the audience to get settled in their seats
   (3) To inform the audience of background information for the play
   (4) To tell the audience things that won't be presented during the play
   (5) To tell the audience what happens after the story

Questions 37–40 refer to the following excerpt of *Journey to the Interior of the Earth*, by Jules Verne.

HOW DO THE OTHER CHARACTERS FEEL ABOUT THE PROFESSOR?

Line

On the 24th of May, 1863, my uncle, Professor Liedenbrock, rushed into his little house, No. 19 Konigstrasse, one of the oldest streets in the oldest portion of the city of Hamburg.

Martha must have concluded that she was very much
(5) behindhand, for the dinner had only just been put into the oven.

"Well, now," said I to myself, "if that most impatient of men is hungry, what a disturbance he will make!"

"M. Liedenbrock so soon!" cried poor Martha in great alarm, half opening the dining-room door.

(10) "Yes, Martha; but very likely the dinner is not half cooked, for it is not two yet. Saint Michael's clock has only just struck half-past one."

"Then why has the master come home so soon?"

"Perhaps he will tell us that himself."

(15) "Here he is, Monsieur Axel; I will run and hide myself while you argue with him."

And Martha retreated in safety into her own dominions.

I was left alone. But how was it possible for a man of my undecided turn of mind to argue successfully with so irascible a person
(20) as the Professor? With this persuasion I was hurrying away to my own little retreat upstairs, when the street door creaked upon its hinges; heavy feet made the whole flight of stairs to shake; and the master of the house, passing rapidly through the dining room, threw himself in haste into his own sanctum.

(25) But on his rapid way he had found time to fling his hazel stick into a corner, his rough broad brim upon the table, and these few emphatic words at his nephew: "Axel, follow me!"

I had scarcely had time to move when the Professor was again shouting after me: "What! not come yet?" And I rushed into my
(30) redoubtable master's study.

Otto Liedenbrock had no mischief in him, I willingly allow that; but unless he very considerably changes as he grows older, at the end he will be a most original character.

He was professor at the Johannaeum, and was delivering a se-
(35) ries of lectures on mineralogy, in the course of every one of which he broke into a passion once or twice at least. Not at all that he was over-anxious about the improvement of his class, or about the degree of attention with which they listened to him, or the success, which might eventually crown his labours. Such little mat-
(40) ters of detail never troubled him much. His teaching was as the German philosophy calls it, 'subjective'; it was to benefit himself, not others. He was a learned egotist. He was a well of science, and the pulleys worked uneasily when you wanted to draw anything out of it. In a word, he was a learned miser.

37. Which of the following is the setting of this passage?

(1) Twentieth-century Germany

(2) Nineteenth-century Germany

(3) Eighteenth-century Germany

(4) At the center of the earth in the nineteenth century

(5) At the center of the earth in the eighteenth century

38. In the line "Martha must have concluded that she was very much behindhand, for the dinner had only just been put into the oven," which of the following is the best meaning for *behindhand*?

(1) Without a hand

(2) In need of a hand

(3) Running behind schedule

(4) Hurting in her hands

(5) Behind closed doors

39. Which of the following is the best interpretation of the line "And Martha retreated in safety into her own dominions"?

(1) Martha locked herself in her room.

(2) Martha retreated to her own house where she was safe.

(3) Martha ran away.

(4) Martha moved to another country.

(5) Martha went back into the kitchen where she was most comfortable.

40. Which of the following best describes the professor?

(1) High strung and demanding

(2) Laid back and relaxed

(3) Dimwitted and confused

(4) Uneducated

(5) Harsh and bitter

Answers

1. **The correct answer is (3), Dark.** This poem has a very dark and sad mood, especially since the theme revolves around death and dying.

2. **The correct answer is (5), Love.** The author states that the only reason that he does not want to die is for his love. His love, therefore, is the only factor motivating the author not to die.

3. **The correct answer is (3), The author believes that expression through art is limited by bureaucracy.** The author uses this language to say that the government limits his ability to express himself freely.

4. **The correct answer is (1), The author is complaining about life.** The author is complaining about all the problems with life and with being alive.

5. **The correct answer is (2), "Captive good" represents the idea that universal good is enslaved, and "captain ill" represents the evil that has enslaved it.** The author uses this symbolic language to say that even the good in life has been tainted because good often is overpowered by and motivated by evil.

6. **The correct answer is (4), "Tired With All These, for Restful Death I Cry."** It is common for the title of a poem to also be the poem's first line. Regardless of the fact that the first line is also the title, choice (4) best summarizes the rest of the poem.

7. **The correct answer is (3), A knight.** This line, along with the rest of the passage, is describing a knight. Even if you couldn't see this based on the line, you can figure it out based on the rest of the passage.

8. **The correct answer is (4), The man loved books, and he loved to read about chivalry.** Throughout the passage, the author mentions and describes the extent to which the main character reads and reads about chivalry in particular.

9. **The correct answer is (1), The man had gone crazy.** The first line of the last paragraph says that the main character's "wits were quite gone," meaning that he had gone crazy.

10. **The correct answer is (2), A knight who performs tasks.** A knight-errant is a knight who performs tasks or errands. The author specifically mentions tasks such as righting wrongs in the text.

11. **The correct answer is (3), The man becomes a knight and has many adventures.** Based on the information in the passage, it is logical that the main character becomes a knight that sets out on a quest for adventures.

12. **The correct answer is (1), The main character is so obsessed with reading about knights that fantasy becomes reality for him.** The main character reads so much about knights and chivalry that he begins to believe that he is a knight-errant. His choice to become a knight-errant is influenced by the books he reads.

13. **The correct answer is (3), The management has a new policy for its employees, which is designed to guide its employees toward appropriate actions concerning the time clock.** The document introduces a new policy or procedure that is designed as a guideline for employees to follow regarding the time clock and time cards. It is the goal of the management to have no employees act inappropriately.

14. **The correct answer is (3), Matter of fact.** Management has very carefully written the document in a very matter of fact, unemotional tone so employees are not offended or made uneasy by the memo.

15. **The correct answer is (5), Some employees of the Smith and Smith Company have exercised poor judgment regarding the time clock and time card procedure, and this poor judgment has caused problems for the Smith and Smith Company.** Based on the information in the memo, the most likely scenario is that the employees of the company have been careless or even deceptive in the past in their actions regarding the time clock and time card.

16. **The correct answer is (5), The accountant.** All of the employees except for the accountant are employees who are paid by the hour or are non-salaried. The accountant, a professional, is most likely on salary. Because an accountant receives a salary, an accountant would not need to punch in and out. Therefore, the memo would not apply to an accountant.

17. **The correct answer is (4), "like the shock of a cannon."** This line is a simile because it uses *like* to make a comparison.

18. **The correct answer is (2), He imagined seeing his home and wife as he was executed.** The images seen by the main character are merely imagined in the instant before he is hanged from a bridge.

19. **The correct answer is (1), Peyton Fahrquhar was injured somehow.** The first line of the passage indicates that he previously sustained some injury that caused him to suffer and fall asleep or pass out.

20. **The correct answer is (2), The passage is written in third person.** The passage is in third person because the story is told by a narrator who observes the actions of the character and knows the thoughts and feelings of the character.

21. **The correct answer is (4), The author of the commentary disliked most of the art at the exhibit.** The author speaks unfavorably about all of the art except for the watercolors.

22. **The correct answer is (2), A commentary.** The author is simply discussing what he saw and his opinion of the sculpture. This passage is a critique of the art exhibition.

23. **The correct answer is (4), Pottery.** Oil paintings, sculptures, and watercolors are all specifically mentioned in the passage. *Landscapes* is an incorrect answer because the author talks about the painted farm scenes he saw at the exhibit.

24. **The correct answer is (3), Simile.** By saying the colors looked *like* shades of brown in a cornfield, the author is using a literary tool called a simile. A simile makes a comparison using *like* or *as*.

25. **The correct answer is (3), Negative and condescending.** The author obviously dislikes the exhibit and insults it by saying that his 11-year-old son could do better.

26. **The correct answer is (2), Greatness.** Grandeur is defined as greatness characterized by dignity of character, largeness of spirit, or significant scope of accomplishment.

27. **The correct answer is (2), His pride.** Mr. Darcy's pride made everyone resent him.

28. **The correct answer is (1), Harsh.** The language used to describe Mr. Darcy is very harsh and sets the tone for the entire passage.

29. **The correct answer is (1), A party.** The setting of the passage is a ball or a large party, as indicated by the first line of the second paragraph.

30. **The correct answer is (5), Hyperbole.** The line is a huge exaggeration, known in literature as a hyperbole.

31. **The correct answer is (4), A public place in Verona.** The play is set in Verona in a public place. Although this information isn't presented in the same place in the play, both *Verona* and *public place* are mentioned to the audience.

32. **The correct answer is (3), To inform the audience about things such as the setting.** The Chorus often acts as a narrator and informs the audience of things such as setting or background information.

33. **The correct answer is (4), Sword.** The word *tool* is used instead of the word *sword*.

34. **The correct answer is (3), Sampson has made a disrespectful gesture.** Sampson "bit his thumb at them" or made a disrespectful gesture at the members of the house of Montague.

35. **The correct answer is (2), The two characters have a confrontation with other characters from the house of Montague.** Based on the tone and the actions of the characters, it is logical that the characters have a fight with the members of the house of Montague whom they have just spotted.

36. **The correct answer is (3), To inform the audience of background information for the play.** The prologue, which is found at the beginning of the work, gives background information that the audience will need to better understand the play.

37. **The correct answer is (2), Nineteenth-century Germany.** The setting is Germany, 1863. You can deduce this from the date, the German names, the mention of Hamburg, and the mention of German philosophy.

38. **The correct answer is (3), Running behind schedule.** Martha was running behind schedule because she had just put dinner in the oven, but the professor was ready to eat.

39. **The correct answer is (5), Martha went back into the kitchen where she was most comfortable.** Martha went back into the kitchen, her dominion, where she was in control and felt the most comfortable.

40. **The correct answer is (1), High strung and demanding.** The professor is portrayed as very high strung and very demanding of the people around him.

SECTION VI

Appendices

Word List A

Use the Words You Learn

Make a deliberate effort to include the new words you're learning in your daily speech and writing. It will impress people (teachers, bosses, friends, and enemies), and it will help your memorize and learn the words and their meanings. Maybe you've heard this tip about meeting new people: if you repeat a new person's name several times, you're unlikely to forget it. The same is true with new words: use them, and you won't lose them.

Create Your Own Word List

Get into the habit of reading a little every day with your dictionary nearby. When you encounter a new word in a newspaper, magazine, or book, look it up. Then jot down the new word, its definition, and the sentence in which you saw it in a notebook set aside for this purpose. Review your vocabulary notebook periodically—say, once a week. Your notebook will reflect the kinds of things you read and the words you find most difficult. The fact that you've taken the time and made the effort to write down the words and their meanings will help to fix them in your memory. Chances are good that you'll encounter a few words from your vocabulary notebook on the GED.

A Sample Word List

A

abbreviate (verb) to make briefer, to shorten. *Because time was running out, the speaker had to abbreviate his remarks.* **abbreviation** (noun).

abrasive (adjective) irritating, grinding, rough. *The manager's rude, abrasive way of criticizing the workers was bad for morale.* **abrasion** (noun).

abridge (verb) to shorten, to reduce. *The Bill of Rights is designed to prevent Congress from abridging the rights of Americans.* **abridgment** (noun).

absolve (verb) to free from guilt, to exonerate. *The criminal jury absolved O. J. Simpson of the murder of his ex-wife and her friend.* **absolution** (noun).

abstain (verb) to refrain, to hold back. *After his heart attack, he was warned by the doctor to abstain from smoking, drinking, and overeating.* **abstinence** (noun), **abstemious** (adjective).

accentuate (verb) to emphasize, to stress. *The overcast skies and chill winds accentuated our gloomy mood.*

acrimonious (adjective) biting, harsh, caustic. *The election campaign became acrimonious, as the candidates traded insults and accusations.* **acrimony** (noun).

adaptable (adjective) able to be changed to be suitable for a new purpose. *Some scientists say that the mammals outlived the dinosaurs because they were more adaptable to a changing climate.* **adapt** (verb), **adaptation** (noun).

adulation (noun) extreme admiration. *Few young actors have received greater adulation than did Marlon Brando after his performance in* A Streetcar Named Desire. **adulate** (verb), **adulatory** (adjective).

adversary (noun) an enemy or opponent. *When the former Soviet Union became an American ally, the United States lost its last major adversary.*

adversity (noun) misfortune. *It's easy to be patient and generous when things are going well; a person's true character is revealed under adversity.* **adverse** (adjective).

aesthetic (adjective) relating to art or beauty. *Mapplethorpe's photos may be attacked on moral grounds, but no one questions their aesthetic value—they are beautiful.* **aestheticism** (noun).

affected (adjective) false, artificial. *At one time, Japanese women were taught to speak in an affected high-pitched voice, which was thought girlishly attractive.* **affect** (verb), **affectation** (noun).

aggressive (adjective) forceful, energetic, and attacking. *A football player needs a more aggressive style of play than a soccer player.* **aggression** (noun).

alacrity (noun) promptness, speed. *Thrilled with the job offer, he accepted with alacrity—"Before they can change their minds!" he thought.*

allege (verb) to state without proof. *Some have alleged that Foster was murdered, but all the evidence points to suicide.* **allegation** (noun).

alleviate (verb) to make lighter or more bearable. *Although no cure for AIDS has been found, doctors are able to alleviate the suffering of those with the disease.* **alleviation** (noun).

ambiguous (adjective) having two or more possible meanings. *The phrase, "Let's table that discussion" is ambiguous; some think it means, "Let's discuss it now," while others think it means, "Let's save it for later."* **ambiguity** (noun).

ambivalent (adjective) having two or more contradictory feelings or attitudes; uncertain. *She was ambivalent toward her impending marriage; at times she was eager to go ahead, while at other times she wanted to call it off.* **ambivalence** (noun).

amiable (adjective) likable, agreeable, friendly. *He was an amiable lab partner, always smiling, on time, and ready to work.* **amiability** (verb).

amicable (adjective) friendly, peaceable. *Although they agreed to divorce, their settlement was amicable and they remained friends afterward.*

amplify (verb) to enlarge, expand, or increase. *Uncertain as to whether they understood, the students asked the teacher to amplify his explanation.* **amplification** (noun).

anachronistic (adjective) out of the proper time. *The reference, in Shakespeare's* Julius Caesar, *to "the clock striking twelve" is anachronistic, since there were no striking timepieces in ancient Rome.* **anachronism** (noun).

anarchy (noun) absence of law or order. *For several months after the Nazi government was destroyed, there was no effective government in parts of Germany, and anarchy ruled.* **anarchic** (adjective).

anomaly (noun) something different or irregular. *The tiny planet Pluto, orbiting next to the giants Jupiter, Saturn, and Neptune, has long appeared to be an anomaly.* **anomalous** (adjective).

antagonism (noun) hostility, conflict, opposition. *As more and more reporters investigated the Watergate scandal, antagonism between Nixon and the press increased.* **antagonistic** (adjective), **antagonize** (verb).

antiseptic (adjective) fighting infection; extremely clean. *A wound should be washed with an antiseptic solution. The all-white offices were bare and almost antiseptic in their starkness.*

apathy (noun) lack of interest, concern, or emotion. *American voters are showing increasing apathy over politics; fewer than half voted in the last election.* **apathetic** (adjective).

arable (adjective) able to be cultivated for growing crops. *Rocky New England has relatively little arable farmland.*

arbiter (noun) someone able to settle dispute; a judge or referee. *The public is the ultimate arbiter of commercial value: It decides what sells and what doesn't.*

arbitrary (adjective) based on random or merely personal preference. *Both computers cost the same and had the same features, so in the end I made an arbitrary decision about which to buy.*

arcane (adjective) little-known, mysterious, obscure. *Eliot's* Waste Land *is filled with arcane lore, including quotations in Latin, Greek, French, German, and Sanskrit.* **arcana** (noun, plural).

ardor (noun) a strong feeling of passion, energy, or zeal. *The young revolutionary proclaimed his convictions with an ardor that excited the crowd.* **ardent** (adjective).

arid (adjective) very dry; boring and meaningless. *The arid climate of Arizona makes farming difficult. Some find the law a fascinating topic, but for me it is an arid discipline.* **aridity** (noun).

ascetic (adjective) practicing strict self-discipline for moral or spiritual reasons. *The so-called Desert Fathers were hermits who lived an ascetic life of fasting, study, and prayer.* **asceticism** (verb).

assiduous (verb) working with care, attention, and diligence. *Although Karen is not a naturally gifted math student, by assiduous study she managed to earn an A in trigonometry.* **assiduity** (noun).

astute (adjective) observant, intelligent, and shrewd. *Safire's years of experience in Washington and his personal acquaintance with many political insiders make him an astute commentator on politics.*

atypical (adjective) not typical; unusual. *In* The Razor's Edge, *Bill Murray, best known as a comic actor, gave an atypical dramatic performance.*

audacious (adjective) bold, daring, adventurous. *Her plan to cross the Atlantic single-handed in a 12-foot sailboat was audacious, if not reckless.* **audacity** (noun).

audible (adjective) able to be heard. *Although she whispered, her voice was picked up by the microphone, and her words were audible throughout the theater.* **audibility** (noun).

auspicious (adjective) promising good fortune; propitious. *The news that a team of British climbers had reached the summit of Everest seemed an auspicious sign for the reign of newly crowned Queen Elizabeth II.*

authoritarian (adjective) favoring or demanding blind obedience to leaders. *Despite Americans' belief in democracy, the American government has supported authoritarian regimes in other countries.* **authoritarianism** (noun)

B

belated (adjective) delayed past the proper time. *She called her mother on January 5th to offer her a belated "Happy New Year."*

belie (verb) to present a false or contradictory appearance. *Lena Horne's youthful appearance belies her long, distinguished career in show business.*

benevolent (adjective) wishing or doing good. *In old age, Carnegie used his wealth for benevolent purposes, donating large sums to found libraries and schools.* **benevolence** (noun).

berate (verb) to scold or criticize harshly. *The judge angrily berated the two lawyers for their unprofessional behavior.*

bereft (adjective) lacking or deprived of something. *Bereft of parental love, orphans sometimes grow up to be insecure.*

bombastic (adjective) inflated or pompous in style. *Old-fashioned bombastic political speeches don't work on television, which demands a more intimate style of communication.* **bombast** (noun).

bourgeois (adjective) middle-class or reflecting middle-class values. *The Dadaists of the 1920s produced art deliberately designed to offend bourgeois art collectors, with their taste for respectable, refined, uncontroversial pictures.* **bourgeois** (noun).

buttress (noun) something that supports or strengthens. *The endorsement of the American Medical Association is a powerful buttress for the claims made about this new medicine.* **buttress** (verb).

C

camaraderie (noun) a spirit of friendship. *Spending long days and nights together on the road, the members of a traveling theater group develop a strong sense of camaraderie.*

candor (noun) openness, honesty, frankness. *In his memoir about the Vietnam War, former defense secretary McNamara describes his mistakes with remarkable candor.* **candid** (adjective).

capricious (adjective) unpredictable, willful, whimsical. *The pop star Madonna has changed her image so many times that each new transformation now appears capricious rather than purposeful.* **caprice** (noun).

carnivorous (adjective) meat-eating. *The long, dagger-like teeth of the Tyrannosaurus make it obvious that this was a carnivorous dinosaur.* **carnivore** (noun).

carping (adjective) unfairly or excessively critical; querulous. *New York is famous for its demanding critics, but none is harder to please than the carping John Simon, said to have single-handedly destroyed many acting careers.* **carp** (verb).

catalytic (adjective) bringing about, causing, or producing some result. *The conditions for revolution existed in America by 1765; the disputes about taxation that arose later were the catalytic events that sparked the rebellion.* **catalyze** (verb).

caustic (adjective) burning, corrosive. *No one was safe when the satirist H. L. Mencken unleashed his caustic wit.*

censure (noun) blame, condemnation. *The news that Senator Packwood had harassed several women brought censure from many feminists.* **censure** (verb).

chaos (noun) disorder, confusion, chance. *The first few moments after the explosion were pure chaos: no one was sure what had happened, and the area was filled with people running and yelling.* **chaotic** (adjective).

circuitous (adjective) winding or indirect. *We drove to the cottage by a circuitous route so we could see as much of the surrounding countryside as possible.*

circumlocution (noun) speaking in a roundabout way; wordiness. *Legal documents often contain circumlocutions that make them difficult to understand.*

circumscribe (verb) to define by a limit or boundary. *Originally, the role of the executive branch of government was clearly circumscribed, but that role has greatly expanded over time.* **circumscription** (noun).

circumvent (verb) to get around. *When Jerry was caught speeding, he tried to circumvent the law by offering the police officer a bribe.*

clandestine (adjective) secret, surreptitious. *As a member of the underground, Balas took part in clandestine meetings to discuss ways of sabotaging the Nazi forces.*

cloying (adjective) overly sweet or sentimental. *The deathbed scenes in the novels of Dickens are famously cloying: as Oscar Wilde said, "One would need a heart of stone to read the death of Little Nell without laughing."*

cogent (adjective) forceful and convincing. *The committee members were won over to the project by the cogent arguments of the chairman.* **cogency** (noun).

cognizant (adjective) aware, mindful. *Cognizant of the fact that it was getting late, the master of ceremonies cut short the last speech.* **cognizance** (noun).

cohesive (adjective) sticking together, unified. *An effective military unit must be a cohesive team, all its members working together for a common goal.* **cohere** (verb), **cohesion** (noun).

collaborate (verb) to work together. *To create a truly successful movie, the director, writers, actors, and many others must collaborate closely.* **collaboration** (noun), **collaborative** (adjective).

colloquial (adjective) informal in language; conversational. *Some expressions from Shakespeare, such as the use of thou and thee, sound formal today but were colloquial English in Shakespeare's time.*

competent (adjective) having the skill and knowledge needed for a particular task; capable. *Any competent lawyer can draw up a will.* **competence** (noun).

complacent (adjective) smug, self-satisfied. *During the 1970s, American automakers became complacent, believing that they would continue to be successful with little effort.* **complacency** (noun).

composure (noun) calm, self-assurance. *The president managed to keep his composure during his speech even when the TelePrompTer broke down, leaving him without a script.* **composed** (adjective).

conciliatory (adjective) seeking agreement, compromise, or reconciliation. *As a conciliatory gesture, the union leaders agreed to postpone a strike and to continue negotiations with management.* **conciliate** (verb), **conciliation** (noun).

concise (adjective) expressed briefly and simply; succinct. *Less than a page long, the Bill of Rights is a concise statement of the freedoms enjoyed by all Americans.* **concision** (noun).

condescending (adjective) having an attitude of superiority toward another; patronizing. *"What a cute little car!" she remarked in a condescending style. "I suppose it's the nicest one someone like you could afford!"* **condescension** (noun).

condolence (noun) pity for someone else's sorrow or loss; sympathy. *After the sudden death of Princess Diana, thousands of messages of condolence were sent to her family.* **condole** (verb).

confidant (noun) someone entrusted with another's secrets. *No one knew about Janee's engagement except Sarah, her confidant.* **confide** (verb), **confidential** (adjective).

conformity (noun) agreement with or adherence to custom or rule. *In my high school, conformity was the rule: everyone dressed the same, talked the same, and listened to the same music.* **conform** (verb), **conformist** (adjective).

consensus (noun) general agreement among a group. *Among Quakers, voting traditionally is not used; instead, discussion continues until the entire group forms a consensus.*

consolation (noun) relief or comfort in sorrow or suffering. *Although we miss our dog very much, it is a consolation to know that she died quickly, without suffering.* **console** (verb).

consternation (noun) shock, amazement, dismay. *When a voice in the back of the church shouted out, "I know why they should not be married!" the entire gathering was thrown into consternation.*

consummate (verb) to complete, finish, or perfect. *The deal was consummated with a handshake and the payment of the agreed-upon fee.* **consummate** (adjective), **consummation** (noun).

contaminate (verb) to make impure. *Chemicals dumped in a nearby forest had seeped into the soil and contaminated the local water supply.* **contamination** (noun).

contemporary (adjective) modern, current; from the same time. *I prefer old-fashioned furniture rather than contemporary styles. The composer Vivaldi was roughly contemporary with Bach.* **contemporary** (noun).

contrite (adjective) sorry for past misdeeds. *The public is often willing to forgive celebrities who are involved in some scandal, as long as they appear contrite.* **contrition** (noun).

conundrum (noun) a riddle, puzzle, or problem. *The question of why an all-powerful, all-loving God allows evil to exist is a conundrum many philosophers have pondered.*

convergence (noun) the act of coming together in unity or similarity. *A remarkable example of evolutionary convergence can be seen in the shark and the dolphin, two sea creatures that developed from different origins to become very similar in form.* **converge** (verb).

convoluted (adjective) twisting, complicated, intricate. *Tax law has become so convoluted that it's easy for people to accidentally violate it.* **convolute** (verb), **convolution** (noun).

corroborating (adjective) supporting with evidence; confirming. *A passerby who had witnessed the crime gave corroborating testimony about the presence of the accused person.* **corroborate** (verb), **corroboration** (noun).

corrosive (adjective) eating away, gnawing, or destroying. *Years of poverty and hard work had a corrosive effect on her beauty.* **corrode** (verb), **corrosion** (noun).

credulity (noun) willingness to believe, even with little evidence. *Con artists fool people by taking advantage of their credulity.* **credulous** (adjective).

criterion (noun) a standard of measurement or judgment. (The plural is criteria.) *In choosing a design for the new taxicabs, reliability will be our main criterion.*

critique (noun) a critical evaluation. *The editor gave a detailed critique of the manuscript, explaining its strengths and its weaknesses.* **critique** (verb).

culpable (adjective) deserving blame, guilty. *Although he committed the crime, because he was mentally ill he should not be considered culpable for his actions.* **culpability** (noun).

cumulative (adjective) made up of successive additions. *Smallpox was eliminated only through the cumulative efforts of several generations of doctors and scientists.* **accumulation** (noun), **accumulate** (verb).

curtail (verb) to shorten. *Because of the military emergency, all soldiers on leave were ordered to curtail their absences and return to duty.*

D

debased (adjective) lowered in quality, character, or esteem. *The quality of TV journalism has been debased by the many new tabloid-style talk shows.* **debase** (verb).

debunk (verb) to expose as false or worthless. *Magician James Randi loves to debunk psychics, mediums, clairvoyants, and others who claim supernatural powers.*

decorous (adjective) having good taste; proper, appropriate. *The once reserved and decorous style of the British monarchy began to change when the chic, flamboyant young Diana Spencer joined the family.* **decorum** (noun).

decry (verb) to criticize or condemn. *Cigarette ads aimed at youngsters have led many to decry the marketing tactics of the tobacco industry.*

deduction (noun) a logical conclusion, especially a specific conclusion based on general principles. *Based on what is known about the effects of greenhouse gases on atmospheric temperature, scientists have made several deductions about the likelihood of global warming.* **deduce** (verb).

delegate (verb) to give authority or responsibility. *The president delegated the vice president to represent the administration at the peace talks.* **delegate** (noun).

deleterious (adjective) harmful. *About thirty years ago, scientists proved that working with asbestos could be deleterious to one's health, producing cancer and other diseases.*

delineate (verb) to outline or describe. *Naturalists had long suspected the fact of evolution, but Darwin was the first to delineate a process—natural selection—through which evolution could occur.*

demagogue (noun) a leader who plays dishonestly on the prejudices and emotions of his followers. *Senator Joseph McCarthy was a demagogue who used the paranoia of the anti-Communist 1950s as a way of seizing fame and power in Washington.* **demagoguery** (noun).

demure (adjective) modest or shy. *The demure heroines of Victorian fiction have given way to today's stronger, more opinionated, and more independent female characters.*

denigrate (verb) to criticize or belittle. *The firm's new president tried to explain his plans for improving the company without seeming to denigrate the work of his predecessor.* **denigration** (noun).

depose (verb) to remove from office, especially from a throne. *Iran was formerly ruled by a monarch called the Shah, who was deposed in 1976.*

derelict (adjective) neglecting one's duty. *The train crash was blamed on a switchman who was derelict, having fallen asleep while on duty.* **dereliction** (noun).

derivative (adjective) taken from a particular source. *When a person first writes poetry, her poems are apt to be derivative of whatever poetry she most enjoys reading.* **derivation** (noun), **derive** (verb).

desolate (adjective) empty, lifeless, and deserted; hopeless, gloomy. *Robinson Crusoe was shipwrecked and had to learn to survive alone on a desolate island. The murder of her husband left Mary Lincoln desolate.* **desolation** (noun).

destitute (adjective) very poor. *Years of rule by a dictator who stole the wealth of the country had left the people of the Philippines destitute.* **destitution** (noun).

deter (verb) to discourage from acting. *The best way to deter crime is to insure that criminals will receive swift and certain punishment.* **deterrence** (noun), **deterrent** (adjective).

detractor (noun) someone who belittles or disparages. *Neil Diamond has many detractors who consider his music boring, inane, and sentimental.* **detract** (verb).

deviate (verb) to depart from a standard or norm. *Having agreed upon a spending budget for the company, we mustn't deviate from it; if we do, we may run out of money soon.* **deviation** (noun).

devious (adjective) tricky, deceptive. *Milken's devious financial tactics were designed to enrich his firm while confusing or misleading government regulators.*

didactic (adjective) intended to teach, instructive. *The children's TV show* Sesame Street *is designed to be both entertaining and didactic.*

diffident (adjective) hesitant, reserved, shy. *Someone with a diffident personality should pursue a career that involves little public contact.* **diffidence** (noun).

diffuse (verb) to spread out, to scatter. *The red dye quickly became diffused through the water, turning it a very pale pink.* **diffusion** (noun).

digress (verb) to wander from the main path or the main topic. *My high school biology teacher loved to digress from science into personal anecdotes about his college adventures.* **digression** (noun), **digressive** (adjective).

dilatory (adjective) delaying, procrastinating. *The lawyer used various dilatory tactics, hoping that his opponent would get tired of waiting for a trial and drop the case.*

diligent (adjective) working hard and steadily. *Through diligent efforts, the townspeople were able to clear away the debris from the flood in a matter of days.* **diligence** (noun).

diminutive (adjective) unusually small, tiny. *Children are fond of Shetland ponies because their diminutive size makes them easy to ride.* **diminution** (noun).

discern (verb) to detect, notice, or observe. *I could discern the shape of a whale off the starboard bow, but it was too far away to determine its size or species.* **discernment** (noun).

disclose (verb) to make known; to reveal. *Election laws require candidates to disclose the names of those who contribute money to their campaigns.* **disclosure** (noun).

discomfit (verb) to frustrate, thwart, or embarrass. *Discomfited by the interviewer's unexpected question, Peter could only stammer in reply.* **discomfiture** (noun).

disconcert (verb) to confuse or embarrass. *When the hallway bells began to ring halfway through her lecture, the speaker was disconcerted and didn't know what to do.*

discredit (verb) to cause disbelief in the accuracy of some statement or the reliability of a person. *Although many people still believe in UFOs, among scientists the reports of "alien encounters" have been thoroughly discredited.*

discreet (adjective) showing good judgment in speech and behavior. *Be discreet when discussing confidential business matters—don't talk among strangers on the elevator, for example.* **discretion** (noun).

discrepancy (noun) a difference or variance between two or more things. *The discrepancies between the two witnesses' stories show that one of them must be lying.* **discrepant** (adjective).

disdain (noun) contempt, scorn. *Millionaire Leona Helmsley was disliked by many people because she treated "little people" with such disdain.* **disdain** (verb), **disdainful** (adjective).

disingenuous (adjective) pretending to be candid, simple, and frank. *When Texas billionaire H. Ross Perot ran for president, many considered his "jest plain folks" style disingenuous.*

disparage (verb) to speak disrespectfully about, to belittle. *Many political ads today both praise their own candidate and disparage his or her opponent.* **disparagement** (noun), **disparaging** (adjective).

disparity (noun) difference in quality or kind. *There is often a disparity between the kind of high-quality television people say they want and the low-brow programs they actually watch.* **disparate** (adjective).

disregard (verb) to ignore, to neglect. *If you don't write a will, when you die, your survivors may disregard your wishes about how your property should be handled.* **disregard** (noun).

disruptive (adjective) causing disorder, interrupting. *When the senator spoke at our college, angry demonstrators picketed, heckled, and engaged in other disruptive activities.* **disrupt** (verb), **disruption** (noun).

dissemble (verb) to pretend, to simulate. *When the police questioned her about the crime, she dissembled innocence.*

dissipate (verb) to spread out or scatter. *The windows and doors were opened, allowing the smoke that had filled the room to dissipate.* **dissipation** (noun).

dissonance (noun) lack of music harmony; lack of agreement between ideas. *Most modern music is characterized by dissonance, which many listeners find hard to enjoy. There is a noticeable dissonance between two common beliefs of most conservatives: their faith in unfettered free markets and their preference for traditional social values.* **dissonant** (adjective).

diverge (verb) to move in different directions. *Frost's poem* The Road Not Taken *tells of the choice he made when "Two roads diverged in a yellow wood."* **divergence** (noun), **divergent** (adjective).

diversion (noun) a distraction or pastime. *During the two hours he spent in the doctor's waiting room, his hand-held computer game was a welcome diversion.* **divert** (verb).

divination (noun) the art of predicting the future. *In ancient Greece, people wanting to know their fate would visit the priests at Delphi, supposedly skilled at divination.* **divine** (verb).

divisive (adjective) causing disagreement or disunity. *Throughout history, race has been the most divisive issue in American society.*

divulge (verb) to reveal. *The people who count the votes for the Oscar awards are under strict orders not to divulge the names of the winners.*

dogmatic (adjective) holding firmly to a particular set of beliefs with little or no basis. *Believers in Marxist doctrine tend to be dogmatic, ignoring evidence that contradicts their beliefs.* **dogmatism** (noun).

dominant (adjective) greatest in importance or power. *Turner's* Frontier Thesis *suggests that the existence of the frontier had a dominant influence on American culture.* **dominate** (verb), **domination** (noun).

dubious (adjective) doubtful, uncertain. *Despite the chairman's attempts to convince the committee members that his plan would succeed, most of them remained dubious.* **dubiety** (noun).

durable (adjective) longlasting. *Denim is a popular material for work clothes because it is strong and durable.*

duress (noun) compulsion or restraint. *Fearing that the police might beat him, he confessed to the crime, not willingly but under duress.*

E

eclectic (adjective) drawn from many sources; varied, heterogeneous. *The Mellon family art collection is an eclectic one, including works ranging from ancient Greek sculptures to modern paintings.* **eclecticism** (noun).

efficacious (adjective) able to produce a desired effect. *Though thousands of people today are taking herbal supplements to treat depression, researchers have not yet proved them efficacious.* **efficacy** (noun).

effrontery (noun) shameless boldness. *The sports world was shocked when a pro basketball player had the effrontery to choke his head coach during a practice session.*

effusive (adjective) pouring forth one's emotions very freely. *Having won the Oscar for Best Actress, Sally Field gave an effusive acceptance speech in which she marveled, "You like me! You really like me!"* **effusion** (noun).

egoism (noun) excessive concern with oneself; conceit. *Robert's egoism was so great that all he could talk about was the importance—and the brilliance—of his own opinions.* **egoistic** (adjective).

egregious (adjective) obvious, conspicuous, flagrant. *It's hard to imagine how the editor could allow such an egregious error to appear.*

elated (adjective) excited and happy; exultant. *When the Green Bay Packers' last, desperate pass was dropped, the elated fans of the Denver Broncos began to celebrate.* **elate** (verb), **elation** (noun).

elliptical (adjective) very terse or concise in writing or speech; difficult to understand. *Rather than speak plainly, she hinted at her meaning through a series of nods, gestures, and elliptical half sentences.*

elusive (adjective) hard to capture, grasp, or understand. *Though everyone thinks they know what "justice" is, when you try to define the concept precisely, it proves to be quite elusive.*

embezzle (verb) to steal money or property that has been entrusted to your care. *The church treasurer was found to have embezzled thousands of dollars by writing phony checks on the church bank account.* **embezzlement** (noun).

emend (verb) to correct. *Before the letter is mailed, please emend the two spelling errors.* **emendation** (noun).

emigrate (verb) to leave one place or country to settle elsewhere. *Millions of Irish emigrated to the New World in the wake of the great Irish famines of the 1840s.* **emigrant** (noun), **emigration** (noun).

eminent (adjective) noteworthy, famous. *Vaclav Havel was an eminent author before being elected president of the Czech Republic.* **eminence** (noun).

emissary (noun) someone who represents another. *In an effort to avoid a military showdown, Carter was sent as an emissary to Korea to negotiate a settlement.*

emollient (noun) something that softens or soothes. *She used a hand cream as an emollient on her dry, work-roughened hands.* **emollient** (adjective).

empathy (noun) imaginative sharing of the feelings, thoughts, or experiences of another. *It's easy for a parent to have empathy for the sorrow of another parent whose child has died.* **empathetic** (adjective).

empirical (adjective) based on experience or personal observation. *Although many people believe in ESP, scientists have found no empirical evidence of its existence.* **empiricism** (noun).

emulate (verb) to imitate or copy. *The British band Oasis admitted their desire to emulate their idols, the Beatles.* **emulation** (noun).

encroach (verb) to go beyond acceptable limits; to trespass. *By quietly seizing more and more authority, Robert Moses continually encroached on the powers of other government leaders.* **encroachment** (noun).

enervate (verb) to reduce the energy or strength of someone or something. *The stress of the operation left her feeling enervated for about two weeks.*

engender (verb) to produce, to cause. *Countless disagreements over the proper use of national forests have engendered feelings of hostility between ranchers and environmentalists.*

enhance (verb) to improve in value or quality. *New kitchen appliances will enhance your house and increase the amount of money you'll make when you sell it.* **enhancement** (noun).

enmity (noun) hatred, hostility, ill will. *Long-standing enmity, like that between the Protestants and Catholics in Northern Ireland, is difficult to overcome.*

enthrall (verb) to enchant or charm. *When the Swedish singer Jenny Lind toured America in the nineteenth century, audiences were enthralled by her beauty and talent.*

ephemeral (adjective) quickly disappearing; transient. *Stardom in pop music is ephemeral; most of the top acts of ten years ago are forgotten today.*

equanimity (noun) calmness of mind, especially under stress. *Roosevelt had the gift of facing the great crises of his presidency—the Depression and World War II—with equanimity and even humor.*

eradicate (verb) to destroy completely. *American society has failed to eradicate racism, although some of its worst effects have been reduced.*

espouse (verb) to take up as a cause; to adopt. *No politician in American today will openly espouse racism, although some behave and speak in racially prejudiced ways.*

euphoric (adjective) a feeling of extreme happiness and well-being; elation. *One often feels euphoric during the earliest days of a new love affair.* **euphoria** (noun).

evanescent (adjective) vanishing like a vapor; fragile and transient. *As she walked by, the evanescent fragrance of her perfume reached me for just an instant.*

exacerbate (verb) to make worse or more severe. *The roads in our town already have too much traffic; building a new shopping mall will exacerbate the problem.*

exasperate (verb) to irritate or annoy. *Because she was trying to study, Sharon was exasperated by the yelling of her neighbors' children.*

exculpate (verb) to free from blame or guilt. *When someone else confessed to the crime, the previous suspect was exculpated.* **exculpation** (noun), **exculpatory** (adjective).

exemplary (adjective) worthy to serve as a model. *The Baldrige Award is given to a company with exemplary standards of excellence in products and service.* **exemplar** (noun), **exemplify** (verb).

exonerate (verb) to free from blame. *Although Jewell was suspected at first of being involved in the bombing, later evidence exonerated him.* **exoneration** (noun), **exonerative** (adjective).

expansive (adjective) broad and large; speaking openly and freely. *The LBJ Ranch is located on an expansive tract of land in Texas. Over dinner, she became expansive in describing her dreams for the future.*

expedite (verb) to carry out promptly. *As the floodwaters rose, the governor ordered state agencies to expedite their rescue efforts.*

expertise (noun) skill, mastery. *The software company was eager to hire new graduates with programming expertise.*

expiate (verb) to atone for. *The president's apology to the survivors of the notorious Tuskegee experiments was his attempt to expiate the nation's guilt over their mistreatment.* **expiation** (noun).

expropriate (verb) to seize ownership of. *When the Communists came to power in China, they expropriated most businesses and turned them over to government-appointed managers.* **expropriation** (noun).

extant (adjective) currently in existence. *Of the seven ancient Wonders of the World, only the pyramids of Egypt are still extant.*

extenuate (verb) to make less serious. *Karen's guilt is extenuated by the fact that she was only twelve when she committed the theft.* **extenuating** (adjective), **extenuation** (noun).

extol (verb) to greatly praise. *At the party convention, speaker after speaker rose to extol their candidate for the presidency.*

extricate (verb) to free from a difficult or complicated situation. *Much of the humor in the TV show* I Love Lucy *comes in watching Lucy try to extricate herself from the problems she creates by fibbing or trickery.* **extricable** (adjective).

extrinsic (adjective) not an innate part or aspect of something; external. *The high price of old baseball cards is due to extrinsic factors, such as the nostalgia felt by baseball fans for the stars of their youth, rather than the inherent beauty or value of the cards themselves.*

exuberant (adjective) wildly joyous and enthusiastic. *As the final seconds of the game ticked away, the fans of the winning team began an exuberant celebration.* **exuberance** (noun).

F

facile (adjective) easy; shallow or superficial. *The one-minute political commercial favors a candidate with facile opinions rather than serious, thoughtful solutions.* **facilitate** (verb), **facility** (noun).

fallacy (noun) an error in fact or logic. *It's a fallacy to think that "natural" means "healthful"; after all, the deadly poison arsenic is completely natural.* **fallacious** (adjective).

felicitous (adjective) pleasing, fortunate, apt. *The sudden blossoming of the dogwood trees on the morning of Matt's wedding seemed a felicitous sign of good luck.* **felicity** (noun).

feral (adjective) wild. *The garbage dump was inhabited by a pack of feral dogs, which had escaped from their owners and become completely wild.*

fervent (adjective) full of intense feeling; ardent, zealous. *In the days just after his religious conversion, his piety was at its most fervent.* **fervid** (adjective), **fervor** (noun).

flagrant (adjective) obviously wrong; offensive. *Nixon was forced to resign the presidency after a series of flagrant crimes against the U.S. Constitution.* **flagrancy** (noun).

flamboyant (adjective) very colorful, showy, or elaborate. *At Mardi Gras, partygoers compete to show off the most wild and flamboyant outfits.*

florid (adjective) flowery, fancy; reddish. *The grand ballroom was decorated in a florid style. Years of heavy drinking had given him a florid complexion.*

foppish (adjective) describing a man who is foolishly vain about his dress or appearance. *The foppish character of the 1890s wore bright-colored spats and a top hat; in the 1980s, he wore fancy suspenders and a shirt with a contrasting collar.* **fop** (noun).

formidable (adjective) awesome, impressive, or frightening. *According to his plaque in the Baseball Hall of Fame, pitcher Tom Seaver turned the New York Mets "from lovable losers into formidable foes."*

fortuitous (adjective) lucky, fortunate. *Although the mayor claimed credit for the falling crime rate, it was really caused by several fortuitous trends.*

fractious (adjective) troublesome, unruly. *Members of the British Parliament are often fractious, shouting insults and sarcastic questions during debates.*

fragility (noun) the quality of being easy to break; delicacy, weakness. *Because of their fragility, few stained glass windows from the early Middle Ages have survived.* **fragile** (adjective).

fraternize (verb) to associate with on friendly terms. *Although baseball players aren't supposed to fraternize with their opponents, players from opposing teams often chat before games.* **fraternization** (noun).

frenetic (adjective) chaotic, frantic. *The floor of the stock exchange, filled with traders shouting and gesturing, is a scene of frenetic activity.*

frivolity (noun) lack of seriousness; levity. *The frivolity of the Mardi Gras carnival is in contrast to the seriousness of the religious season of Lent that follows.* **frivolous** (adjective).

frugal (adjective) spending little. *With our last few dollars, we bought a frugal dinner: a loaf of bread and a piece of cheese.* **frugality** (noun).

fugitive (noun) someone trying to escape. *When two prisoners broke out of the local jail, police were warned to keep an eye out for the fugitives.* **fugitive** (adjective).

G

gargantuan (adjective) huge, colossal. *The building of the Great Wall of China was one of the most gargantuan projects ever undertaken.*

genial (adjective) friendly, gracious. *A good host welcomes all visitors in a warm and genial fashion.*

grandiose (adjective) overly large, pretentious, or showy. *Among Hitler's grandiose plans for Berlin was a gigantic building with a dome several times larger than any ever built.* **grandiosity** (noun).

gratuitous (adjective) given freely or without cause. *Since her opinion was not requested, her harsh criticism of his singing seemed a gratuitous insult.*

gregarious (adjective) enjoying the company of others; sociable. *Marty is naturally gregarious, a popular member of several clubs and a sought-after lunch companion.*

guileless (adjective) without cunning; innocent. *Deborah's guileless personality and complete honesty make it hard for her to survive in the harsh world of politics.*

gullible (adjective) easily fooled. *When the sweepstakes entry form arrived bearing the message, "You may be a winner!" my gullible neighbor tried to claim a prize.* **gullibility** (noun).

H

hackneyed (adjective) without originality, trite. *When someone invented the phrase, "No pain, no gain," it was clever, but now it is so commonly heard that it seems hackneyed.*

haughty (adjective) overly proud. *The fashion model strode down the runway, her hips thrust forward and a haughty expression, like a sneer, on her face.* **haughtiness** (noun).

hedonist (noun) someone who lives mainly to pursue pleasure. *Having inherited great wealth, he chose to live the life of a hedonist, traveling the world in luxury.* **hedonism** (noun), **hedonistic** (adjective).

heinous (adjective) very evil, hateful. *The massacre by Pol Pot of more than a million Cambodians is one of the twentieth century's most heinous crimes.*

hierarchy (noun) a ranking of people, things, or ideas from highest to lowest. *A cabinet secretary ranks just below the president and vice president in the hierarchy of the executive branch.* **hierarchical** (adjective).

hypocrisy (noun) a false pretense of virtue. *When the sexual misconduct of the television preacher was exposed, his followers were shocked at his hypocrisy.* **hypocritical** (adjective).

I

iconoclast (noun) someone who attacks traditional beliefs or institutions. *Comedian Dennis Miller enjoys his reputation as an iconoclast, though people in power often resent his satirical jabs.* **iconoclasm** (noun), **iconoclastic** (adjective).

idiosyncratic (adjective) peculiar to an individual; eccentric. *Cyndi Lauper sings pop music in an idiosyncratic style, mingling high-pitched whoops and squeals with throaty gurgles.* **idiosyncrasy** (noun).

idolatry (noun) the worship of a person, thing, or institution as a god. *In Communist China, Chairman Mao was the subject of idolatry; his picture was displayed everywhere, and millions of Chinese memorized his sayings.* **idolatrous** (adjective).

impartial (adjective) fair, equal, unbiased. *If a judge is not impartial, then all of her rulings are questionable.* **impartiality** (noun).

impeccable (adjective) flawless. *The crooks printed impeccable copies of the Super Bowl tickets, making it impossible to distinguish them from the real ones.*

impetuous (adjective) acting hastily or impulsively. *Ben's resignation was an impetuous act; he did it without thinking, and he soon regretted it.* **impetuosity** (noun).

impinge (verb) to encroach upon, touch, or affect. *You have a right to do whatever you want, so long as your actions don't impinge on the rights of others.*

impute (verb) to credit or give responsibility to; to attribute. *Although Sarah's comments embarrassed me, I don't impute any ill will to her; I think she didn't realize what she was saying.* **imputation** (noun).

inarticulate (adjective) unable to speak or express oneself clearly and understandably. *A skilled athlete may be an inarticulate public speaker, as demonstrated by many post-game interviews.*

incisive (adjective) expressed clearly and directly. *Franklin settled the debate with a few incisive remarks that summed up the issue perfectly.*

incompatible (adjective) unable to exist together; conflicting. *Many people hold seemingly incompatible beliefs: for example, supporting the death penalty while believing in the sacredness of human life.* **incompatibility** (noun).

inconsequential (adjective) of little importance. *When the stereo was delivered, it was a different shade of gray than I expected, but the difference was inconsequential.*

incontrovertible (adjective) impossible to question. *The fact that Sheila's fingerprints were the only ones on the murder weapon made her guilt seem incontrovertible.*

incorrigible (adjective) impossible to manage or reform. *Lou is an incorrigible trickster, constantly playing practical jokes no matter how much his friends complain.*

incremental (adjective) increasing gradually by small amounts. *Although the initial cost of the Medicare program was small, the incremental expenses have grown to be very large.* **increment** (noun).

incriminate (adjective) to give evidence of guilt. *The Fifth Amendment to the Constitution says that no one is required to reveal information that would incriminate him in a crime.* **incriminating** (adjective).

incumbent (noun) someone who occupies an office or position. *It is often difficult for a challenger to win a seat in Congress from the incumbent.* **incumbency** (noun), **incumbent** (adjective).

indeterminate (adjective) not definitely known. *The college plans to enroll an indeterminate number of students; the size of the class will depend on the number of applicants and how many accept offers of admission.* **determine** (verb).

indifferent (adjective) unconcerned, apathetic. *The mayor's small proposed budget for education suggests that he is indifferent to the needs of our schools.* **indifference** (noun).

indistinct (adjective) unclear, uncertain. *We could see boats on the water, but in the thick morning fog their shapes were indistinct.*

indomitable (adjective) unable to be conquered or controlled. *The world admired the indomitable spirit of Nelson Mandela; he remained courageous despite years of imprisonment.*

induce (verb) to cause. *The doctor prescribed a medicine that was supposed to induce a lowering of the blood pressure.* **induction** (noun).

ineffable (adjective) difficult to describe or express. *He gazed in silence at the sunrise over the Taj Mahal, his eyes reflecting an ineffable sense of wonder.*

inevitable (adjective) unable to be avoided. *Once the Japanese attacked Pearl Harbor, American involvement in World War II was inevitable.* **inevitability** (noun).

inexorable (adjective) unable to be deterred; relentless. *It's difficult to imagine how the mythic character of Oedipus could have avoided his evil destiny; his fate appears inexorable.*

ingenious (adjective) showing cleverness and originality. *The Post-It note is an ingenious solution to a common problem—how to mark papers without spoiling them.* **ingenuity** (noun).

inherent (adjective) naturally part of something. *Compromise is inherent in democracy, since everyone cannot get his way.* **inhere** (verb), **inherence** (noun).

innate (adjective) inborn, native. *Not everyone who takes piano lessons becomes a fine musician, which shows that music requires innate talent as well as training.*

innocuous (adjective) harmless, inoffensive. *I was surprised that Andrea took offense at such an innocuous joke.*

inoculate (verb) to prevent a disease by infusing with a disease-causing organism. *Pasteur found he could prevent rabies by inoculating patients with the virus that causes the disease.* **inoculation** (noun).

insipid (adjective) flavorless, uninteresting. *Most TV shows are so insipid that you can watch them while reading without missing a thing.* **insipidity** (noun).

insolence (noun) an attitude or behavior that is bold and disrespectful. *Some feel that news reporters who shout questions at the president are behaving with insolence.* **insolent** (adjective).

insurgency (noun) uprising, rebellion. *The angry townspeople had begun an insurgency bordering on downright revolution; they were collecting arms, holding secret meetings, and refusing to pay certain taxes.* **insurgent** (adjective).

integrity (noun) honesty, uprightness; soundness, completeness. *"Honest Abe" Lincoln is considered a model of political integrity. Inspectors examined the building's support beams and foundation and found no reason to doubt its structural integrity.*

interlocutor (noun) someone taking part in a dialogue or conversation. *Annoyed by the constant questions from someone in the crowd, the speaker challenged his interlocutor to offer a better plan.* **interlocutory** (adjective).

interlude (noun) an interrupting period or performance. *The two most dramatic scenes in King Lear are separated, strangely, by a comic interlude starring the king's jester.*

interminable (adjective) endless or seemingly endless. *Addressing the United Nations, Castro announced, "We will be brief"—then delivered an interminable 4-hour speech.*

intransigent (adjective) unwilling to compromise. *Despite the mediator's attempts to suggest a fair solution, the two parties were intransigent, forcing a showdown.* **intransigence** (noun).

intrepid (adjective) fearless and resolute. *Only an intrepid adventurer is willing to undertake the long and dangerous trip by sled to the South Pole.* **intrepidity** (noun).

intrusive (adjective) forcing a way in without being welcome. *The legal requirement of a search warrant is supposed to protect Americans from intrusive searches by the police.* **intrude** (verb), **intrusion** (noun).

intuitive (adjective) known directly, without apparent thought or effort. *An experienced chess player sometimes has an intuitive sense of the best move to make, even if she can't explain it.* **intuit** (verb), **intuition** (noun).

inundate (verb) to flood; to overwhelm. *As soon as playoff tickets went on sale, eager fans inundated the box office with orders.*

invariable (adjective) unchanging, constant. *When writing a book, it was her invariable habit to rise at 6 and work at her desk from 7 to 12.* **invariability** (noun).

inversion (noun) a turning backward, inside-out, or upside-down; a reversal. *Latin poetry often features inversion of word order; for example, those in the first line of Vergil's* Aeneid: *"Arms and the man I sing."* **invert** (verb), **inverted** (adjective).

inveterate (adjective) persistent, habitual. *It's very difficult for an inveterate gambler to give up the pastime.* **inveteracy** (noun).

invigorate (verb) to give energy to, to stimulate. *As her car climbed the mountain road, Lucinda felt invigorated by the clear air and the cool breezes.*

invincible (adjective) impossible to conquer or overcome. *For three years at the height of his career, boxer Mike Tyson seemed invincible.*

inviolable (adjective) impossible to attack or trespass upon. *In the president's remote hideaway at Camp David, guarded by the Secret Service, his privacy is, for once, inviolable.*

irrational (adjective) unreasonable. *Charles knew that his fear of insects was irrational, but he was unable to overcome it.* **irrationality** (noun).

irresolute (adjective) uncertain how to act, indecisive. *When McGovern first said he supported his vice presidential candidate "one thousand percent," then dropped him from the ticket, it made McGovern appear irresolute.* **irresolution** (noun).

J

jeopardize (verb) to put in danger. *Terrorist attacks jeopardize the fragile peace in the Middle East.* **jeopardy** (noun).

juxtapose (verb) to put side by side. *It was strange to see the old-time actor Charlton Heston and rock icon Bob Dylan juxtaposed at the awards ceremony.* **juxtaposition** (noun).

L

languid (adjective) without energy; slow, sluggish, listless. *The hot, humid weather of late August can make anyone feel languid.* **languish** (verb), **languor** (noun).

latent (adjective) not currently obvious or active; hidden. *Although he had committed only a single act of violence, the psychiatrist who examined him said he had probably always had a latent tendency toward violence.* **latency** (noun).

laudatory (adjective) giving praise. *The ads for the movie are filled with laudatory comments from critics.*

lenient (adjective) mild, soothing, or forgiving. *The judge was known for his lenient disposition; he rarely imposed long jail sentences on criminals.* **leniency** (noun).

lethargic (adjective) lacking energy; sluggish. *Visitors to the zoo are surprised that the lions appear so lethargic, but, in the wild, lions sleep up to 18 hours a day.* **lethargy** (noun).

liability (noun) an obligation or debt; a weakness or drawback. *The insurance company had a liability of millions of dollars after the town was destroyed by a tornado. Slowness afoot is a serious liability in an aspiring basketball player.* **liable** (adjective).

lithe (adjective) flexible and graceful. *The ballet dancer was almost as lithe as a cat.*

longevity (noun) length of life; durability. *The reduction in early deaths from infectious diseases is responsible for most of the increase in human longevity over the past two centuries.*

lucid (adjective) clear and understandable. *Hawking's* A Short History of the Universe *is a lucid explanation of modern scientific theories about the origin of the universe.* **lucidity** (noun).

lurid (adjective) shocking, gruesome. *While the serial killer was on the loose, the newspapers were filled with lurid stories about his crimes.*

M

malediction (noun) curse. *In the fairy tale "Sleeping Beauty," the princess is trapped in a death-like sleep because of the malediction uttered by an angry witch.*

malevolence (noun) hatred, ill will. *Critics say that Iago, the villain in Shakespeare's* Othello, *seems to exhibit malevolence with no real cause.* **malevolent** (noun).

malinger (verb) to pretend incapacity or illness to avoid a duty or work. *During the labor dispute, hundreds of employees malingered, forcing the company to slow production and costing it millions in profits.*

malleable (adjective) able to be changed, shaped, or formed by outside pressures. *Gold is a very useful metal because it is so malleable. A child's personality is malleable and deeply influenced by the things her parents say and do.* **malleability** (noun).

mandate (noun) order, command. *The new policy on gay people in the military went into effect as soon as the president issued his mandate about it.* **mandate** (verb), **mandatory** (adjective).

maturation (noun) the process of becoming fully grown or developed. *Free markets in the former Communist nations are likely to operate smoothly only after a long period of maturation.* **mature** *(adjective and verb)*, **maturity** *(noun)*.

mediate (verb) to act to reconcile differences between two parties. *During the baseball strike, both the players and the club owners were willing to have the president mediate the dispute.* **mediation** (noun).

mediocrity (noun) the state of being middling or poor in quality. *The New York Mets, who finished in ninth place in 1968, won the world's championship in 1969, going from horrible to great in a single year and skipping mediocrity.* **mediocre** (adjective).

mercurial (adjective) changing quickly and unpredictably. *The mercurial personality of Robin Williams, with his many voices and styles, made him perfect for the role of the ever-changing genie in* Aladdin.

meticulous (adjective) very careful with details. *Repairing watches calls for a craftsperson who is patient and meticulous.*

mimicry (noun) imitation, aping. *The continued popularity of Elvis Presley has given rise to a class of entertainers who make a living through mimicry of "The King."* **mimic** (noun and verb).

misconception (noun) a mistaken idea. *Columbus sailed west with the misconception that he would reach the shores of Asia.* **misconceive** (verb).

mitigate (verb) to make less severe; to relieve. *Wallace certainly committed the assault, but the verbal abuse he'd received helps to explain his behavior and somewhat mitigates his guilt.* **mitigation** (noun).

modicum (noun) a small amount. *The plan for your new business is well designed; with a modicum of luck, you should be successful.*

mollify (verb) to soothe or calm; to appease. *Carla tried to mollify the angry customer by promising him a full refund.*

morose (adjective) gloomy, sullen. *After Chuck's girlfriend dumped him, he lay around the house for a couple of days, feeling morose.*

mundane (adjective) everyday, ordinary, commonplace. *Moviegoers in the 1930s liked the glamorous films of Fred Astaire because they provided an escape from the mundane problems of life during the Great Depression.*

munificent (adjective) very generous; lavish. *Ted Turner's billion-dollar donation to the United Nations is probably the most munificent act of charity in history.* **munificence** (noun).

mutable (adjective) likely to change. *A politician's reputation can be highly mutable, as seen in the case of Harry Truman—mocked during his lifetime, revered afterward.*

N

narcissistic (adjective) showing excessive love for oneself; egoistic. *Andre's room, decorated with photos of himself and the sports trophies he has won, suggests a narcissistic personality.* **narcissism** (noun).

nocturnal (adjective) of the night; active at night. *Travelers on the Underground Railroad escaped from slavery to the North by a series of nocturnal flights. The eyes of nocturnal animals must be sensitive in dim light.*

nonchalant (adjective) appearing to be unconcerned. *Unlike the other players on the football team, who pumped their fists when their names were announced, John ran on the field with a nonchalant wave.* **nonchalance** (noun).

nondescript (adjective) without distinctive qualities; drab. *The bank robber's clothes were nondescript; none of the witnesses could remember their color or style.*

notorious (adjective) famous, especially for evil actions or qualities. *Warner Brothers produced a series of movies about notorious gangsters such as John Dillinger and Al Capone.* **notoriety** (noun).

novice (noun) beginner, tyro. *Lifting your head before you finish your swing is a typical mistake committed by the novice at golf.*

nuance (noun) a subtle difference or quality. *At first glance, Monet's paintings of water lilies all look much alike, but the more you study them, the more you appreciate the nuances of color and shading that distinguish them.*

nurture (verb) to nourish or help to grow. *The money given by the National Endowment for the Arts helps nurture local arts organizations throughout the country.* **nurture** (noun).

O

obdurate (adjective) unwilling to change; stubborn, inflexible. *Despite the many pleas he received, the governor was obdurate in his refusal to grant clemency to the convicted murderer.*

objective (adjective) dealing with observable facts rather than opinions or interpretations. *When a legal case involves a shocking crime, it may be hard for a judge to remain objective in his rulings.*

oblivious (adjective) unaware, unconscious. *Karen practiced her oboe with complete concentration, oblivious to the noise and activity around her.* **oblivion** (noun), **obliviousness** (noun).

obscure (adjective) little known; hard to understand. *Mendel was an obscure monk until decades after his death, when his scientific work was finally discovered. Most people find the writings of James Joyce obscure; hence the popularity of books that explain his books.* **obscure** (verb), **obscurity** (noun).

obsessive (adjective) haunted or preoccupied by an idea or feeling. *His concern with cleanliness became so obsessive that he washed his hands twenty times every day.* **obsess** (verb), **obsession** (noun).

obsolete (adjective) no longer current; old-fashioned. *W. H. Auden said that his ideal landscape would include water wheels, wooden grain mills, and other forms of obsolete machinery.* **obsolescence** (noun).

obstinate (adjective) stubborn, unyielding. *Despite years of effort, the problem of drug abuse remains obstinate.* **obstinacy** (noun).

obtrusive (adjective) overly prominent. *Philip should sing more softly; his bass is so obtrusive that the other singers can barely be heard.* **obtrude** (verb), **obtrusion** (noun).

ominous (adjective) foretelling evil. *Ominous black clouds gathered on the horizon, for a violent storm was fast approaching.* **omen** (noun).

onerous (adjective) heavy, burdensome. *The hero Hercules was ordered to clean the Augean Stables, one of several onerous tasks known as "the labors of Hercules."* **onus** (noun).

opportunistic (adjective) eagerly seizing chances as they arise. *When Princess Diana died suddenly, opportunistic publishers quickly released books about her life and death.* **opportunism** (noun).

opulent (adjective) rich, lavish. *The mansion of newspaper tycoon Hearst is famous for its opulent decor.* **opulence** (noun).

ornate (adjective) highly decorated, elaborate. *Baroque architecture is often highly ornate, featuring surfaces covered with carving, sinuous curves, and painted scenes.*

ostentatious (adjective) overly showy, pretentious. *To show off his wealth, the millionaire threw an ostentatious party featuring a full orchestra, a famous singer, and tens of thousands of dollars worth of food.*

ostracize (verb) to exclude from a group. *In Biblical times, those who suffered from the disease of leprosy were ostracized and forced to live alone.* **ostracism** (noun).

P

pallid (adjective) pale; dull. *Working all day in the coal mine had given him a pallid complexion. The new musical offers only pallid entertainment: the music is lifeless, the acting dull, the story absurd.*

parched (adjective) very dry; thirsty. *After two months without rain, the crops were shriveled and parched by the sun.* **parch** (verb).

pariah (noun) outcast. *Accused of robbery, he became a pariah; his neighbors stopped talking to him, and people he'd considered friends no longer called.*

partisan (adjective) reflecting strong allegiance to a particular party or cause. *The vote on the president's budget was strictly partisan: every member of the president's party voted yes, and all others voted no.* **partisan** (noun).

pathology (noun) disease or the study of disease; extreme abnormality. *Some people believe that high rates of crime are symptoms of an underlying social pathology.* **pathological** (adjective).

pellucid (adjective) very clear; transparent; easy to understand. *The water in the mountain stream was cold and pellucid. Thanks to the professor's pellucid explanation, I finally understand relativity theory.*

penitent (adjective) feeling sorry for past crimes or sins. *Having grown penitent, he wrote a long letter of apology, asking forgiveness.*

penurious (adjective) extremely frugal; stingy. *Haunted by memories of poverty, he lived in penurious fashion, driving a 12-year-old car and wearing only the cheapest clothes.* **penury** (noun).

perceptive (adjective) quick to notice, observant. *With his perceptive intelligence, Holmes was the first to notice the importance of this clue.* **perceptible** (adjective), **perception** (noun).

perfidious (adjective) disloyal, treacherous. *Although he was one of the most talented generals of the American Revolution, Benedict Arnold is remembered today as a perfidious betrayer of his country.* **perfidy** (noun).

perfunctory (adjective) unenthusiastic, routine, or mechanical. *When the play opened, the actors sparkled, but, by the thousandth night, their performance had become perfunctory.*

permeate (verb) to spread through or penetrate. *Little by little, the smell of gas from the broken pipe permeated the house.*

persevere (adjective) to continue despite difficulties. *Although several of her teammates dropped out of the marathon, Laura persevered.* **perseverance** (noun).

perspicacity (noun) keenness of observation or understanding. *Journalist Murray Kempton was famous for the perspicacity of his comments on social and political issues.* **perspicacious** (adjective).

peruse (verb) to examine or study. *Mary-Jo perused the contract carefully before she signed it.* **perusal** (noun).

pervasive (adjective) spreading throughout. *As news of the disaster reached the town, a pervasive sense of gloom could be felt.* **pervade** (verb).

phlegmatic (adjective) sluggish and unemotional in temperament. *It was surprising to see Tom, who is normally so phlegmatic, acting excited.*

placate (verb) to soothe or appease. *The waiter tried to placate the angry customer with the offer of a free dessert.* **placatory** (adjective).

plastic (adjective) able to be molded or reshaped. *Because it is highly plastic, clay is an easy material for beginning sculptors to use.*

plausible (adjective) apparently believable. *The idea that a widespread conspiracy to kill President Kennedy has been kept secret for over thirty years hardly seems plausible.* **plausibility** (noun).

polarize (adjective) to separate into opposing groups or forces. *For years, the abortion debate polarized the American people, with many people voicing extreme views and few trying to find a middle ground.* **polarization** (noun).

portend (verb) to indicate a future event; to forebode. *According to folklore, a red sky at dawn portends a day of stormy weather.*

potentate (noun) a powerful ruler. *Before the Russian Revolution, the Tsar was one of the last hereditary potentates of Europe.*

pragmatism (noun) a belief in approaching problems through practical rather than theoretical means. *Roosevelt's approach toward the Great Depression was based on pragmatism: "Try something," he said; "If it doesn't work, try something else."* **pragmatic** (adjective).

preamble (noun) an introductory statement. *The preamble to the Constitution begins with the famous words, "We the people of the United States of America . . ."*

precocious (adjective) mature at an unusually early age. *Picasso was so precocious as an artist that, at nine, he is said to have painted far better pictures than his teacher.* **precocity** (noun).

predatory (adjective) living by killing and eating other animals; exploiting others for personal gain. *The tiger is the largest predatory animal native to Asia. Microsoft has been accused of predatory business practices that prevent other software companies from competing with them.* **predation** (noun), **predator** (noun).

predilection (noun) a liking or preference. *To relax from his presidential duties, Kennedy had a predilection for spy novels featuring James Bond.*

predominant (adjective) greatest in numbers or influence. *Although hundreds of religions are practiced in India, the predominant faith is Hinduism.* **predominance** (noun), **predominate** (verb).

prepossessing (adjective) attractive. *Smart, lovely, and talented, she has all the prepossessing qualities that mark a potential movie star.*

presumptuous (adjective) going beyond the limits of courtesy or appropriateness. *The senator winced when the presumptuous young staffer addressed him as "Chuck."* **presume** (verb), **presumption** (noun).

pretentious (adjective) claiming excessive value or importance. *For a shoe salesman to call himself a "Personal Foot Apparel Consultant" seems awfully pretentious.* **pretension** (noun).

procrastinate (verb) to put off, to delay. *If you habitually procrastinate, try this technique: never touch a piece of paper without either filing it, responding to it, or throwing it out.* **procrastination** (noun).

profane (adjective) impure, unholy. *It seems inappropriate to have such profane activities as roller blading and disco dancing in a church.* **profane** (verb), **profanity** (noun).

proficient (adjective) skillful, adept. *A proficient artist, Louise quickly and accurately sketched the scene.* **proficiency** (noun).

proliferate (verb) to increase or multiply. *Over the past fifteen years, high-tech companies have proliferated in northern California, Massachusetts, and other regions.* **proliferation** (noun).

prolific (adjective) producing many offspring or creations. *With more than three hundred books to his credit, Isaac Asimov was one of the most prolific writers of all time.*

prominence (noun) the quality of standing out; fame. *Kennedy's victory in the West Virginia primary gave him a position of prominence among the Democratic candidates for president.* **prominent** (adjective).

promulgate (verb) to make public, to declare. *Lincoln signed the proclamation that freed the slaves in 1862, but he waited several months to promulgate it.*

propagate (verb) to cause to grow; to foster. *John Smithson's will left his fortune for the founding of an institution to propagate knowledge, without saying whether that meant a university, a library, or a museum.* **propagation** (noun).

propriety (noun) appropriateness. *Some people had doubts about the propriety of Clinton's discussing his underwear on MTV.*

prosaic (adjective) everyday, ordinary, dull. *"Paul's Case" tells the story of a boy who longs to escape from the prosaic life of a clerk into a world of wealth, glamour, and beauty.*

protagonist (noun) the main character in a story or play; the main supporter of an idea. *Leopold Bloom is the protagonist of James Joyce's great novel* Ulysses.

provocative (adjective) likely to stimulate emotions, ideas, or controversy. *The demonstrators began chanting obscenities, a provocative act that they hoped would cause the police to lose control.* **provoke** (verb), **provocation** (noun).

proximity (noun) closeness, nearness. *Neighborhood residents were angry over the proximity of the sewage plant to the local school.* **proximate** (adjective).

prudent (adjective) wise, cautious, and practical. *A prudent investor will avoid putting all of her money into any single investment.* **prudence** (noun), **prudential** (adjective).

pugnacious (adjective) combative, bellicose, truculent; ready to fight. *Ty Cobb, the pugnacious outfielder for the Detroit Tigers, got into more than his fair share of brawls, both on and off the field.* **pugnacity** (noun).

punctilious (adjective) very concerned about proper forms of behavior and manners. *A punctilious dresser like James would rather skip the party altogether than wear the wrong color tie.* **punctilio** (noun).

pundit (noun) someone who offers opinions in an authoritative style. *The Sunday afternoon talk shows are filled with pundits, each with his or her own theory about the week's political news.*

punitive (adjective) inflicting punishment. *The jury awarded the plaintiff one million dollars in punitive damages, hoping to teach the defendant a lesson.*

purify (verb) to make pure, clean, or perfect. *The new plant is supposed to purify the drinking water provided to everyone in the nearby towns.* **purification** (noun).

Q

quell (verb) to quiet, to suppress. *It took a huge number of police to quell the rioting.*

querulous (adjective) complaining, whining. *The nursing home attendant needed a lot of patience to care for the three querulous, unpleasant residents on his floor.*

R

rancorous (adjective) expressing bitter hostility. *Many Americans are disgusted by recent political campaigns, which seem more rancorous than ever before.* **rancor** (noun).

rationale (noun) an underlying reason or explanation. *At first, it seemed strange that several camera companies would freely share their newest technology; but their rationale was that offering one new style of film would benefit them all.*

raze (verb) to completely destroy; demolish. *The old coliseum building will soon be razed to make room for a new hotel.*

reciprocate (verb) to make a return for something. *If you'll baby-sit for my kids tonight, I'll reciprocate by taking care of yours tomorrow.* **reciprocity** (noun).

reclusive (adjective) withdrawn from society. *During the last years of her life, actress Greta Garbo led a reclusive existence, rarely appearing in public.* **recluse** (noun).

reconcile (verb) to make consistent or harmonious. *Roosevelt's greatness as a leader can be seen in his ability to reconcile the demands and values of the varied groups that supported him.* **reconciliation** (noun).

recriminate (verb) to accuse, often in response to an accusation. *Divorce proceedings sometimes become bitter, as the two parties recriminate each other over the causes of the breakup.* **recrimination** (noun), **recriminatory** (adjective).

recuperate (verb) to regain health after an illness. *Although she left the hospital two days after her operation, it took her a few weeks to fully recuperate.* **recuperation** (noun), **recuperative** (adjective).

redoubtable (adjective) inspiring respect, awe, or fear. *Johnson's knowledge, experience, and personal clout made him a redoubtable political opponent.*

refurbish (verb) to fix up; renovate. *It took three days' work by a team of carpenters, painters, and decorators to completely refurbish the apartment.*

refute (adjective) to prove false. *The company invited reporters to visit their plant in an effort to refute the charges of unsafe working conditions.* **refutation** (noun).

relevance (noun) connection to the matter at hand; pertinence. *Testimony in a criminal trial may be admitted only if it has clear relevance to the question of guilt or innocence.* **relevant** (adjective).

remedial (adjective) serving to remedy, cure, or correct some condition. *Affirmative action can be justified as a remedial step to help minority members overcome the effects of past discrimination.* **remediation** (noun), **remedy** (verb).

remorse (noun) a painful sense of guilt over wrongdoing. *In Poe's story "The Tell-Tale Heart," a murderer is driven insane by remorse over his crime.* **remorseful** (adjective).

remuneration (noun) pay. *In a civil lawsuit, the attorney often receives part of the financial settlement as his or her remuneration.* **remunerate** (verb), **remunerative** (adjective).

renovate (verb) to renew by repairing or rebuilding. *The television program "This Old House" shows how skilled craftspeople renovate houses.* **renovation** (noun).

renunciation (noun) the act of rejecting or refusing something. *King Edward VII's renunciation of the British throne was caused by his desire to marry an American divorcee, something he couldn't do as king.* **renounce** (verb).

replete (adjective) filled abundantly. *Graham's book is replete with wonderful stories about the famous people she has known.*

reprehensible (adjective) deserving criticism or censure. *Although Pete Rose's misdeeds were reprehensible, not all fans agree that he deserves to be excluded from the Baseball Hall of Fame.* **reprehend** (verb), **reprehension** (noun).

repudiate (verb) to reject, to renounce. *After it became known that Duke had been a leader of the Ku Klux Klan, most Republican leaders repudiated him.* **repudiation** (noun).

reputable (adjective) having a good reputation; respected. *Find a reputable auto mechanic by asking your friends for recommendations based on their own experiences.* **reputation** (noun), **repute** (noun).

resilient (adjective) able to recover from difficulty. *A pro athlete must be resilient, able to lose a game one day and come back the next with confidence and enthusiasm.* **resilience** (adjective).

resplendent (adjective) glowing, shining. *In late December, midtown New York is resplendent with holiday lights and decorations.* **resplendence** (noun).

responsive (adjective) reacting quickly and appropriately. *The new director of the Internal Revenue Service has promised to make the agency more responsive to public complaints.* **respond** (verb), **response** (noun).

restitution (noun) return of something to its original owner; repayment. *Some Native American leaders are demanding that the U.S. government make restitution for the lands taken from them by white settlers.*

revere (verb) to admire deeply, to honor. *Millions of people around the world revered Mother Teresa for her saintly generosity.* **reverence** (noun), **reverent** (adjective).

rhapsodize (verb) to praise in a wildly emotional way. *That critic is such a huge fan of Toni Morrison that she will surely rhapsodize over the writer's next novel.* **rhapsodic** (adjective).

S

sagacious (adjective) discerning, wise. *Only a leader as sagacious as Nelson Mandela could have united South Africa so successfully and peacefully.* **sagacity** (noun).

salvage (verb) to save from wreck or ruin. *After the earthquake destroyed her home, she was able to salvage only a few of her belongings.* **salvage** (noun), **salvageable** (adjective).

sanctimonious (adjective) showing false or excessive piety. *The sanctimonious prayers of the TV preacher were interspersed with requests that the viewers send him money.* **sanctimony** (noun).

scapegoat (noun) someone who bears the blame for others' acts; someone hated for no apparent reason. *Although Buckner's error was only one reason the Red Sox lost, many fans made him the scapegoat, booing him mercilessly.*

scrupulous (adjective) acting with extreme care; painstaking. *Disney theme parks are famous for their scrupulous attention to small details.* **scruple** (noun).

scrutinize (verb) to study closely. *The lawyer scrutinized the contract, searching for any sentence that could pose a risk for her client.* **scrutiny** (noun).

secrete (verb) to emit; to hide. *Glands in the mouth secrete saliva, a liquid that helps in digestion. The jewel thieves secreted the necklace in a tin box buried underground.*

sedentary (adjective) requiring much sitting. *When Officer Samson was given a desk job, she had trouble getting used to sedentary work after years on the street.*

sequential (adjective) arranged in an order or series. *The courses for the chemistry major are sequential; you must take them in the order, since each course builds on the previous ones.* **sequence** (noun).

serendipity (noun) the ability to make lucky accidental discoveries. *Great inventions sometimes come about through deliberate research and hard work, sometimes through pure serendipity.* **serendipitous** (adjective).

servile (adjective) like a slave or servant; submissive. *The tycoon demanded that his underlings behave in a servile manner, agreeing quickly with everything he said.* **servility** (noun).

simulated (adjective) imitating something else; artificial. *High-quality simulated gems must be examined under a magnifying glass to be distinguished from real ones.* **simulate** (verb), **simulation** (noun).

solace (verb) to comfort or console. *There was little the rabbi could say to solace the husband after his wife's death.* **solace** (noun).

spontaneous (adjective) happening without plan or outside cause. *When the news of Kennedy's assassination broke, people everywhere gathered in a spontaneous effort to share their shock and grief.* **spontaneity** (noun).

spurious (adjective) false, fake. *The so-called "Piltdown Man," supposed to be the fossil of a primitive human, turned out to be spurious, although who created the hoax is still uncertain.*

squander (verb) to use up carelessly, to waste. *Those who had made donations to the charity were outraged to learn that its director had squandered millions on fancy dinners and first-class travel.*

stagnate (verb) to become stale through lack of movement or change. *Having had no contact with the outside world for generations, Japan's culture gradually stagnated.* **stagnant** (adjective), **stagnation** (noun).

staid (adjective) sedate, serious, and grave. *This college is no "party school"; the students all work hard, and the campus has a reputation for being staid.*

stimulus (noun) something that excites a response or provokes an action. *The arrival of merchants and missionaries from the West provided a stimulus for change in Japanese society.* **stimulate** (verb).

stoic (adjective) showing little feeling, even in response to pain or sorrow. *A soldier must respond to the death of his comrades in stoic fashion, since the fighting will not stop for his grief.* **stoicism** (noun).

strenuous (adjective) requiring energy and strength. *Hiking in the foothills of the Rockies is fairly easy, but climbing the higher peaks can be strenuous.*

submissive (adjective) accepting the will of others; humble, compliant. *At the end of Ibsen's play* A Doll's House, *Nora leaves her husband and abandons the role of submissive housewife.*

substantiated (adjective) verified or supported by evidence. *The charge that Nixon had helped to cover up crimes was substantiated by his comments about it on a series of audio tapes.* **substantiate** (verb), **substantiation** (noun).

sully (verb) to soil, stain, or defile. *Nixon's misdeeds as president did much to sully the reputation of the American government.*

superficial (adjective) on the surface only; without depth or substance. *Her wound was superficial and required only a light bandage. His superficial attractiveness hides the fact that his personality is lifeless and his mind is dull.* **superficiality** (noun).

superfluous (adjective) more than is needed, excessive. *Once you've won the debate, don't keep talking; superfluous arguments will only bore and annoy the audience.*

suppress (verb) to put down or restrain. *As soon as the unrest began, thousands of helmeted police were sent into the streets to suppress the riots.* **suppression** (noun).

surfeit (noun) an excess. *Most American families have a surfeit of food and drink on Thanksgiving Day.* **surfeit** (verb).

surreptitious (adjective) done in secret. *Because Iraq has avoided weapons inspections, many believe it has a surreptitious weapons development program.*

surrogate (noun) a substitute. *When the congressman died in office, his wife was named to serve the rest of his term as a surrogate.* **surrogate** (adjective).

sustain (verb) to keep up, to continue; to support. *Because of fatigue, he was unable to sustain the effort needed to finish the marathon.*

T

tactile (adjective) relating to the sense of touch. *The thick brush strokes and gobs of color give the paintings of Van Gogh a strongly tactile quality.* **tactility** (noun).

talisman (noun) an object supposed to have magical effects or qualities. *Superstitious people sometimes carry a rabbit's foot, a lucky coin, or some other talisman.*

tangential (adjective) touching lightly; only slightly connected or related. *Having enrolled in a class on African-American history, the students found the teacher's stories about his travels in South America only of tangential interest.* **tangent** (noun).

tedium (noun) boredom. *For most people, watching the Weather Channel for 24 hours would be sheer tedium.* **tedious** (adjective).

temerity (noun) boldness, rashness, excessive daring. *Only someone who didn't understand the danger would have the temerity to try to climb Everest without a guide.* **temerarious** (adjective).

temperance (noun) moderation or restraint in feelings and behavior. *Most professional athletes practice temperance in their personal habits; too much eating or drinking, they know, can harm their performance.* **temperate** (adjective).

tenacious (adjective) clinging, sticky, or persistent. *Tenacious in pursuit of her goal, she applied for the grant unsuccessfully four times before it was finally approved.* **tenacity** (noun).

tentative (adjective) subject to change; uncertain. *A firm schedule has not been established, but the Super Bowl in 2002 has been given the tentative date of January 20.*

terminate (verb) to end, to close. *The Olympic Games terminate with a grand ceremony attended by athletes from every participating country.* **terminal** (noun), **termination** (noun).

terrestrial (adjective) of the earth. *The movie* Close Encounters of the Third Kind *tells the story of the first contact between beings from outer space and terrestrial humans.*

therapeutic (adjective) curing or helping to cure. *Hot-water spas were popular in the nineteenth century among the sickly, who believed that soaking in the water had therapeutic effects.* **therapy** (noun).

timorous (adjective) fearful, timid. *The cowardly lion approached the throne of the wizard with a timorous look on his face.*

toady (noun) someone who flatters a superior in hopes of gaining favor; a sycophant. *"I can't stand a toady!" declared the movie mogul. "Give me someone who'll tell me the truth—even if it costs him his job!"* **toady** (verb).

tolerant (adjective) accepting, enduring. *San Franciscans have a tolerant attitude about lifestyles: "Live and let live" seems to be their motto.* **tolerate** (verb), **toleration** (noun).

toxin (noun) poison. *DDT is a powerful toxin once used to kill insects but now banned in the United States because of the risk it poses to human life.* **toxic** (adjective).

tranquillity (noun) freedom from disturbance or turmoil; calm. *She moved from New York City to rural Vermont seeking the tranquility of country life.* **tranquil** (adjective).

transgress (verb) to go past limits; to violate. *If Iraq has developed biological weapons, then it has transgressed the UN's rules against weapons of mass destruction.* **transgression** (noun).

transient (adjective) passing quickly. *Long-term visitors to this hotel pay at a different rate than transient guests who stay for just a day or two.* **transience** (noun).

transitory (adjective) quickly passing. *Public moods tend to be transitory; people may be anxious and angry one month, but relatively content and optimistic the next.* **transition** (noun).

translucent (adjective) letting some light pass through. *Blocks of translucent glass let daylight into the room while maintaining privacy.*

transmute (verb) to change in form or substance. *In the Middle Ages, the alchemists tried to discover ways to transmute metals such as iron into gold.* **transmutation** *(noun)*.

treacherous (adjective) untrustworthy or disloyal; dangerous or unreliable. *Nazi Germany proved to be a treacherous ally, first signing a peace pact with the Soviet Union, then invading. Be careful crossing the rope bridge; parts are badly frayed and treacherous.* **treachery** (noun).

tremulous (adjective) trembling or shaking; timid or fearful. *Never having spoken in public before, he began his speech in a tremulous, hesitant voice.*

trite (adjective) boring because of over-familiarity; hackneyed. *Her letters were filled with trite expressions, like "All's well that ends well" and "So far so good."*

truculent (adjective) aggressive, hostile, belligerent. *Hitler's truculent behavior in demanding more territory for Germany made it clear that war was inevitable.* **truculence** (noun).

truncate (verb) to cut off. *The manuscript of the play appeared truncated; the last page ended in the middle of a scene, halfway through the first act.*

turbulent (adjective) agitated or disturbed. *The night before the championship match, Martina was unable to sleep, her mind turbulent with fears and hopes.* **turbulence** (noun).

U

unheralded (adjective) little known, unexpected. *In a year of big-budget, much-hyped mega-movies, this unheralded foreign film has surprised everyone with its popularity.*

unpalatable (adjective) distasteful, unpleasant. *Although I agree with the candidate on many issues, I can't vote for her, because I find her position on capital punishment unpalatable.*

unparalleled (adjective) with no equal; unique. *Tiger Woods's victory in the Masters golf tournament by a full twelve strokes was an unparalleled accomplishment.*

unstinting (adjective) giving freely and generously. *Eleanor Roosevelt was much admired for her unstinting efforts on behalf of the poor.*

untenable (adjective) impossible to defend. *The theory that this painting is a genuine Van Gogh became untenable when the artist who actually painted it came forth.*

untimely (adjective) out of the natural or proper time. *The untimely death of a youthful Princess Diana seemed far more tragic than Mother Teresa's death of old age.*

unyielding (adjective) firm, resolute, obdurate. *Despite criticism, Cuomo was unyielding in his opposition to capital punishment; he vetoed several death penalty bills as governor.*

usurper (noun) someone who takes a place or possession without the right to do so. *Kennedy's most devoted followers tended to regard later presidents as usurpers, holding the office they felt he or his brothers should have held.* **usurp** (verb), **usurpation** (noun).

utilitarian (adjective) purely of practical benefit. *The design of the Model T car was simple and utilitarian, lacking the luxuries found in later models.*

utopia (noun) an imaginary, perfect society. *Those who founded the Oneida community dreamed that it could be a kind of utopia—a prosperous state with complete freedom and harmony.* **utopian** (adjective).

V

validate (verb) to officially approve or confirm. *The election of the president is validated when the members of the Electoral College meet to confirm the choice of the voters.* **valid** (adjective), **validity** (noun).

variegated (adjective) spotted with different colors. *The brilliant, variegated appearance of butterflies makes them popular among collectors.* **variegation** (noun).

venerate (verb) to admire or honor. *In Communist China, Chairman Mao Zedong was venerated as an almost god-like figure.* **venerable** (adjective), **veneration** (noun).

verdant (adjective) green with plant life. *Southern England is famous for its verdant countryside filled with gardens and small farms.* **verdancy** (noun).

vestige (noun) a trace or remainder. *Today's tiny Sherwood Forest is the last vestige of a woodland that once covered most of England.* **vestigial** (adjective).

vex (verb) to irritate, annoy, or trouble. *Unproven for generations, Fermat's last theorem was one of the most famous, and most vexing, of all mathematical puzzles.* **vexation** (noun).

vicarious (adjective) experienced through someone else's actions by way of the imagination. *Great literature broadens our minds by giving us vicarious participation in the lives of other people.*

vindicate (verb) to confirm, justify, or defend. *Lincoln's Gettysburg Address was intended to vindicate the objectives of the Union in the Civil War.*

virtuoso (noun) someone very skilled, especially in an art. *Vladimir Horowitz was one of the great piano virtuosos of the twentieth century.* **virtuosity** (noun).

vivacious (adjective) lively, sprightly. *The role of Maria in* The Sound of Music *is usually played by a charming, vivacious young actress.* **vivacity** (noun).

volatile (adjective) quickly changing; fleeting, transitory; prone to violence. *Public opinion is notoriously volatile; a politician who is very popular one month may be voted out of office the next.* **volatility** (noun).

W

whimsical (adjective) based on a capricious, carefree, or sudden impulse or idea; fanciful, playful. *Dave Barry's* Book of Bad Songs *is filled with the kind of goofy jokes that are typical of his whimsical sense of humor.* **whim** (noun).

Z

zealous (adjective) filled with eagerness, fervor, or passion. *A crowd of the candidate's most zealous supporters greeted her at the airport with banners, signs, and a marching band.* **zeal** (noun), **zealot** (noun), **zealotry** (noun).

About the GED B

What to Expect on the GED

Now that you have prepared for the GED Language Arts, Reading Test, Let's look at the other tests you will have to take in order to receive your GED:

- Language Arts, Writing
- Social Studies
- Science
- Mathematics

On every test (except for Language Arts, Writing) all the questions will be multiple choice. Each multiple-choice question will have five possible answer choices. For each question, you must choose the best answer of the five possible choices. The multiple-choice questions may be based on a graphic, a text, or a mathematics problem, or they may just test your knowledge of a particular subject. Let's take a look at the kinds of questions asked on each subject area test:

Language Arts, Writing

The multiple-choice section of the Writing exam tests English grammar and usage. It contains several passages and questions about those passages in which you find errors or determine the best way to rewrite particular sentences. The essay section will require you to write a 200- to 250-word essay on a particular topic in 45 minutes. This question won't test your knowledge of a particular subject, such as the War of 1812 or the Pythagorean Theorem. Instead, you will write about your own life experiences. The readers of the essay will not be grading the essay based on how much you know or don't know about the topic but rather on how well you use standard English.

Social Studies

The Social Studies Test contains multiple-choice questions on history, economics, political science, and geography. In the United States, the test focuses on U.S. history and government, while the test in Canada focuses on Canadian history and government. World history will be included, too. Some of the questions will be based on reading passages, and some questions will be based on graphics such as maps, charts, illustrations, or political cartoons.

Science

The Science Test contains multiple-choice questions on physical and life sciences. You will also see questions on earth science, space science, life science, health science, and environmental science. As with the Social Studies Test, some of the Science questions will be based upon reading passages and some of the questions will be based upon graphics such as scientific diagrams.

Mathematics

There are two parts to the Mathematics Test. You can use a calculator on Part I, but not on Part II. The Mathematics Test uses multiple-choice questions to measure your skills in arithmetic, algebra, geometry, and problem solving. Some of the questions will ask you to find the answer to a problem, while others will require you to find the best way to solve the problem. Many of the questions will be based upon diagrams. Some of the questions will be grouped into sets that require you to draw upon information from a number of sources, such as graphs and charts.

The majority of GED questions on all five of the tests measure your skills and test-taking abilities. What does this mean for you? This means that if you work hard to sharpen your test-taking skills, you will be much more prepared for success on the tests than if you sat down and memorized names, dates, facts, properties, charts, or other bits of information. Basically, you will have more success on the GED if you know how to take the tests than if all you know is information about reading, writing, science, social studies, and math. Let's look at some strategies for answering multiple-choice questions.

Answering Multiple-Choice Questions

The key to success on multiple-choice tests is understanding the questions and how to find the correct answer. Each multiple-choice question on the GED will be followed by five answer choices: (1), (2), (3), (4), and (5). There will be no trick questions and no questions intended to confuse you. If you use the strategies that follow, you will be very successful on the multiple-choice questions.

Strategies for Attacking Multiple-Choice Questions

- **Read the question carefully and make sure you know what it is asking.** Read each question slowly. If you rush through the question, you might miss a key word that could cost you the correct answer. You might want to run your pencil under the question as you read it to be sure that you don't miss anything in the question. If you don't understand the question after the first time you read it, go back and read it another time or two until you do understand it.

- **Don't overanalyze the question or read something into the question that just isn't there.** Many test-takers make the mistake of over-analyzing questions, looking for some trick or hidden meaning that the test creators added for the sake of confusion. The GED Test creators can't do that on any of the questions, so take each question at face value. Each question will say exactly what it means, so don't try to interpret something unusual into the questions.

- **Circle or underline the key words in the question.** As you read through the question, locate any important words in the question and either circle or underline the word or words. Important words will be anything taken directly from the chart, table, graph, or reading passage on which the question is based. Other important words will be words like *compare*, *contrast*, *similar*, *different*, or *main idea*. By circling or underlining the key words, you will understand the question better and will be more prepared to recognize the correct answer.

- **After you read the question, try to answer the question in your head before you look at the answer choices.** If you think you know the answer to the question without even looking at the answer choices, then you most likely will recognize the correct answer right away when you read the possible answer choices. Also, if you think you know the correct answer right away, then you should be very confident in your answer when you find it listed among the possible answer choices.

- **Try covering the answer choices while you are reading the question.** To try answering the question in your head without being influenced by the answer choices, cover the answer choices with your hand as you read the question. This technique will also help prevent you from reading something into the question that isn't there based on something you saw in one of the answer choices first. Covering the answer choices may also help you concentrate only on the question to make sure you read it carefully and correctly.

- **Carefully read all the answer choices before answering the question.** You need to look at all the possibilities before you choose the best or correct answer. Even if you think you know the answer before looking at the possible answer choices, read all of the answer choices anyway. If you read through two of the answer choices and you find that choice (3) is a good answer, keep reading because choices (4) or (5) may very well be a better answer. Finally, by reading all the answer choices, you can be more confident in your answer because you will see that the others are definitely incorrect.

- **Eliminate answer choices that you know are wrong.** As you read through all the choices, some will obviously be incorrect. When you find those answer choices, mark through them. This will help you narrow the possible choices. In addition, marking through incorrect answers will prevent you from choosing an incorrect answer by mistake.

- **Don't spend too much time on one question.** If you read a question and you just can't seem to find the best or correct answer, circle the question, skip it, and come back to it later. Your time will be better spent answering questions that you can answer. Your time is limited, so don't struggle with one question if you could correctly answer three others in the same amount of time.

- **Go with your first answer.** Once you choose an answer, stick to it. A test-taker's first hunch is usually the correct one. There is a reason why your brain told you to choose a particular answer, so stand by it. Also, don't waste time debating over whether the answer you chose is correct. Go with your first answer and move on.

- **Don't go back and change your answer unless you have a good, solid reason to do so.** Remember that your first hunch is usually the best, so don't change your answer on a whim. One of the only times you should change your answer on a previous question is if you find something later in the test that contradicts what you chose. The only other time you should change an answer is if you remember very clearly a teacher's lecture, a reading passage, or some other reliable source of information to the contrary of what you chose.

- **Look for hints within the answer choices.** For example, some sets of answer choices may contain two choices that vary by only a word or two. Chances are that the correct answer is one of those two answers.

- **Watch out for absolutes.** Other hints within answer choices can be words called absolutes. These words include *always*, *never*, *only*, or *completely*. These words severely limit the possibility of that answer choice being right because the absolutes make answer choices that include them correct under certain, very limited circumstances.

- **If you just don't know the correct answer, guess.** That's right, guess. The GED Tests are scored based on how many questions you answer correctly, and there is no point penalty for answering incorrectly. Therefore, why leave questions unanswered? If you do, you have no chance at getting any points for those. However, if you guess, you at least have a chance to get some points. Before you guess, try to eliminate as many wrong answer choices as possible. You have a much greater chance of choosing the correct answer if you can weed out some that are incorrect. This strategy is especially helpful if you have several questions left for which you are going to guess.

- **Be aware of how much time you have left on the test.** However, don't glance down at your watch or up at the clock after every question to check the time. You will be instructed at the beginning of the test as to the amount of time you have to complete the test. Just be aware of that amount of time. The creators of the GED Tests designed the tests and the test times so that you will have ample time to complete the tests. As you approach the point at which you have 10 minutes left, make sure that you are not spending your time answering the difficult questions if you still have other questions ahead of you that you can answer. If you have answered all the questions that you can with relatively little difficulty, go back and work on those that gave you trouble. If you come down to the wire and have a few left, guess at the answers. There is no penalty for wrong answers on the GED.

- **If you have time left at the end of the test, go back to any questions that you skipped.** As you just read, after you finish all the questions that you can without too much difficulty, you should go back over the test and find the ones you skipped. The amount of time you have left should determine the amount of time you spend on each unanswered question. For example, if you have 10 questions left and 10 minutes left, try to work on a few of them. However, if you have 10 questions left and 2 minutes left, go through and guess on each of the remaining questions.

What's Next?

Working with this book is the first step toward getting your GED. But what should you do next? Many people find it helpful to take a GED test-preparation course. Call your local high school counselor or the Adult Education or Continuing Education Department at your local community college, college, or university. The people in those offices can tell you where courses are offered and how to enroll. In addition to taking a GED course, continue studying on your own with this book and others in the ARCO line of books.

Once you feel ready to take the tests, contact the GED Testing Service to find out when and where the exams will be administered next:

General Educational Development
GED Testing Service
American Council on Education
One Dupont Circle, NW
Washington, D.C. 20036
Phone: 800-626-9433 (toll-free)
Web site: www.gedtest.org

Good luck!

Test-Taking Tips and Strategies   C

I. Prepare Your Mind

Being mentally ready to take a test is very important. You must walk into any test with a positive mental attitude. YOU CAN DO IT!

This should be easy. You've studied this book, and maybe others. You're comfortable with the material on the test. You won't run into any surprises. So take some deep breaths and walk into the test room knowing that you can succeed!

Be relaxed. Be confident.

II. The Night Before

Cramming doesn't work for any kind of test. So the night before the test, you should briefly review some of the concepts that you're still unsure of. Then go straight to bed. Make sure you get enough sleep. You'll be glad you did the next morning.

III. The Morning of the Test

Did you know that you think better when you have a full stomach? So don't skip breakfast the morning of the test. Get to your test site early (you should make a practice run before the test if the test site is in an unfamiliar area).

Come prepared with all the materials you'll need. These might include number 2 pencils or identification. You might want to wear a watch too, in case the room you're in doesn't have a clock.

IV. Test Time

Before the test begins, make sure you have everything you need. This will keep your test anxiety low.

Choose a comfortable seat (if possible!) and in a spot where you will not be distracted, cold, hot, etc.

Try not to talk to other test-takers before the test. Anxiety is contagious.

V. Managing Time

Scan through the test quickly before starting it. Be familiar with the time for each section and the time the test should be over. Look at how many questions there are, and where the answers are filled in.

READ ALL DIRECTIONS VERY CAREFULLY.

VI. Know Your Test

On the GED, test questions are arranged in order of difficulty. This means the easier questions come first. So the more time you spend on the easier early questions, the less time you'll have for the harder questions later in the section. If you're stuck, don't get worried or frustrated. Circle the question and move on. Go back to it later, once you've finished the rest of the test. And make sure that you skip space on the answer sheets for every question you skip on the test.

VII. Test Review

Once you've finished taking the test, look back over the exam to review what you've done. Resist the urge to run away as fast as you can once you mark your last answer. Some things to look for:

Make sure you've answered all the questions.

Proofread (when you're doing any written work).

Answer any questions you skipped.

Practice makes perfect!

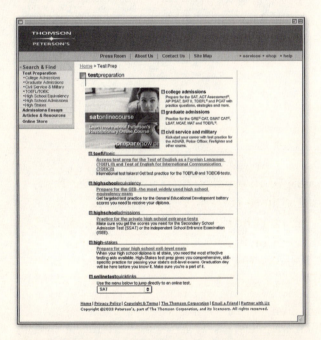

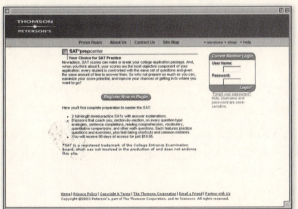

Improve your scores from the comfort of your own computer.

Online Practice Tests for the SAT*, ACT Assessment®, GRE® CAT, GMAT CAT®, TOEFL®, and ASVAB

No matter what test you're taking, the best ways to improve your scores are through repeated practice and a solid understanding of how the test works. Whether you're headed for college, graduate school, or a new career, if your test is computer-adaptive or paper-based, Peterson's online practice tests give you the convenience you crave. Each is completely self-directed. And you get 90 days access so you can log on and off whenever you like. Plus, automated essay question scoring for the GRE, GMAT, and TOEFL!

 Visit the Test Preparation Channel of **www.petersons.com**, select your test, and get started.

*SAT is a registered trademark of the College Entrance Examination Board, which was not involved in the production of and does not endorse this product.

*ACT Assessment is a registered trademark of ACT™ Inc., which has no connection with this product.

*GRE and TOEFL are registered trademarks of Educational Testing Service (ETS). These products are not endorsed or approved by ETS.

*GMAT and GMAT CAT are registered trademarks of the Graduate Management Admission Council (GMAC). This product does not contain any actual GMAT test items, nor is it endorsed or approved by GMAC.

www.petersons.com

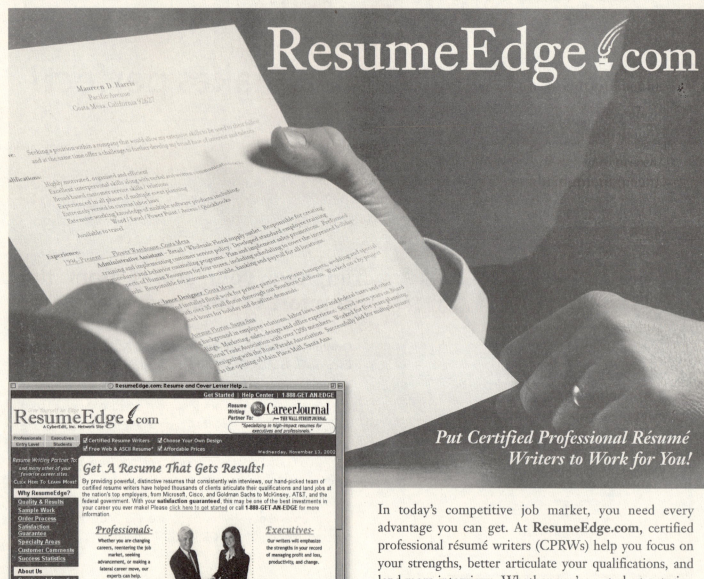